The Tipping Point: The Noah Hunter

"Best novel I have read in 2021! An outs[...] incredible author." - *Jonas Saul, author of the Sarah Roberts Series.*

"Loved this book, it was interesting from page one to the end. Never knowing what was going to happen next. Kept me on the edge page after page." - *Elaine C. Stewart, Amazon Review*

"Darling's story telling is edge-of-your seat, what's going to happen next, tension-filled and intriguing." – *SteVen Hendricks*

Grave Choices: The Noah Hunter Series: Book 2

"*Grave Choices* is right up your alley if you enjoy terrifyingly suspenseful thrillers that leave you gasping at the end with cliffhanger reveals and utter desperation to find out more." - *Kashif Hussain, reviewer from Best Thriller Books.*

"Darling writes one heck of a police thriller that will leave you up all night telling yourself "Just one more chapter". This one grabs you from the first chapter and does not let go until the last page and will have you begging for the next book." – *Troy Pool*

"Reading Grave Choices is like watching a high action police drama with characters that you become invested in the more you read, and become emotionally attached to as the story progresses. Through the highs and lows of this roller coaster of a story you will feel the full range of emotions up until the jaw dropping cliff hanger of an ending." – *Mark Elliott*

Eighteen years after four-year-old Angela Taylor was kidnapped, Detective Noah Hunter receives information that the girl may be alive. The cold case is reopened, but someone would rather see the police detective dead than publicly reveal what happened all those years ago.

Dodging government agents and hired contractors, a small-town police officer pits himself against those responsible. But powerful people are interested in the outcome, controlling the narrative—something he could not imagine.

This time Noah will solve the case, no matter the cost.

Course of Action, The Noah Hunter Series: Book 3

Novels by David Darling

The Noah Hunter Series

The Tipping Point

Grave Choices

Course of Action

Hunter's Gambit (forthcoming)

Standalone

Serve in the Shadows: Recruitment

Novella

Grim Measures

In loving memory of my cousins, Susan and Nicole. The separate blows to the family are devastating and break our hearts.

"… sing your death song and die like a hero going home."

- *Chief Tecumseh 1813*

Course of Action

THE NOAH HUNTER SERIES: BOOK 3

David Darling

Chapter 1

Noah Hunter stood beside the front door in full tactical gear with his Glock 17 ready. When he nodded to the US Marshal, he counted down, "Breach in three, two ...."

On *one*, Sedore swung the battering ram, and it collided with the door just under the locking mechanism. The thirty-five-pound Enforcer shattered the wooden frame and bent the dead bolt—it didn't stand a chance against the four tons of force generated.

Noah threw the flash-bang grenade and leaned away from the opening. The loud explosion resonated throughout the house, and despite the fact he was around the corner, Noah's ears rang from the concussive wave. Anyone inside would stagger from the noise and be temporarily blinded by the light, which gave them an advantage.

A plume of smoke shot out the door and began to fill the interior room. Sergeant Angie Dickinson took a deep breath and tapped her hand on Noah's left shoulder, and they entered the small home in a rush.

Noah cleared the left corner while his partner swept the living room's right side. "Clear."

Despite his ears ringing from the grenade, he still heard a young baby shriek down the hall.

Dickinson stepped to the side at the doorway to the kitchen, brought her Glock 19 to shoulder height, and fired two rounds at the older man with the knife.

Noah crouched and peered around the corner when the blade hit the floor. "Covering."

"Moving." Angie stayed to the right with her back to the kitchen wall, barrel trained to the man's head. Her shots had hit an inch apart, dead center of his chest.

"Clear."

Smoke filtered into the remainder of the home as Noah moved through the kitchen and down the hall. The sound of the child crying intensified, and he gestured to the first bedroom on the right. Angie stood at his back and covered the two closed doors down the hall. "Ready."

With a surge of energy, Detective Hunter flung the door open. He didn't hesitate when spotting the shotgun. A three-round burst from his pistol hit the woman in the head, and she flew back into the curtains, then toppled sideways across the nightstand. The baby continued to scream on the bed as the sound of small-arms fire filled the bedroom.

"Clear!"

There was no time to deal with the infant as they proceeded down the hall, Dickinson in the lead. When the door at the end flung open, Angie fired at the same time as she reeled from a hit to her shoulder. Her shot went wide and into the top of the door frame. The large man wore a balaclava and had withdrawn into the room while she swore and fell against the wall.

"Stay here." Noah stepped around his partner and attempted to slow his heart rate. He couldn't let the excitement impair his judgment. When a figure leaned around the open doorway in the last bedroom, Noah squeezed the trigger in reflex, and his Glock jumped in his hands with the recoil.

By then, it was too late.

The woman in the gray dress slumped to the floor, the warning klaxon sounded, and the bright overhead lights came on.

Noah couldn't help but groan, and Angie swore under her breath as she regained her feet.

"It's okay. Everyone falls for the switch with the first run through here."

The US Marshal had followed several steps behind and punched him in the shoulder as they turned and filed out of the training house. Angie kicked the mannequin in the kitchen as she walked past and holstered her pistol. The exhaust fans turned on while the crew prepared for the next team.

They had received permission to train at the Federal Law Enforcement Training Center (FLETC) in Glynco, Georgia. Over the ten-day session, they took advanced evasive and defensive driving techniques classes, electronic countermeasures, and enhanced communications lectures. Noah had recognized Marshal Daryl Sedore, who volunteered to work with them for the house clearing (CQB) drills. FLETC was also home to the US Marshal's training center, and Daryl had taken them under his wing.

"Hunter and Dickinson, briefing room Charlie."

Noah's instructor leaned over the observation platform and pointed at the set of offices toward the far end of the warehouse. Noah gave him the thumbs-up.

"Good luck. Will I see you for dinner?"

"Sounds good." Sedore removed the training vest and glasses before going to the storeroom. It had been half a year since they worked with him in Arrow Point. His knowledge and expertise were essential to their last case. They had almost captured the serial killer before a hangman's noose solved the issue of a trial.

"I should have covered the door better." Sergeant Dickinson was the most demanding critic of her performance.

"You were fine. I was the one to shoot the hostage. I didn't verify my target."

Angie nodded, but Noah could tell she wasn't thrilled. The debriefing room had several desks that faced a large display monitor where the instructor would play back and analyze their last session. The Arrow Point Police Department lacked a tactical division or a quick reaction force where this training type would be standard. Long as the budget allowed, the chief would authorize cross-training of this nature.

Noah had done such room-clearing drills while in the military as part of his work-up training before deployment. That was over twenty years ago, however, their techniques hadn't changed.

Angie collapsed behind a desk and pulled out her notebook to go over the two-person room-clearing drills yet again.

When Noah's phone vibrated, he answered when Steve Hutchings's name popped on the screen. They talked for a minute when Noah abruptly stood. The chair tipped over onto the floor and was ignored.

"You have to be kidding me ..."

He couldn't help but grin at the news and scratched his new short dark beard. Angie gave up studying, closed her manual, and waited.

Hunter looked at his watch. "Give me sixty minutes, and then I'll be at the airport and back in Wyoming soon. You better wait for me. We've waited eighteen years for this, so a few more hours won't kill you."

After he disconnected the call, Noah closed his eyes and took a few deep breaths.

Angie placed the manual off to the side and smiled. "So, are you going to let me in on this, or will I have to guess?"

The excitement was too much, and Noah grinned. "New information on an old abduction cold case. The first investigation I worked on, actually."

Noah had been a rookie and with the Arrow Point Police Department for two weeks when the call came in. They hadn't found the little girl that went missing, and despite the eighteen years that passed, he had never forgotten.

Angie took off her training gear. "There isn't a chance I'll be staying here. They better have room for us both on this flight."

Noah gave her a wink and immediately called the airline while his right foot tapped as he waited to connect. Dickinson left to find their instructor and turn in the gear.

His mind spun with the possibilities, and he was ready to re-open the case. This time he would find answers, and the likelihood that the little girl could still be alive fueled hope.

After eighteen years, he knew Angela's parents hadn't given up on finding their daughter, and neither would he.

Chapter 2

The next flight from Georgia to Cheyenne wasn't until the following morning. However, Noah found a direct flight to Denver International Airport that same afternoon. There wasn't a chance of waiting until the next day. Noah tried to rest during the three-hour flight and go over all the details from the missing child case.

"I was only gone for a minute! When I turned around, my daughter was missing." Sergeant Steve Hutchings and Constable Noah Hunter heard the mother scream when they first arrived at the motel. Unfortunately, that wasn't the last time Noah listened to a similar statement from a parent. Those words and that moment in time still resonate eighteen years later.

The Taylor family was on holiday and passing through Yellowstone National Park. They stopped at the Travel Resort Motel in Arrow Point and would continue their drive the next morning. Leslie Taylor brought in the luggage had let her daughter Angela sleep in the car while her husband, Joe, went to the motel office.

Leslie had thrown the suitcases on the bed, and when she returned to the car, the door was wide open, and her daughter was missing. The four-year-old couldn't reach to unbuckle the harness from the car seat, which only left one option. Someone had taken her.

They had quickly set up a perimeter search, and the highway patrol and the county sheriffs arrived on the scene within thirty minutes. The FBI was called as well. After several days of searching, they slowly called personnel away for other tasks due to the lack of viable leads. The various statements from the witness in the area and the road drivers didn't provide any credible information. Leslie and Joe Taylor eventually returned to Washington, D.C., heartbroken. Their life and hearts had shattered. Regardless, there wasn't anything the police could do without new information.

Noah opened his eyes when the flight attendant asked him to raise his seat fully. They began their descent into Denver, and he looked out the small window at the countryside. The early fall weather had turned the trees brilliant oranges and yellows, and winter would not be far away. The farmer's fields were bare and ready for spring planting.

Georgia was humid and warm, but they had to wear a light jacket when they got off the plane. The Colorado autumn weather hinted at an early winter.

In a rental vehicle, they took Interstate-25 north from Denver. Construction outside of the city slowed them down, but he relied on his badge to get him out of trouble if it came to it, and he quickly made up the time.

Two-and-a-half hours after they left, the Chevy Equinox nearly sighed in relief when he closed the car door. "Much better than a four-hour drive."

Angie stepped out of the car and stretched as the engine ticked. "I think you've set a new record."

She stood two inches taller than Noah at six-foot-one and had recently cut her long brown hair to shoulder length. Angie looked much younger and had a few problems with her apparent youth despite being twenty-eight. After four years with the APPD, she was the youngest officer promoted to sergeant. Despite her misgivings, she had scored perfect on her exam and was excellent at her job. Noah didn't hesitate to choose her as a partner, a decision he never regretted.

Eight hours after receiving the phone call, Noah walked through the police department's doors, eager to find answers.

~

The FD-258 fingerprint card was standard for background checks through any government agency with the FBI. Noah remembered the application process as part of his police department background check.

He held the form up to the light and tried to read the blacked-out, redacted text. "Have we verified this with the Feds? Why would that information be left out?"

Staff Sergeant Steve Hutchings took the form, held it up to the light, and squinted, but he couldn't see anything. He sighed. "This didn't arrive through the regular channels. Someone wanted us to see this."

The top half of the fingerprint sheet had an area for name, address, aliases, etc. There were only two pieces of information not redacted: the gender marked as female and the state of Florida.

It arrived with the daily mail to the police station, care of Noah Hunter, with no return address. Since 9/11, the staff sergeant processed all incoming mail and packages as a security precaution. Hutchings ran the prints in their system and got a match within minutes.

"Do you think it's real?" Noah handed the form over to Dickinson as he sat behind the conference room table.

The staff sergeant nodded. "Without a doubt."

The prints matched those of Angela Taylor, but as an adult. They had dusted and found a complete set of fingerprints from the four-year-old at the scene, but nothing else. The abductor must have worn gloves.

"Who do you think sent this? They must have known I worked the case."

Hutchings shook his head. "Not sure, but the good news is she's alive."

10

"Do you still have the envelope it came in?" Angie slid the prints across the table and took out her notebook while Hutchings removed the large manila envelope from a folder.

She examined the paper at the corner. "This didn't run through the post office. There isn't a postal meter. Hand-delivered?"

Hutchings ran a hand through his short white hair and shook his head. "No. It was in the pile of mail early this morning."

"What about this?" One end gaped opened, the other sealed by the sender. "Any chance of prints on the inside?"

"We can send this to the lab to look for trace, but I wouldn't put much hope in it. More importantly, this is a solid lead. Review the files and go over the evidence. Start from square one."

Angie grinned at Noah, and the dimples deepened. "Maybe your new girlfriend can help?"

"We're just friends."

Even Hutchings smirked.

Noah and Jessica Ross had a casual relationship, but he enjoyed her company despite the age difference—she was easy to talk with and twelve years older. Jessica was focused on her work at the lab and side business. Noah realized he wouldn't get anywhere without some type of answer. "We went on a couple of dates, but that's it. First, I need to sign out the evidence and go over the files."

Steve picked up the paperwork. "I'll have the FBI run the prints through their system. It's their form, and they should know more. I want to put this one to bed before I retire. Get crackin' rookie."

Once they were alone, Angie asked. "How much longer is he going to call you that?"

Noah chuckled. "Rest of my career, most likely. It's his way of saying he cares. Maybe."

Despite the long day and drive, he was anxious and filled with energy. "I'm going to need my own office before we begin. We won't be able to work in the general area properly."

The second floor's main workspace had a large open area filled with desks, which all the officers shared. The only rooms on the second floor were the captain's office and the conference room. Captain Haslam preferred to work the night shift, and Lieutenant Bydal worked days. Rarely was there a problem sharing an office. It had been done this way for decades due to lack of space.

Angie frowned. "Not too sure where you want to set up. Not much free room left."

Noah stood. "How many times have we used all three holding cells at once?"

"You want to have an office in lockup? There's a definite odor there." Angie tapped her pen on the table while she thought. "How about the travel trailer in the parking lot?"

The twenty-eight-foot trailer was a mobile command unit and rarely used, except for a recruitment information center at Casper College this last spring.

"At least it wouldn't smell like disinfectant. I think it'll work. Call Bruce and see if he can set up a phone and at least two computers. I have some more driving to do tonight."

Noah wanted to get to work right away, but he still had to go to Cheyenne Regional Airport and get his truck and return the rental. With a quick look at his watch, he figured he would be lucky to get a few hours of sleep. After eighteen years, a night without rest would be a small price to pay.

Chapter 3

Noah was on his fifth black coffee by three o'clock the next afternoon as he toured Dickinson around the Travel Resort Motel property. He used to wear a suit while he worked, but it wasn't practical in the end. His default uniform was jeans, running shoes, a dress shirt, and a suit jacket. The shoulder harness was replaced with a holster for the Glock 17 on his right hip. Since Angie's promotion to sergeant, she had worn much the same clothing, opting for comfort and practicality.

He passed her the photos and the AS-32(a) report (initial form including sketches and distances) as they stood in front of the motel room.

"The Taylor family arrived at 18:53 on August third and checked in with the office. Joe Taylor moved their vehicle and parked in front of room eight, ten minutes later."

Angie studied the eight-by-ten pictures, then the building. "Not much has changed."

The motel's shape resembled a long L, with twenty-four rooms that faced the parking lot. The office was next to the road, with ice and vending machines underneath the overhang—the sign on the road advertised air-conditioning and free Wi-Fi with each room. The red sheet-metal roof had faded with time, giving the building a worn-down look.

"Why did Joe go back to the office after he parked the car?" Angie looked across the parking lot. The office was one hundred feet away at the end of the building.

Noah read the report typed from his notes. "The couple in room nine was loud, and he wanted to see if there was another room available."

The rooms were in numerical order, and room nine shared the same wall as eight.

"Do you think we can see inside?"

"Let's see if it's vacant, just to have a quick peek."

Despite having the interior pictures, it didn't compare with seeing it in person. When they walked into the office, silver bells hanging off the hinge rang, announcing a customer.

A chest-height check-in counter stood next to a display filled with local attractions and restaurants pamphlets. Large windows showed views of the interstate on one side and the parking lot on the opposite.

Noah eyed the coffeemaker and stepped forward but was interrupted when a young blonde woman came out of the offices.

"Detective Hunter and Sergeant Dickinson, APPD."
Noah flashed his badge and identification. "Could we get the key
to room eight? It will be only for a few minutes."

The nametag on the woman's shirt read *Sandy*. "Is there
something wrong? That unit has been vacant for weeks."

"We're following up on an old case."

Sandy frowned but nodded. "That won't be a problem."

Noah walked across the parking lot two minutes later
with a white security key card. Inside the room, two double beds
were on the north wall with a nightstand between them. A large
dresser filled the opposite wall, with a flat-screen television next
to a small coffeemaker. A small pedestal table and chairs were
inside the door, underneath the front window.

Noah headed to the closet next to the bathroom door.
"This is where Leslie Taylor placed the bags, then washed her
hands. When she returned to the car, she found the rear door
open, and Angela was missing. The call came in at 19:04, and we
were on scene within six minutes."

Dickinson opened the closet door before inspecting the
standard motel bathroom. "Are the curtains open all the time, or
would they be closed when she first walked into the room?"

Noah flipped through the typed notes and reports. The
half-inch stack was freshly printed. "Not recorded. Hold on."

There was only one other car in the parking lot. He
walked under the overhang and checked a few different rooms
before returning.

"It looks like the vacant rooms have the curtains drawn. But, I'm not sure how they were eighteen years ago."

Noah wasn't sure of his memory. The minor details had faded or were misremembered. Angie opened the drapes above the small table and stood in front of the closet. Noah could see her reflection in the mirrored door.

"Because, if I'm standing here, with the curtains open, I can see where they parked. Same as the bathroom."

Straight ahead inside the bathroom, a large mirror ran the length of the wall above the sink and counter. Glasses with paper caps and wrapped soaps awaited the next occupant.

Noah stood at the sink. "They would have had a full visual and even partial if the door was left open from this angle."

"Stay there for a second, and I'll move the cruiser." Noah left the door and curtains open. Seconds later, he stood at the vehicle's rear door and left it open. He could see straight into the bathroom from that location, and when Dickinson stood near the closet, he could see her through the window.

Noah looked around the parking lot and at the front office as he stood outside. He could see the young woman behind the counter watching. There were no blinds or curtains in the office. Anyone behind or in front of the counter would have a full view of the parking lot.

Angie joined him beside the cruiser. "Unless things have changed in the last eighteen years, they should have seen everything."

17

Noah slowly nodded. He should have noticed this eighteen years ago, and the fact that the girl's parents didn't mention they had line-of-sight to their vehicle raised a red flag. His sense of unease increased.

"I can only guess that the curtains were closed, and the clerk was busy. Let's head back to the station and start going through the full file, step by step."

*****

Dress shoes clicked against the polished stone floor as she strode around the older man with the red dust broom and his veteran's ballcap.

"Sorry, Andy."

"No problem, ma'am."

He had kept the lobby clean for over thirty years, and everyone knew Andy. However, she didn't have time to talk. The woman absently smoothed the gray dress suit and tucked the file folder under her left arm as she continued.

She passed the one-hundred and thirty-three stars engraved into the marble wall, as well as the black book encased in a display of steel and glass. Her passing caused the American flag to stir as she reached for the myriad of security passes and identifications that hung around her neck. Next to the staircase, the black security door had a card reader and a biometric scanner, and it took the woman a few seconds to find the correct card before she was through.

18

The thirty-foot hallway ended at the door with a wooden plaque. The Latin motto was engraved in large letters, *Tertia Optio*. Directly translated, 'a third alternative,' more commonly known as 'the third option.'

Yet another security card opened the door, and she walked into the small set of offices. She took a moment to look in the mirror behind the display cabinet and fix her hair. The stress of the job had aged her. Despite being sixty-five years old, the woman could have passed for seventy on a good day, but typically older. Her once long blond hair was now short, streaked with gray, and cut over her ears. The lines on her face had deepened over the years, and her oval glasses would slide down her nose when she bent forward. She would always stand with her shoulders back, and head held high to avoid this.

The woman knocked on the middle office door, looked up at the wall and ceiling corner, and waited. It was hard to see the camera inside the black housing, but she knew it was there.

The lock clicked, and she stepped inside.

"It's been a while since you've been here, Miriam. To what do I owe the pleasure?"

The large office hadn't changed in over two decades, and it still resembled a 1940's cigar lounge with dark leather chairs. Law books and encyclopedias filled the floor-to-ceiling shelves. Six TV screens decorated the south wall and there was a small mahogany bar-cart beside the sizeable executive desk's right side. This was the only office with a twenty-by-twenty-foot area rug in the entire building. Somehow it seemed to fit.

The gentleman stood when she entered, walked around the desk to give her a brief hug, and gestured to take a seat.

He was in his late seventies and wore his usual dark slacks and a golf shirt, and his short white hair resembled a military brush-cut.

"Is the room secure, Walter?"

He held a finger in the air, sat behind his desk, and flicked a switch inside the top drawer before nodding. "We're good."

All electronic communication now ended at the walls. Nothing could be broadcasted nor be received. They couldn't do anything about internal recording devices, but a crew swept the room weekly.

Miriam relaxed into the comfortable leather chair while Walter sat across from her. He gestured to the bar, and she shook her head. "I only have a few minutes before I have to go."

She handed him the file folder while he pulled a pair of reading glasses out of his breast pocket and studied the reports.

When he frowned, the lines on his forehead deepened. Miriam knew he had finished the first-page summary.

Once he completed the remainder, he folded his glasses and rubbed his eyes. "How many others know this information?"

"Including us, only four."

Walter nodded before he passed over the paperwork. "All roads will lead to a dead end. I'll make sure the Florida field office acts accordingly."

Miriam stood. "I thought you should be aware."

"I appreciate the heads-up. It's been a while. Dinner sometime?"

Walter gave her another brief hug after they stood. A sheet of paper fell out of the folder and landed at his feet. He picked up the FD-258 form and handed it over.

"I'll give you a call if there is any new information. No need to wait for our next meeting." With a half-smile, she left without a response to his question. Some things she wasn't willing to forget.

However, Miriam could not see the cold, deadpan look that overcame Walter's face as he watched her leave. Not looking back would cost her dearly.

Chapter 4

Bruce transformed the trailer into an acceptable office, and the computer system was up and running and tied into the station. He changed the door lock and installed secure filing cabinets to store sensitive material. The APPD didn't have the budget for all new furniture. The desks and chairs looked like they had been salvaged from a thrift store, but they were functional.

Noah stopped at the store, made a few purchases, and once unboxed, the mugs were lined up in front of a new coffeemaker like soldiers—ready to go. The desk drawer already held a stash of protein bars, and water bottles were stocked in the small fridge. Priorities.

Dickinson finished setting up a long table in the secondary office and spread out the evidence boxes and reports. She was reading through the material to familiarize herself with the case.

Noah's first order of business was to electronically forward the DNA sample to Jessica at Casper's FSL laboratory.

Eighteen years ago, hair and skin cell samples were collected from the car seat hoping the kidnapper had left evidence. They had matched the child's hair and toothbrush samples, but there wasn't anything else left behind. They didn't find the abductor's prints on the door handle or the buckle.

Jessica wrote back immediately and told him it wouldn't take long to complete an analysis. Most of the work involved separating the DNA, but that was already done and digitally recorded. Revisiting old cases and using modern technology to help law enforcement or give families closure was why she worked at FSL and was more than happy to help out.

In the basement of the police station was a storage facility for documents and files that stretched back decades. It took several trips to the trailer and a few hours to go over all the material gathered for the case. Noah refreshed his memory on what attempts to locate the child had been made, and the steps law-enforcement officers had taken. That alone filled countless reports.

The only information worth revisiting was the witness statements. Leslie Taylor had moved the luggage into the motel room, and Joe went to the office. Kendra Plummer and her husband, Ethan, argued next door, and the couple could not hear or see a thing. The young man who worked behind the counter and a businessman who arrived in the parking lot had nothing to add.

"Do you think it's worth doing a follow-up interview to see if any of the witnesses would remember anything else?" Angie pushed the reports back and rubbed her eyes.

Noah shook his head. "After this long, it's doubtful." When his computer chimed, he checked his emails.

After reading the message twice, he leaned back in the chair. "Holy crap."

With the tone of his voice, Angie spun her chair around. "What's wrong?"

"Just a second." He quickly scanned the email and reports once again before grinning. "Information from Jessica at FSL."

Noah rotated the monitor when she sat beside him. "This is on the child's grandparents?"

"Angel Taylor would be twenty-two years old by now. If she had submitted her DNA for ancestry tracking, we could contact her. It's a whole new science that's gaining ground. However, we don't know if she's alive or not." He opened the family tree. "This is the interesting part."

The maternal chart showed a couple had married in western Ukraine in 1954, Zoya and Petro Chupryna. They had six children, five boys, and one girl.

"Angela's mother, listed as Leslie Taylor, but this chart shows Zoya only had one daughter, named Tetyana Chupryna, born in 1970."

Angie scanned the information and shrugged. "People change their names."

Noah scrolled and showed her the composition ancestry chart for Angela; 42% percent Ukrainian and, 49% percent eastern Slavic, 9% other.

"I would have to go over the file one more time, but I thought Leslie and Joe Taylor were from Washington D.C., and it appears the father's side of the family was *also* from the Soviet Union."

Angie opened the folders and quickly returned with a photocopy of Noah's notebook. "According to your notes, they were from Alexandria, Virginia."

She passed over the photocopy of their driver's licenses and detailed statements. Noah entered the information into the computer and located Leslie at the same address, but the computer didn't show any data for Joe.

Noah pulled out his cell phone and dialed the long-distance number. He placed the call on speaker and waited while it rang.

Noah added two hours for the time difference. It would be seven o'clock at night in Virginia.

A woman answered on the third ring. "Hello?"

She had a deep, throaty voice and seemed out of breath. "Leslie Taylor?"

Dickinson slid her cell phone beside his and activated the voice recorder. He nodded in approval. It was best to keep a record of all the conversations, something he should have thought of beforehand.

"Yes, how can I help you?"

25

"This is Detective Noah Hunter from Arrow Point Police Department. Do you have a moment?"

There were a few seconds of silence, and then they heard a sharp draw of breath. "Is this about my daughter?"

"Yes, is your husband available? I want to go over some information with both of you if possible."

There was a moment of silence before she continued. "Joe passed away two years ago."

"My condolences, Mrs. Taylor."

Angie sat down at the desk and worked on the computer while listening.

"I'm not able to confirm. However, we may have information that leads me to believe Angela is alive."

"Oh, my God." Leslie cried into the phone, and her sobs tore at Noah's heartstrings.

"I have re-opened the case, and I'll keep you informed of any details as they arrive."

"Thank you."

There was an awkward moment of silence, and Angie cleared her throat. "Mrs. Taylor, this is Sergeant Dickinson. Is it okay to ask a few questions?"

Leslie paused to blow her nose away from the phone. "Sorry about that. The news hit me rather hard after all these years. Anything I can do to help, let me know."

"First, have you recalled any other details on the day of the abduction that may be of assistance?"

"Joe and I went over this a hundred times. Sorry, I can't be of more help."

Noah turned his monitor and tapped the ancestry chart on the screen.

"I had another question." Dickinson made sure her phone was recording before she continued. "When did you change your name from Tetyana Chupryna?"

The moment of silence stretched on for fifteen seconds.

"Mrs. Taylor?"

Noah leaned forward, and he thought he could hear muttering on the other end.

"That's a long story. I wish I could talk about—"

After they heard the click, Angie reached for the cell phone, "Disconnected."

Noah quickly redialed the number, and it rang a few times before the call disconnected once again. On the next attempt, they heard a computer recording, *The number you have reached is no longer in service.*

Angie turned off the voice recorder, and the trailer filled with the sound of Noah's fingers as he drummed the death march on the desk.

*****

It took Leslie a few seconds to realize she was talking to dead air. She tried to call the detective back, but there wasn't a ring tone.

The lines were down.

She dug in her purse, pulled out her cell, and tried to look up the Arrow Point Police Department's phone number, but there wasn't a signal. The internet wasn't working on her laptop, either.

Leslie tried to slow her breathing and control the rapid pounding of her heart against her ribs. She glanced around her small home and made a decision.

She ran upstairs to the bedroom and changed out of her work clothes. Once dressed in jeans and a T-shirt, she pulled her long blond hair into a ponytail and grabbed a navy-blue ballcap.

"Am I doing the right thing?" Leslie closed her eyes and thought about what was at stake. After a slow breath in, she listened to her heart. Nothing else mattered but her daughter. Leslie flicked the exhaust fan switch in the guest bathroom before darting downstairs.

She slipped on a pair of running shoes and a hooded sweatshirt from the front hall closet. She pulled down a heavy green backpack from the top shelf and emptied her purse on the couch. The money from her wallet and the spare change went into the pocket of her jeans.

Leslie took two steps away and, with a change of heart, she opened her wallet and removed a small picture from the plastic sleeve. A brief smile lit up her face, and she placed the photo in the front center pocket of the backpack. With a last look at her credit cards, bank card, and driver's license, she left them all behind.

She still had time until it was dark outside. There was no point in leaving early. It didn't take long to make a few roast beef sandwiches and place two water bottles in the pack before she sat at the kitchen table and waited.

Once the sun had set, Leslie slipped out the back door and disappeared into the streets of Alexandria.

Her cell phone sat on the kitchen table, next to her wedding ring and a red, White House identification security badge.

Chapter 5

Noah immediately placed a call to the Alexandria City Police Department and asked for an officer to do a wellness check on Leslie Taylor at her residence.

"I know how you feel about coincidences." Angie paced the small trailer. "What's our next step?"

"We need to find where this came from." Noah held the fingerprint form and placed it on top of the file. "I also want to send the last picture of Angela and her parents to the FBI for their Aging Program to find out what she would look like today. The technology has changed in the last two decades. We may as well make use of it."

Noah had collected several pictures of the young girl before the family had gone on vacation. It would be a good starting point.

"We may not need the FBI's program." Dickinson took a picture of the four-year-old with her phone and ran it through an application on a social media site. Within a minute, she showed Noah the results.

The young woman had high cheekbones, a thin nose, and dimples, with a definite resemblance to Leslie. The blue eyes were the same, and the hairstyle hadn't changed—shoulder-length blond. Angela seemed to stare right at him through the screen. "With these looks, she could be a model."

"I'm not too sure how accurate this free application is, but it would be interesting to compare it to the FBI's results."

Noah handed the phone back. "Can you get that printed out?"

A few minutes later he added the photo to the file and sent the FBI a request for processing. Everything was done through email, and they would respond with a link. Noah would be able to download and print the pictures or share them with law enforcement across the country.

"They have a fairly quick turnaround time. It shouldn't take long."

Dickinson tapped the pile of folders. "I'll start with the current addresses of everyone that was interviewed."

"Make sure to include the highway patrol and the sheriff's officers. Even if to just follow up and see if they recall any other details the reports didn't cover."

After a few minutes of sorting through the folders on the table, Noah pulled out the witness statements. "While we're waiting on the feds, I wanted to contact the highway patrol. I want to see if anyone was pulled over for speeding at that time. Someone screwed up somewhere. We'll get them."

*****

The black Chevy Tahoe parked in front of the end unit townhouse at ten p.m. The nearest streetlamp was seventy-five feet away, and the dim light flickered and warred with the shadows. The interior of the house was dark, as well as the neighbors' houses. When two men in dark suits approached the front door, a security sensor tripped, and the front porch light turned on before they knocked.

The men were in their mid-thirties, fit with short crew-cut hair. They couldn't hide the bulges in their suit jackets from the holstered Sig Sauer P226 pistols.

One man had a short goatee and a deep tan, and the other looked like his nose had broken many years ago, and it never healed straight. Otherwise, they could have been brothers. Short-goatee Man pulled out a five-inch metal rod and a set of keys. The key selected had the ridges filed, making them all a low uniform height. Once placed in the front door lock, he applied pressure until it halted. With the rod, he struck the butt-end of the key and smoothly finished the turn. The door was unlocked without effort. A bump-key entry was faster than picking a lock or kicking down a door. To the casual observer, everything would appear normal.

32

One minute after the vehicle was parked, both men stood inside the home. Jackets were unbuttoned, and calloused hands hovered above the pistol grips while they listened. The man with the short goatee whispered to his partner. "Check upstairs. I'll clear the main floor."

The men separated and LED flashlights flickered to life as they searched the home. The White House ID security badge was discovered on the kitchen table as the doorbell rang.

Seconds later, both stood to the side of the living room window and pulled the curtain back just enough to see a police cruiser parked in front of their vehicle. An officer stood at the front door.

"He will head out soon."

When someone also banged on the back door, one man sighed. "Let's make this quick."

After reaching into his jacket pocket, the man with goatee turned on the living room overhead light and opened the front door.

Startled, the police officer took a step back, and one hand drifted near his holstered pistol. "ACDP doing a wellness check. Can I speak to Mrs. Leslie Taylor, please?"

The young officer wore his patrol blues and black vest. The name tag was velcroed on the front with his rank on the shoulder flashes. His eyes narrowed, and he took a second step back as he noticed a second large man.

The man with a goatee opened a wallet and flashed a badge and ID. "Austin Gordon, Secret Service, and this is agent

Dylan Noland." His partner's wallet held the same gold badge. Special Agent was engraved in the blue banner across the bottom. The officer verified both men matched the photos. "I'd like to ask you a few questions, Constable Simmonds. If you could have your partner join us out front?"

Gordon knew the best line of defense was a solid offense. That technique had worked for most of his career and on the field at Michigan State.

Simmonds paused, and his eyes flicked back and forth between the two agents, then nodded.

The police officer spoke into the microphone on his right shoulder, and his partner quickly joined them. Constable Gibson stood six-foot-eight-inches, and Gordon's neck strained to look him in the eyes. He felt like standing on the last step to even the score.

Noland pulled out his cell phone and showed both officers a recent picture of Leslie Taylor. "Have either of you seen this woman?"

Both officers shook their heads. Simmonds asked, "What's this about?"

Gordon jerked a thumb over his shoulder at the small townhouse. "We have reason to believe Mrs. Taylor has been abducted." He pulled out her security badge. "With her clearance and position, it's considered a matter of national security."

"We were told to check this place out by our staff sergeant and report back. We haven't seen her."

Noland put his phone away. "Do you know who your staff serge—"

His words were lost as the second floor of the townhouse exploded. The windows shattered outward above their heads as they dropped to the ground. A shower of glass and debris rained down over the cruiser and Tahoe. No one was hurt, but the ringing in their ears would last for days.

"Jesus Christ!" Gordon covered his head with his jacket as embers landed around them. Had they been in the house, Dylan would have been dead.

The four men scrambled away from the front door as a second explosion almost lifted the roof.

Flames shot out of the second-floor window, and smoke billowed into the night sky. Alarms sounded from inside the home and a neighbor's parked car. The officers screamed into their radios for assistance as they ran down the pathway. Simmonds immediately moved to the attached townhome and pounded on the front door to wake the neighbors.

Gordon glanced at Noland and shook his head. "Nothing covert about this now."

Dozens of people poured out of their homes. Cell phones recorded the fire, and he knew their images were captured.

"I'll move the car."

Gordon nodded to his partner while he pulled out his cell phone. As the mayhem grew and various neighbors called out to each other, the distant sounds of sirens were clear.

Fuck.

A simple investigation turned into a shit-show. Gordon called in the report as he walked down the street, and the wailing drew closer.

Chapter 6

Noah woke early the next morning, dressed in his gym shorts and a gray T-shirt, and went for a run. After a day of being stuck in the trailer and paperwork, he needed the exercise. It also gave him time to think about what had happened and the phone call he made to the FBI.

He knew it was a simple matter for the automated-aging progression software to develop a new picture. However, after eight hours, Noah called Quantico to find out if there were any problems.

There wasn't a request for processing.

He sent a screenshot attached to a follow-up email proving he had initially sent the request. That was over eleven hours ago, and he hadn't heard back from them yet.

Noah tried to put the computer error out of his mind as he turned north on Pine Street and made his way to the bicycle paths at Rotary Park. The sun had risen only fifteen minutes ago, and for now, he was alone. Most would be getting ready for work or school, and Noah enjoyed the solitude. Soon he was lost in the rhythm, and he slowly increased the pace.

It only took ten minutes to run through the park, over the pedestrian bridge north to cross Main Street. The circuit was four miles, with the last quarter downhill until he returned home.

Noah had garnered a habit over the years to scan vehicles and identify the make, model, and year, while at work. It kept his mind sharp during long shifts, even when not on patrol. Once he was close enough, he would read the plates, and if he were parked at a light or following someone, he would run them. A habit that was encouraged for all officers.

After crossing Main Street and following the sidewalk east, he picked out the three vehicles parked in front of the coffee shop. The first stood out with the Colorado plates, a brown two-year-old Toyota Sienna. The windows were tinted, and he couldn't tell if anyone was in the back seat or not.

The other two vehicles were an older Malibu and an Accord, and both looked familiar. They must have been locals.

As he passed the donut shop, a man and a woman stepped outside, carrying a coffee and a paper bag each. They were dressed in dark suits and headed for the minivan. As Noah ran around them, he caught the woman's eye. He had never seen the middle-aged female before, but her eyes widened in recognition.

He had taken another ten steps when she called out. "Noah Hunter?"

The man and woman stood shoulder to shoulder and faced him. The coffee and bags were placed on the ground behind them. Noah wasn't sure of their intent, and his right hand twitched for a pistol that wasn't there. "How can I help you?"

Despite the run, his adrenaline levels had just spiked.

"We just want to ask you a few questions." The man in the suit spoke in a baritone voice that was deep and methodical. The man stood a few inches taller than Noah with a deep barrel chest and approximately the same age, thirty-eight years old. The woman could have been anywhere between twenty-five and forty-five years old, with a smooth face and upturned nose. Her dark brown hair was pulled back in a severe braid. Noah didn't see any tell-tail bulges of a weapon. As they both took another step toward him, Noah held out a hand.

"That's close enough. What questions do you have?"

The two shared a quick look, then the woman spoke. "Allison Parke, and this is Gary Beaton, Homeland Security."

"Identifications." Noah shifted his weight to the balls of his feet, ready for fight or flight. Allison reached into her jacket and produced a long slim wallet.

A familiar badge and ID were held straight out from the shoulder. Beaton's badge was silver, not gold.

"Why is yours different?"

Beaton gave a half-smile as he placed his wallet back in his pocket. "Office of Operations and Co-ordinations, mid-west region. Someone in headquarters that had always sat behind a desk decided we needed a different color."

The threat level lowered, and Noah relaxed just a little. It wasn't totally gone, only slightly improved. He was never much for coincidences, and *literally* running into two people in town looking for him, seemed too much.

"How can I help you? How do you know me?"

Beaton turned to pick up their drinks and bags while Parke tried to smile. It came across as half grimace before she abandoned that tactic.

"What's your connection to Leslie and Angela Taylor?"

Noah paused. Something didn't seem right. "I'm not at liberty to talk about an active case. If you wish, you can arrange a meeting through the department, and should the chief agree, we can share any information. If there's a need to know."

It was clear Agent Parke wasn't used to being stonewalled, and when her brow furrowed, Noah revised her age closer to fifty. Her cheeks flushed as she stepped toward him. "I strongly suggest you co-operate now and save yourself trouble later on."

"How about you call the station and make an appointment. I'll be free next week." He nodded to Agent Beaton only. "Nice to meet you."

As her mouth opened, Noah spun on his heel and continued his run. Parke swore as she got in the minivan and slammed the door.

Soon as he was out of sight, Noah pulled out his cell phone and activated the security system at his home just in case.

He sent a quick text to the staff sergeant and friend, Steve Hutchings.

>>Feds are sniffing around our case, asking questions.
Stall them if they show up at the station. Omw.

Noah chuckled at the reply as he headed home. Hutchings's response involved sex and travel for the G-men. Not in so many words.

*****

Leslie dropped the backpack and looked along the wide laneway in both directions. At six o'clock in the morning, Sentinel Security Storage was empty.

She was exhausted after a sleepless night, but determination and willpower kept her going. Leslie had paid cash for the local bus and traveled north of Washington to Silver Spring. However, at one in the morning, anyone on foot drew attention. She spent five hours in Jesup Blair Park, sipping on a bottle of water under a spruce tree. With every noise, she was prepared to run. She was wired and couldn't control the tremor in her hands.

Traffic had started at six o'clock in the morning, and she felt safe enough to walk east past the college and Highway 410, blending into the foot traffic. The two-acre lot of storage units were secured with a tall fence and barbed wire. Control was granted through a gate with a passcode. Once through, it quickly closed behind her, and she was lost in the maze of orange-colored doors. Some units were large enough to fit a pickup truck, and others were barely four feet by three.

She pulled out a set of keys from the pack's front pocket and opened the large Master lock at a smaller storage unit. The door was quickly lifted, and she slipped underneath.

A false lock with Velcro was secured on the outside latch. To all appearances, it would look locked. Someone would have to handle the padlock to know it was a decoy.

The interior was five feet by ten, and the only contents were a large green army duffel bag against the far wall. The overhead light worked, but it wasn't worth the risk. A flashlight flickered over the layers of dust on the canvas and floor. No one had been here in a while.

Inside the bag were several smaller containers with different labels: medical kits, freeze-dried food, and a compression bag with clothing. There was also enough backpacking and lightweight camping equipment to make any outdoor enthusiast happy.

A series of titanium poles quickly made the frame, and Leslie stretched the material over the ends to form the cot. A small, waxed canvas bag held a Glock 19, with two loaded magazines and a silencer. With a deft movement, she loaded the pistol and engaged the slide. Loading a round in the chamber brought a sense of relief, and some of the tension eased in her shoulders.

Exhausted, Leslie lay on the cot with her pack as a pillow. She held the small picture of her daughter in the glow of the flashlight.

"Momma's coming, sweetheart. This time, no one is stopping me."

She patted the Glock and rested her hand on the grip as she waited to fall asleep.

One eye remained on the door.

She was ready.

Chapter 7

Noah paced within the conference room's small confines at the station, dressed in jeans and a collared shirt. His suit jacket lay over the back of a chair. He could have passed for a civilian, except for the holstered Glock and badge on his belt. Forty years ago, the room would have been filled with cigarette smoke and the table littered with Styrofoam coffee cups next to overflowing ashtrays, while police officers would have ignored the feds and carried on. Today, the hum of the air conditioner and the crisp sound of papers turning were the only tell-tale signs of action.

Police Chief Jason Birch sat at the head of the table and looked over Noah's statement. After returning home from his run, Noah immediately went to the station and typed up the report. Despite the Homeland Security agent's hidden threats, they had not contacted the station or Noah. When he was done, a second statement had come in. Together they painted a different picture.

Birch cleared his throat and pushed the report across the table while adjusting his dark suit.

Once Angie picked up the papers, Birch shook his head. "I think a hornet's nest has been kicked. As to what it means, I don't know."

The second report was sent from Alexandria Police for the wellness check on Leslie Taylor. It also included a statement from the fire marshal and witnesses on the blast at her residence. The cause of the explosion was unknown. Preliminary investigation led the marshal to believe it was a gas leak.

"The last names are making me question what's going on." Noah pointed at Agent Gordon and Noland's statement. "I was only able to verify they worked for Homeland Security, but that's it. Same as the two agents that I ran into this morning. I couldn't find anything else about them."

Dickinson looked up from the pages. "Wouldn't they find it strange that during a check on the home, it blew up?"

Noah was about to speak when the chief caught his eye and beat him to the punch. "Yes, it stinks of a coverup. The good news is they didn't find a body in the home. Leslie Taylor may still have answers."

"In the meantime?"

Birch gestured to the growing case file. "Start with the fingerprints. They are the only tangible evidence." The chief's phone rang inside his jacket, and he stood. "I have to get back to my office. Keep me informed of any developments."

As he stepped outside the conference room to take the call, Noah sat across from his partner and opened the folder. He held up the large envelope. "The form was delivered by hand or mixed in with the daily mail. We need to know who dropped it off. Follow the paperwork."

Angie agreed. "I'll talk with Bruce and go over the security footage around the station."

"Doesn't the coffee shop across the street have a security camera as well?" Noah wasn't sure what the angle or quality of the recording would be, but better than nothing. "I'll check that out. May as well grab a coffee while I'm there. Do you want one?"

"I'm okay. I just—"

When the loud crash sounded throughout the station, Noah spun around.

The police chief had kicked a chair across the cube, and it crashed into an empty desk. Red-faced, he yelled into the phone. "I won't forget this!"

A dozen officers stood in silence as they watched the drama unfold, but no one moved to step in.

Noah knew without a doubt that the phone call involved the case. When the chief hung up and stared at him through the glass, he realized his hunch was correct. Birch had a haunted look in his eyes, and it spelled trouble.

"Oh, shit ..." Angie whispered.

When the conference room door opened, Noah felt the anger radiate off the chief. He had only seen him this mad once before, and he didn't want to be on the receiving end.

"That was Mayor Cavanaugh. He's ordering the APPD off the case as an official waste of resources. Failure to comply will result in me being fired as chief."

What the hell?

"Can he do that, sir?" Noah couldn't believe the mayor's orders. Chief Birch had less than eight months until retirement, with thirty-six years of service.

"My rank and position are an appointment from the municipality and the council. They can easily remove me with a majority vote."

Noah stood with clenched fists. "Who has the authority to order the mayor?"

Birch took a deep breath and slowly let it out, but it did nothing to change his flushed face. "Ultimately, it's the governor."

Angie spoke through clenched teeth. "Someone *very* high up has sent an order, and they made the governor dance. That narrows it to a small playing field."

Birch agreed. "For now, I have to comply. Officially, you're off the case."

Noah got the hint. "Don't mess up your career, chief. Report that you've given the order."

Noah watched the fire fade from his eyes, and Birch pointed a finger. "CYA."

Noah nodded, and his boss walked out of the meeting room.

Angie looked confused and waited until the door closed. "CYA?"

"Cover your ass. He's telling us to be careful."

She chuckled. "Easy enough. We won't get caught."

"You have one part correct. *I* won't get caught. You are young and have a full career ahead of you." Her eyes widened, and Dickinson started to object, but Noah cut her off. "There isn't a chance, sorry."

Angie frowned and collapsed back into the chair. "I don't like this." She wasn't pouting. A twenty-eight-year-old woman and police officer didn't pout, but she came close. "If you need me, I'm here."

"I know, and I appreciate it."

Noah collected all the paperwork and folders before heading to the administration offices. Susan handled the digitizing of documents, and he would need it done quickly for what he had in mind.

Time for a coffee and then shopping.

Noah would rather be in a shoot-out than go to a busy store, but there wasn't time to order what he needed. Keeping the department at arm's length would be critical for the next stage.

Chapter 8

Noah handed an absence without pay request to HR, and the chief approved it immediately. There was one other stop he had to make before he left the station, and it was going to be painful.

Behind the staff sergeant's desk, Steve Hutchings coordinated the cars on patrol and fielded incoming calls off the station's main lobby. He had pulled himself off the streets when his hip affected his performance, and he could no longer keep up. The image of an old warrior, past his prime, was most people's first impression. Steve could still hold his own if required. The short white hair resembled a crew cut, and, with a stern look, he could head off most trouble before it began.

"Yes, ma'am. I'll send a car over right away. Stay inside." Hutchings rolled his eyes as he hung up. "An elk wandered into a woman's backyard and was sleeping in her flower bed."

Noah chuckled. He had taken many of those calls over the years. Banging garbage can lids would do the job if the cruiser's horn didn't move them. "Welcome to Wyoming."

"Okay, rookie. What's up?" Hutchings sat on the edge of the desk. When he crossed his arms and stared, Noah couldn't hide anything from him. They had known each other too long.

"I've been ordered off the case from the mayor's office. The chief had to comply or be replaced."

When the staff sergeant frowned, Noah could see his teeth grind as his jaw worked back and forth. "I could have retired over a year ago. I'm done with political bullshit."

"Hold on. I want you to hear me out."

Hutchings had already taken the badge off his belt, and his hand hovered over the holster. "Better be quick, Hunter."

"I'm on a leave of absence. I plan on two stops, the first in Alexandria and the next in the Miami FBI field office. That's the processing hub for Florida. I can't let this go."

"I'm coming with you." Noah's hand rose in the air as he objected, and Hutchings batted it down. "Don't be an idiot. You can't stop me. I've waited too long to finish this case. I want this done, and then I can retire."

It was Noah's turn to be stern, but the look did nothing to faze the grizzled sergeant. Hutchings picked up the phone and dialed the duty captain.

"Sir, I'm not feeling well. I should be back to work in a month or so. I have almost three years of sick time saved up. I need you to approve." He waited for a moment to listen. "Immediately."

Noah heard the yelling over the phone from four feet away, but Hutchings just shrugged. "No offense, Captain, but I'm informing you what's happening, not asking for permission. Not feeling well. I have to go."

When he hung up, Noah realized his jaw had dropped. "Seriously?"

"Don't pull a stunt like that unless you've been here thirty years or more. Come on, rookie. We have things to do." Hutchings called Lieutenant Bydal to fill the staff position. Moments later, Noah left the station, back with his first partner on an unofficial case.

*****

Terry Clarke had worked for Knight Security for eight years. His dreams of working for the Alexandria Police Department were sunk for the second time twelve months ago. He had the height and muscle required for the position at six-foot-one-inches, but he couldn't pass the physical portion despite passing the written exam with flying colors.

The last year wasn't wasted.

Terry worked out twice a day, stopped the junk food, and at twenty-nine years old, he was in the best shape of his life.

Next week, he would apply for the third time, and he was more than prepared.

However, there were bills to pay until he was accepted, and he didn't want to give up the security job. Terry drove the patrol car, cruising through construction sites and office buildings during his shift, making sure doors were locked.

At four in the morning, he drove through Sentinel Storage. The Tahoe's spotlight swung back and forth from a practiced hand as he scanned the shadows and checked the locker doors. The security gates wouldn't stop someone from climbing over, and a cordless grinder would make the best padlocks open—hence the need for boots on the ground. Thefts had dropped since the patrols had started, and the storage company owners had increased security.

The midnight to eight o'clock shift was usually quiet, and at the mid-point, Terry would stop for his lunch. The back corner of the two-acre lot had a picnic table next to Q Block where he usually took a break.

As he ate the salad and hard-boiled eggs, he flipped through examples of the police exam on his phone. He knew the answers by heart and looked forward to retaking the test.

Thirty minutes later, his break over, Terry climbed back into the vehicle and called headquarters over the radio.

"HQ, this is Rover One. All clear, over."

"Rover One, roger. Out."

When the headlights swept across the front of T Block, one padlock looked out of place. It hung at an angle and looked open. The gap between the shackle and the body was obvious.

He threw the vehicle in park, and the tactical flashlight came to life as he stepped outside. The radio handset squelched as other patrols reported, and the sound echoed down the rows of storage units.

The flashlight scanned the area. Terry couldn't hear anything, and the other units were intact. Storage locker T-12 wasn't secure. The lock was held on with Velcro but had slipped at an angle.

It rolled upward easily when he tested the door, like a garage door on tracks.

A pair of hands grabbed his ankles and pulled sharply at the two-foot mark. Terry fell flat on his back and with a cry of fear as he was dragged inside the unit. The flashlight spun in a circle as the door slammed closed.

Anyone outside would have heard a hollow thump as Terry's struggles ceased, but there were no witnesses. Moments later, the storage unit door opened, and a woman stepped outside. She shouldered a large duffel bag and darted away from the scene.

The patrol car's dash security camera recorded the assault and the look of anger on the woman's face. The police would be on scene within the hour when Terry failed to check in with HQ. Two hours after that, law enforcement would be reviewing footage and the screenshots uploaded while the security officer was recovering in the hospital.

One man struggled to suppress the image from spreading from an office eight miles away.

It was too late.

A White House reporter recognized the woman, and every news outlet picked up the story for the morning news cycle.

Chapter 9

Leslie Taylor is wanted for questioning by the secret service and the FBI, scrolled across the bottom of the news feed, and two pictures flashed across the screen. The first photo was a stock image taken by White House security, and the second was from a dash camera earlier in the morning.

"Are you seeing this?" Noah pulled the phone out of his suit pocket and verified the story.

The plane landed at Ronald Regan Airport mid-morning, and the two police officers dressed smartly in dark suits debarked from their direct flight. Noah hated wearing a suit and tie, but he deferred to his partner's opinion. A suit in Washington helped you blend in, and they didn't want to be noticed.

Hutchings nodded. "She's on the run."

Noah found the developing story all over social media and news websites. "Leslie was holed up in a storage unit and assaulted a security guard."

"Definitely running." Hutchings followed as they made their way to the procession of rental companies.

"How this relates to her daughter and the explosion, I don't know." Noah ran a hand through his short hair and shook his head in disbelief.

"Same here, rookie. Let's go."

A new Suburban SUV rental easily held their carry-on bags, and Noah punched in the address in the navigation system. Despite the late morning hour, traffic was bad, and it took them sixty minutes instead of twenty.

The neighborhood was mainly townhomes, with a small dog park near the bus stop. The last house was surrounded by yellow barricade tape, and the lingering smell of burnt wood carried half a block.

A red minivan from the Alexandria Fire Marshal blocked the end of the driveway next to a police cruiser.

Two men dressed in dark blue coveralls and white hard hats looked over a clipboard next to the van while the cop sat behind the wheel, engaged on his phone. After he parked next to the cruiser, the young Alexandria officer finally noticed them, quickly exited, and waited.

There was no hiding the look Noah and Hutchings carried despite the suits.

They were cops.

Noah pulled out his wallet, and when he flashed the gold badge, the officer didn't notice a finger blocking *Arrow Point*.

"Detective Hunter and Sergeant Hutchings."

Steve also flashed his badge in the same manner. They didn't want to let others know an out-of-state police officer was asking questions until required as they had no real authority to work outside their jurisdiction.

"Officer Cranston. How can I help you?"

The tall man looked to be in his mid-twenties and new to the job. However, his gray shirt and dark blue pants were pressed and sharp. Watch duty for a crime scene was usually given to the new officers, regardless of the city. Noah counted on that.

"We're here to see if there are any new developments from the marshal."

Cranston shrugged. "They don't tell me much. The deputy marshal is here now. Go on in."

Noah ducked under the tape. The technician entered the van to work on a laptop while the deputy marshal waited for them.

As they walked toward the smaller dark-skinned man, he barked, "Are you the guys that got me called in on my day off?"

The Italian accent was thick, and Noah didn't understand him for a moment. He spoke in a rush, so all the words blended.

"Sorry, nothing to do with us." Noah introduced them again but kept the badges away. "We're the initial investigators, and we are looking for any information or developments."

The deputy marshal tapped his pen on the clipboard and studied them. "Reports were filed late last night. Someone didn't like the answers, and I was called in, *on my day off,* to verify the findings."

Hutchings stepped forward to talk to him while Noah examined the home. Noah found it strange that after eighteen years, they fell back into the old habits without conscious thought.

The townhome was the last unit at the end of a row, and the top floor was partially intact. Crumbled brick and glass were scattered over the lawn and road. The ground was still soaked from the fire crews a day and a half ago, and the interior hadn't dried out. Large holes gaped in the roof where the flames had burned through, but the adjoining home didn't have any damage.

As Noah stepped through the doorway, the deputy marshal called out. "You're going to get your suit dirty."

He waved his hand in acknowledgment and stepped through the door. The interior was destroyed by water on the lower level, and crews had torn large holes in the wall to check for lingering hot spots. Most of the living room ceiling had collapsed. The investigators had cleared a path.

Despite the fire and the thirty-six hours, a distinct scent hit Noah when he climbed the stairs to the second floor.

When he was in the military, explosives were used on many UXOs (unexploded ordinances) at the range and in Afghanistan. A faint hint of sulfur mixed with tar clung to the surface for days after use, and it wasn't an odor he would forget.

The home's second floor took the brunt of the explosion, including a hole in the ceiling the size of a king bed. Noah could see where the blast originated in the second-floor laundry room despite his lack of training. A blind man would have spotted it.

The investigators had placed temporary flooring down so they wouldn't fall through to the living room, but there was no need for Noah to go farther. Either Leslie tried to cover her tracks or she set a trap. The other option was someone had made an attempt on her life, and it failed.

That would explain the coverup.

"Hey, rookie. You done?"

"Ya, coming down." Noah took one last look and willingly left. There wouldn't be anything to find in the rubble. Hutchings stood in the doorway as he came down the stairs into the living room. The couch and recliner were littered with drywall and still wet from the water. On the middle couch cushion, a handle from a purse stuck in the air. Noah shifted a chunk of drywall and lifted the bag.

Empty.

Hutchings looked over his shoulder. "I'll block. Hurry."

Noah didn't waste time and flipped debris until he found the scattered contents. Wedged between the cushions was a woman's wallet, burgundy with a gold clasp and a long zipper along the back. There were other items, but he didn't have time to go through them. Hutchings was talking with the deputy marshal right outside the front door.

He tucked the wallet inside the suit jacket, and once outside, he brushed imaginary dirt from his clothes.

It isn't much, but it may help.

*****

A young man sat on a bench across the street at the dog park and flipped through a tablet while reading. White earbuds were hidden by long brown hair. Dressed in jeans and a collared shirt, he looked comfortable with legs crossed and his jacket on the seat beside him.

The short beard and sunglasses hid his features, but he never looked around. His eyes were glued to the tablet's screen.

Underneath the jacket, a Sigma 150-600m lens had a clear view of the home and the new visitors. Thick fingers tapped the screen, and several dozen closeup pictures were captured. The older man with white hair and suit shook the investigator's hand while the younger man started the SUV.

The man shifted his right hand on the jacket, and the front of the Suburban came into focus. There were a few more taps on the screen, and the plate number was recorded.

Seconds later, the images were uploaded, and it didn't take the facial recognition software long to find a match.

Chapter 10

"Are you sure this is going to work?"

Noah had parked in the Walmart parking lot, next to a Wendy's restaurant. They had a full view of the Sunoco gas station at the end of the strip plaza, one hundred and twenty feet away. The parking spaces around them began to fill up by mid-afternoon as people stopped by on their way home to grab some groceries or fast food. The gas station had a steady stream of customers coming and going.

Leslie Taylor's wallet contained everything a modern human needed to survive in the industrial world—a library card, credit and debit cards, and a driver's license. Anything that was personal and could be used to identify or trace her whereabouts was left behind.

Before they had parked, Hutchings had gone to the station and left the debit card on top of pump six. It had a *tap to pay* under a certain amount and didn't require a PIN.

"We're about to find out." Hutchings took the large cowboy hat and threw it in the backseat. The wide brim kept his face from being recorded by the overhead cameras. A minivan pulled in for gas. The driver, an older woman, was not tall enough to see on top of the pump, and after filling up, she drove off.

They didn't have to wait long for another customer. A gray Hyundai SUV now occupied the same spot, and a teenager got out and opened the filler cap. When he picked up the debit card, he looked around the station for the owner, but no one ran forward. With a smile on his face, the card tapped against the reader and filled the tank.

"Bingo." Hutchings grinned. "It's a nice neighborhood, but in the end, people are all the same."

"*Some* people. Not all."

"True enough."

Noah glanced at the time. Four-thirty in the afternoon. "Best guess for a response time?"

Hutchings shrugged and leaned back in the seat. "I would say between fifteen to twenty minutes? Even if someone is monitoring, they have to send the call, and a team is deployed."

They didn't have that long to wait. Only two minutes after the card was tapped, things started happening. The concussive thump of rotor-wash was almost felt as the UH-60M tactical helicopter flew in low, barely over the buildings, and hovered twenty feet over the gas station. In the distance, the wail of sirens drew close.

Noah's jaw dropped, and he glanced at Hutchings. "You have to be kidding me."

The side door of the helicopter swung open, and a figure dressed in green combat fatigues leaned out with the butt of an H&K MP5 jammed into his shoulder. The muzzle swept the crowd for a target. Many had stepped out of the restaurant and stood in the parking lot as the drama unfolded like an action movie before their eyes. Cell phones appeared and recorded the scene from dozens of angles.

Virginia Avenue traffic came to a standstill at the three-minute mark as two unmarked SUVs screeched through the intersection and blocked access to the parking lot. Strobe lights flashed behind tinted windows as men in suits got out and sprinted toward the gas station.

"I've heard of a Quick Reaction Force, but this is ridiculous." Noah shook his head. "Are they even allowed to fly here?"

The White House was within fifteen miles, and the area was a well-known no-fly zone.

Hutchings jerked a thumb toward a series of people that didn't want to stick around and watch the show. Many had forgone their cars and made their way on foot. The parking lot was quickly emptying. "We got our answer. Fairly sure we don't want to get caught here, rookie."

All the customers at the gas station, including the young woman who worked inside, were face down on the ground as more suits arrived. Everyone was being detained, and they would sort it out later.

The helicopter slowly circled the area, and Noah could feel the unease in his stomach. "This is several pay grades above us, Hutch."

For the first time, Noah noticed his old partner looked nervous as they shook their heads at the confusion they had created.

"You can say that again."

"I'm thinking we rely on good old-fashioned police work. You up for it?"

The staff sergeant nodded and kept his gaze fixed on the side mirror as they exited the parking lot from the east exit. Noah couldn't help but wonder how badly they kicked the hornet's nest.

Chapter 11

When Noah raised his eyebrows, the woman nodded again. "Honest, I told the other officers everything I knew."

Carol worked at the Sentinel Storage offices, and a series of law enforcement officials from various departments had questioned her all yesterday and early this morning at her home. The woman was in her mid-forties and had platinum hair tied to the side, with large, hooped earrings. Her makeup was applied heavily with dark eyeshadow and bright red lipstick. She wore a denim shirt with the company logo on the breast pocket, a stylized white "S" over a dark padlock.

Hutchings stood to the side and looked through the display case's rent rates and unit sizes.

"You've never met the person that rented the unit?"

She shook her head, and the earrings clinked like miniature wind chimes. "The unit was rented out several years ago, long before I started working here. I've never seen her before."

Noah pulled out a notebook and pen from inside his suit pocket and took brief notes.

Hutchings tapped the Plexiglas over the unit rates. "How far in advance was that storage unit paid?"

Carol turned to the computer to call up the answer. "It was a fifteen-year contract. Due to rate changes, there were only four years left."

Noah thought through various scenarios. "What was the method of payment?"

Her nails clicked on the keyboard once more. "It wasn't recorded, so I'm guessing someone paid cash at the time."

After some scribbling on the paper, Noah did the math. "She would have paid over five thousand dollars in cash?"

"I'm not sure if it was rented to a he or she. As I told the other officers, it was rented long-term to a corporation. Only a nine-digit business code."

30995818-5

Noah copied it down and thanked her. "Hopefully, there are no more questions from other agencies. There isn't much communication between various officers, so we all have to follow up."

Carol grinned. "That's okay. You can visit any time."

Noah ignored the muffled chuckle from his partner and took a business card off the counter. "If I have any more questions, I'll give you a call."

Hutchings held the door for him as they made their way back to the Suburban.

Noah only took a few steps before they both halted. "Shit."

Noah's stomach dropped when he saw a black Tahoe parked next to their rental.

There were three large men in dark blue suits, sunglasses, and a coiled earpiece standing by the driver's door. Noah noted the bulge in the jackets and the holstered pistols at their hips.

"We knew it was coming. Ready, rookie?"

He was about to reply when one of the men opened the SUV's rear door, and an older man stepped out dressed in dark pants and a green golf shirt. His short white hair and bearing reminded Noah of a military officer.

Someone used to authority.

"Ah, Noah Hunter and Steven Hutchings. I figured it's time we talked."

Chapter 12

Miriam Davis closed the briefing notes on the conference table as President Monroe rose and shook hands with the Canadian ambassador. That was the signal everyone waited for, and the remainder also stood. The afternoon briefing with Homeland Security and the Canadian Security Intelligence Service (CSIS) filled the JFK conference room, along with a team of photographers. The annual Joint Border Threat and Risk Assessment meeting was mostly posturing for the media, but the Quebec border's increased security would be welcome.

She slid her glasses back up her nose and shook the hand of her counterpart, Patrick LeBlanc, the CSIS deputy director. "Nice to meet you, Mr. LeBlanc."

"Call me Patrick. You as well."

They posed for the typical photos, and she stood off to the side, out of the limelight. The disaster prevention and management director within Homeland Security kept her in the spotlight more than she cared. Director Johnson was overseas coordinating with the US counterparts on operational security measures and information sharing. He usually dealt with high-profile meetings.

After nearly two decades in the Office of Special Operations, she was well prepared for whatever Homeland Security could throw at her. The transfer from the CIA was natural and a stepping stone. She had risen through the ranks for the last eighteen years soon after HLS was formed from the ashes of 9/11.

As everyone made their way out of the conference room, her cell vibrated. Miriam braced both hands on the table to hold herself up when the codes flashed on the screen.

Her blood pressure spiked, and the pounding in her ears drowned out the dull roar of the dozen conversations in the room. Before she left the meeting, she fired off a quick text. It took several deep breaths to calm down as a shaking hand slid the phone into her briefcase. When she straightened out the dress suit and adjusted her glasses once again, only her flushed cheeks and darting glances gave away the inner turmoil.

Several minutes later, her driver navigated the staff car south to the Homeland Security building on 7th Street. During the ten-minute commute, she calmed enough to start thinking properly again. Miriam turned off her phone and removed the battery as she watched the sunset across the Washington Canal.

As they arrived in front of the offices, she changed her mind. "It's been a long day. Can you just drop me off at home, Juan?"

The driver glanced in the rearview mirror and smiled. "No problem, ma'am."

Miriam was about to correct him yet again when she saw the twinkle in his eyes. She had tried to get him to call her Miriam for the past eight years, but he'd never done so.

A few miles west of Arlington National Cemetery was a small subdivision called Virginia Square. She had bought a two-story Victorian home in dire need of repairs many years ago. Slowly, the renovations had restored the house to its natural beauty, and it was one treasure she cherished. She had sat on the front porch swing many evenings and watched the neighborhood kids play baseball in Quincy Park across the street. It was her calming island in a sea of turmoil.

Miriam never married and had no children. There had been several short-term relationships during her career, but her first love was the job.

When Juan pulled into her driveway, she caught his eye in the mirror. "Take the rest of the evening and all of tomorrow off. You'll not be needed."

"Thank you, ma'am."

Once inside, she threw her case into the office before darting upstairs to change. A glance out the second-floor window showed the sun would set in a few minutes.

"Hurry up, old lady."

From the back of her closet, she dug out a silver-gray tracksuit and sweater that had never been worn.

"It's never too late to start working out." She paused in the mirror and added, "As well as, start talking to yourself."

She couldn't help but let out a nervous chuckle as she dressed in several layers. Miriam also ignored the shaking in her hands as she sat behind the desk and fired up the computer. The alert codes from earlier had started a chain reaction out of her control, which was more than unusual. What was about to happen couldn't be stopped, but it could be guided like a missile strike.

A flurry of emails were sent, and transactions finished before her watch chimed.

9:30 p.m.

After she stood and closed everything down, Miriam glanced around at her beautiful home one last time and let out a sigh. She was never one to shirk from duty.

The antique walnut desk top drawer tended to stick, but with a squeak, it opened.

A large black box filled the drawer with a single button on top. Once pressed, the LED screen lit up, and she placed her thumb on the reader. When the single *beep* filled the office, Miriam removed her glasses and left them on the desk.

Her blood pressure spiked once again, and the pounding in her ears matched the rhythm in her chest as she unlocked the front door.

The lights across the street from the baseball diamond were off, and only a few distant streetlamps pushed back the shadows. She knew it wouldn't matter.

Miriam left the lights on, the door unlocked behind her, and crossed the road to the park.

By the time her watch sounded a single chime, she stood on second base and stared out into the darkness.

"Just get this over with before I die of old age!" Her shout carried across the outfield and park. A lone dog barked in response.

When the single flash of rifle fire caught her eye three hundred yards out, she wasn't surprised. Miriam had no time to react. Her feet left the ground as she was hurtled backward from the force of the impact.

The residents of Virginia Square never heard the shot, let alone the sound of a body collapsing into the dirt.

When the sun came up the next morning, there was only a small disturbance on the ground.

Chapter 13

"Keys." The taller man, who opened the rear door, held out a hand, palm up.

Noah had a quick look at the others. They were ready to handle any situation he could create. He wasn't armed, having left his Glock in Wyoming. Even if he was, this wasn't the time or place to start a scene.

It isn't worth it—time to see who's pulling strings.

He pulled out the rental keys and passed them over without a word.

The man gave him a brief nod of acceptance while the man in the golf shirt gestured to the rear seat of the Tahoe. "Gentlemen, after you."

The bench was suddenly crowded with Noah against the passenger door and one guard squeezed in tight. Hutchings was pressed against the driver's side door after being slammed closed.

73

The man in the golf shirt got in the front seat while the last suit monkey got behind the wheel. The older man in front turned toward them while he talked.

"First, I applaud your efforts. Well, done. Second, both of you are jeopardizing a national security situation by making it worse."

"I don't mean to be rude. But who the hell are you?" Noah shifted to free his right hand and rested it on his lap. Ready to open the door if required. However, they were now on the interstate and going too fast to bail.

The man chuckled. "I'm the one who has to piece together this whole operation while trying to contain it."

Hutchings had enough. "Since I don't see any identification, I'm considering this an unlawful abduction of two police officers."

The man between them tensed as his eyes flicked back and forth. Noah could see the grip of a Sig Sauer 226 in a shoulder harness when his jacket gapped open. Wedged tight, he wouldn't be able to draw the pistol at his hip.

The man in the front chuckled. "Consider it all you want, but you both are working, not just outside your pay grade, but jurisdiction as well."

When the older man reached into his jacket pocket and pulled out a cell phone, he flipped through the images before chuckling. "I'm impressed, and not much does that anymore." He turned the screen so Noah and Steve could see. A large cowboy hat rested on the backseat of the Suburban. "You should have ditched the hat as soon as possible. It was evidence. But today's show kept many people on their toes. Well, done."

Noah remained silent. With the gas station's information and knowledge, this man would have to be high up on the food chain. How high or what the repercussions would be, Noah couldn't guess. FBI or Homeland Security were his top choices.

But when he saw the signs on the interstate, the tension in his stomach didn't go away completely, but it eased.

Washington Dulles International Airport, 2 miles.

Hutchings continued to stare straight ahead into the back of the driver's head, his fists clenched tight. Noah took the time to study the driver's profile and burn their faces into his memory. There was nothing he could do now but prepare for next time. If there was a next time. The adage *you never learn while talking* came to mind, and he kept silent.

When they pulled into the departure drop-off, their rental driver already had their carry-on bags sitting on the curb. Yet another man dressed in a similar suit waited for them, but this guy looked like a professional wrestler squeezed into a jacket. He must have stood six-foot-seven inches with a goatee and shaved head.

"Gentlemen, we have arrived. Enjoy your flight home, and any attempt to return will be dealt with harshly. The security of the country depends on this." The man in the front of the car didn't even bother turning around to talk with them. Noah's door was opened, and shortly, he stood next to his bag.

Hutchings slid out and joined him.

He leaned down inside the car. "Have a good *fucking* day, asshole," then he slammed the door. Noah couldn't help but grin as he heard the taller man chuckle.

"This way, please."

The two men escorted them through the airport and straight through security. They arrived at the gate for United as they were boarding.

The tall man handed them each a pass. "Sorry about this. There isn't much we can do. I did upgrade your seats, though."

Noah knew they were under orders and just doing their job. It wasn't their fault the boss was a dick. "Thank you."

"We have to confirm you are on board and leaving."

Hutchings nodded. "Understood. Tell your boss to watch his ass if he ever comes to Wyoming."

Both men grinned while Noah shouldered his bag and handed his pass to the attendant at the counter. Moments later, under escort, he buckled into his seat. Hutchings handed their carry-on bags to an attendant and ordered a scotch on the rocks. "If they are paying for this, may as well enjoy it."

Their escorts left, and Noah unbuckled. The curtain was still open to the main cabin, and he noticed a young army soldier in his combat uniform halfway back on the full flight. The idea firmed in his mind, and he turned to Hutchings.

"We were firmly told *not* to return. Correct?"

Steve winced and nodded. "What are you thinking, rookie?"

"Sorry, Hutch. This is the part that you won't like ..."

Chapter 14

Noah pulled out his phone and made sure it was on before passing it to Hutchings. "I need whatever cash you have on hand."

"Do I want to know what's going on?" Hutchings handed over sixty dollars.

He shook his head and grabbed his small bag. "I'll call you on your cell and keep you updated if I can. I'll send something to your work email."

"I don't like this, Hunter. Be careful."

With boarding pass in hand, Noah made his way down the aisle to the rear of the plane. He stopped in front of the soldier. "Excuse me, can I see your pass?"

Confused, the man handed it over, and Noah slid it into his suit pocket. "Ah. I see the problem." Noah handed him *his* boarding pass. "It seems you are in the wrong seat Corporal Frith. You're now in first class. Thank you for your service."

The young soldier grinned as a few people around them smiled at the situation. "Are you serious?"

"As a heart attack. Enjoy it." Noah shook his hand and escorted Frith to his former seat. Then, with a nod to Hutchings, he waited until the attendant moved into the galley. When another woman took her place at the door, he stepped forward.

"Excuse me, but there's been a family emergency, and I have to leave."

"So sorry to hear. In another minute, it would have been too late. Do you have any checked luggage?" Noah handed her the boarding pass and shook his head. She used the radio to call the service desk. "I have a Ben Frith, seat 23B departing due to an emergency."

Moments later, Noah stood on the walkway back into the terminal while the doors to the plane closed behind him. The airline attendant who checked his boarding pass at the gate briskly walked down the hall, and Noah pulled out his wallet. A quick flash of the badge and identification was enough to give her pause.

"The men that escorted us inside. Are they still here?"

"They're at the window. Is there something wrong?"

The radio rose in her hand, and Noah quickly reassured her. "I have reason to believe they may not be federal agents. I've been ordered to follow at a distance. They can't know I have left the plane. This is a matter of national security."

He didn't mind borrowing the standard line. However, the effect on the woman was evident. Her eyes widened, and she grinned. "Really? This is just like the movies."

Noah tucked the wallet back in his pocket and nodded. "Except real lives are on the line."

Face flushed with excitement, she nodded. "Follow me."

The woman brought the radio up and made a call. "United 454 is cleared. I'm taking a quick break, Cynthia."

"United 454 is cleared," came over the speaker as the woman opened a service door with her badge. She led Noah down the steps and opened another door that led into the terminal. He stood in the area where the handlers loaded the baggage, and several gave him a curious look as he was escorted to the employee door.

"Thank you so much. I appreciate it."

"No problem. Flight 545 should be taxiing on the runway and ready for takeoff." The woman seemed to be enjoying the situation. "Good luck."

Noah gave her a wink as he opened the door and, after leaving another hallway, merged with a crowd of people at the taxi stand. Eighty feet ahead was the Tahoe parked against the curb. He could see the driver still behind the wheel, but the tint was too dark to view in the back.

The number of people being dropped off and those waiting on taxis acted as camouflage. Noah easily blended in with the suit and small bag. As he stood next in line, the two men that had escorted him on the plane exited the building. The tall bald man stood out from the crowd as the setting sun gleamed off his bald head.

"Where to?"

Noah slid into the backseat and flashed his badge to the driver. "Right now, we are going to follow that SUV at a safe distance."

The older cabbie didn't even blink at the request, but he readjusted his ballcap. "That ain't a problem. You *are* paying. Right?"

Noah chuckled. "Only if cash is good enough for you."

"Perfect."

The driver didn't engage the meter when they pulled away from the curb.

True to the instructions, the taxi remained several vehicles back as they got on the 267 East. "If they get on the toll, you're paying extra."

When they merged on the I-66 East, the cabbie nodded. "They're going downtown."

"You're doing good and earning your tip. Thanks."

Once they crossed the Potomac River, the Tahoe took the first exit on the right. Noah wasn't familiar with the area, and when they turned south on 23rd Street NW, the cabbie pulled over. The SUV went through the controlled gates on the west side of the road. He didn't see any signs. "What's that place?"

The cabbie glanced in the rearview mirror. "Executive entrance for the White House."

How could the spooks be involved with Leslie Taylor and her daughter?

Noah shook his head. "Good job. Thanks. Can you drop me off at a shopping center? I have some things to pick up."

He had the resources, and despite his misgivings about how they were secured, it was time to use them.

Chapter 15

Noah stood outside Chase Bank on Wisconsin Avenue, in the heart of Georgetown. The cobblestone streets and architecture enhanced the fashion and designer shops, and upscale restaurants were on every block. The sun had set, but the area was well lit for all the foot traffic. He didn't choose this bank at random, but because of its hours of operation. At nine p.m. on a Friday, Chase Bank was the only option. Noah was glad he wore a suit as he opened the glass doors and stepped inside. First impressions were everything in this city, and the clothes helped him blend in.

When Noah helped his former fiancée take down her uncle, a mafia boss in Chicago, she had drained the hidden bank accounts. Then, after the US Marshals had taken her uncle and lawyer into custody, Megan disappeared into the witness protection program. And if Noah knew Megan, and he did, there was no doubt she had vanished from there as well. He recovered from his wounds and found out what she had done.

Megan had transferred ninety-two million dollars into various accounts worldwide, with Noah as the sole owner. Over the last year, Noah had slowly filtered some of the money back into Arrow Point. As a result, the homeless shelter and church received sizeable donations. The local food bank could now afford to pay their volunteers with the influx of money. Noah didn't want fame or recognition. He just wanted to remain anonymous.

The FBI would have gone through all the financial records and attempted to track all funds. Megan had shifted accounts and filtered it enough that it would be near-impossible to trace, but he knew he would be under scrutiny for years to come. That only left him one option—a false identity.

John Visser, an entrepreneur from Canada, was born.

The money was transferred into various accounts several times before it was deposited in the JPT Institution in the Caribbean. The Caribbean banking laws have been more secure than Switzerland in later years. The corporations were created and owned by more corporations and eventually a trust. The layering effect kept prying eyes from finding out any details. Through a lawyer in Montreal, Quebec, properties and assets were purchased. In order to access any money, financial loans were arranged through US banks against properties for cash to be accessible. Noah only needed an authorization code and an email with the transaction details required, and it would be done. The lawyer had never spoken to John Visser, and Noah intended they never had to do so. Everything had been arranged by email, and all invoices were promptly paid.

On paper, a second corporation was based out of Dayton, Ohio, to avoid law enforcement scrutiny. So long as taxes were covered, the CD Consulting Firm flew under the radar as they bought real estate and sold for profit. As Noah tried to burn through the money, even with donations, the nest egg continued to grow as property values sky-rocketed.

None of that included the small bag of cash stored away in a shed on a remote property Megan had secured as a fallback position. Almost another two million dollars.

This method got around foreign funds being tracked by the IRS and Homeland Security. Transfers over ten thousand dollars were flagged by the financial institutions for the IRS, but they could not pierce the veil of an off-shore trust.

The anti-fraud courses he had attended year after year came in handy at times.

He had stepped over the line, but he justified the wealth by giving it away and using it for good. The money would have lined politicians' pockets and solidified the mafia's organization in ways he couldn't imagine. So that balanced the internal war of right versus wrong in his mind.

For now, he needed to draw on the funds to further the investigation. Buying the burner phone and the taxi used up the last of his cash, and credit cards were not an option. Besides a few changes of clothes and the suit, Noah had nothing.

His dress shoes clicked against the polished stone floors as he approached the service desk. "I'm here to pick up a package for CD Consulting."

The woman behind the desk smiled. "Just one moment, sir." She pulled up the information with a series of fingernails clicking on a keyboard. "I have to get the bank manager to authorize release. I'll be right back."

The young woman soon returned with a middle-aged dark-skinned gentleman dressed in a similar suit, dark blue with a red tie. "Thank you for doing business with Chase Bank. If you will come around and enter your transaction code and password."

Moments after entering the information, Noah shook his hand and walked out of the bank with a large manila envelope clutched in his left hand. Nine-thousand dollars cash and a corporate credit card tied to a newly opened bank account. The lawyer had come through in record time.

Noah opened his wallet and removed a business card.

Despite the late hour, it was time to go back to work.

Chapter 16

"Thank you for staying late. It's appreciated."

Once again, Noah leaned entered the Sentinel Storage offices while Carol locked the office door behind him. "Not a problem, honey. Glad to help."

"I just need to confirm all bases were covered."

Carol grinned. "Which base are you on now?"

Noah tried not to wince as he looked at his notebook. "Going back fifteen years, how many other units have been rented out long-term?"

Noah's military career was only two years and two tours, but the infantry unit and training had left a lasting impression. During the patrol briefings, in case of contact or separation, a rendezvous point was always designated, as well as a fallback or secondary position. The storage unit could have been considered an RV point, and if Noah had time to plan, he would have had a secondary place nearby. The next storage facility was six miles away, leaving few options.

"We're not supposed to give out customer information." Carol gave him a wink as she scrolled through the rental agreements. "This won't take long."

She wrote down a series of numbers and dates on a notepad while one finger tapped against a keyboard. "There are quite a few long-term agreements, but these are the ones from ten to sixteen years ago." Finished, she tore the page off the pad and passed it over. "You can't mention where you got this. It isn't much, but I need this job."

"You have my promise." Noah scanned the notes and smiled. Six units with dates were more than he hoped.

"Thank you so much. Hopefully, there won't be any problems. I'll be back in the morning or the next day."

Noah headed to the parking lot after saying good night and got in a compact rental car. Having a vehicle was essential, and the risk was low. While he did have to show a driver's license, it was paid for with the corporate credit card. Someone would have to search each rental agreement in the state for his name. One day, it may come to that, but he would deal with it then. For now, he was under the radar.

After starting the car, he didn't travel far. A small plaza with a dry cleaner and nail salon was a hundred yards down the road. The empty parking lot had a direct line of sight to the Sentinel Storage.

A minute later, Carol turned off the office lights and locked the front door. She climbed in her small Honda and headed home. Noah turned on the dome light and looked at the list.

Three of the units were only four by three feet and were dismissed. The next two were larger and paid monthly by credit card. Five of the six units had a first and last name attached. The last on the list was the exception.

6634990-8

A corporate account paid in full for twenty years for locker seven on T Block—an eight by twelve-foot heated room.

Noah didn't believe in coincidences as a general rule.

The familiar sense of excitement made Noah grin as he pulled the small bag out of the backseat. He didn't have time to buy more appropriate attire, but jeans and a green T-shirt with running shoes would do the job. After changing, Noah locked the car and made his way along the side of the property. He had spotted security cameras at the front gate, and they were easily avoided.

However, it left him with a daunting task. The eight-foot fence had a foot of barbed wire along the top. Moving between a spruce tree and the lot's rear corner, Noah planted the running shoe's toe in the diamond-shaped opening. Then, with a grunt of effort, he began the slow climb. Old injuries made his right shoulder ache, but Noah was physically fit and could ignore it. At the top, he carefully stepped over the barbed wire and dropped down onto the grass near a picnic table. Unsure of what may happen next, he moved the table closer to the corner in case he had to leave in a hurry.

Security lights illuminated the main gate and the interior aisles. Staying close to the building and away from the fence, Noah followed the letter sequence north until he found T Block.

He had to get within arm's length to read the numbers.

At number seven, he paused and took a deep breath before he gently knocked against the metal door and whispered. "Leslie Taylor, open up. It's Detective Noah Hunter. I'm alone."

Chapter 17

Noah couldn't help but glance over his shoulder as he tilted an ear to listen. Gently he pressed his fingertips against the cold steel door and waited. He was about to knock again when the muffled noise of a foot scraping against concrete sounded from inside.

"I promise there's no one else with me. We need to talk."

With startling speed, the door was flung upward. Despite taking a step back, Noah found himself staring into the muzzle of a silencer—mere inches from his face.

"Step inside, and face the wall." Leslie gestured with her chin, and the weapon didn't waver. A dim flashlight illuminated the small ten by twelve locker propped in the rear corner. A large duffel bag and backpack were the only items inside he could see.

Noah felt the weapon pressed into his lower back as he was guided to face the wall. After Leslie lowered the door, deft fingers checked his pockets and frisked him from head to toe.

"Are you wearing a wire?"

"No one knows I'm here. No wire." Noah turned around and left his hands open at shoulder height when she stepped away.

She moved to the rear wall, and the pistol remained pointed in his direction, tucked in close to her hip. "How did you find me?"

Noah slowly lowered his hands. "In this case, it was old-fashioned police work. Fortunately, there are only so many long-term rentals that have paid cash over fifteen years ago."

Leslie winced and slowly nodded. "Now what?"

"My main goal is to find your daughter. That's never changed. However, I believe you haven't told me everything."

She shook her head. "I still can't tell you much. There's too much at stake."

In the dim light, Noah studied her as best he could. Leslie hadn't physically changed in the last eighteen years. The last time they had met, she was distraught and an emotional wreck. Now the woman appeared focused and not nervous in the slightest. By the way she handled her pistol and controlled the situation reaffirmed his suspicions.

"I'm going to make a few guesses. Tell me if I'm wrong." Noah crossed his arms and leaned against the wall. "You were handpicked to come to the United States at a young age and haven't been called Tetyana Chupryna since you left the Soviet Union. I'm not sure about Joe, but you both would have been a package deal. I don't know what your assignment would have been, but I'm guessing the US government knew and kept track of you."

Her mouth had opened as Noah spoke, and the barrel tilted downward.

"Far as I can figure, there are a few possibilities. But what comes to mind is that the Soviet agents took Angela to keep you on assignment, or it was staged to throw off your minders. Maybe Joe never died, and he raised Angela elsewhere."

Leslie took a deep breath and shook her head. Her voice was barely above a whisper, but it reached his ears. "My daughter really was kidnapped. I have no idea how you learned my real name. That alone places you in great danger."

The silenced pistol now pointed at the ground, and her head leaned back on the wall as she was lost in memories. Noah didn't want to break the silence, but he knew time was of the essence. If a detective from Arrow Point could find her location, government law enforcement wouldn't be far behind.

"Let's work together and share information. But first, I think it's time we left."

Leslie Taylor nodded and bent to pick up the backpack when they both heard the slight squeal as a vehicle braked and a door opened.

Footsteps sounded on the concrete and halted outside the locker door.

Chapter 18

Agent Gordon took a sip of coffee and leaned back behind the wheel of the undercover Ford Taurus to get comfortable. After the home explosion, Gordon and Noland were on the shit list and drew the detail. Noland was in a similar vehicle and had a view of the rear fence at Sentinel Storage. They were not dressed in their usual suits but wore black tactical gear and vests. Where the nametag and Homeland Security would have been across the front and back was blank. There were no markings or identification of any kind on the uniforms.

Once the sun had set, Austin slipped out of the vehicle to relieve himself in the alley. A result of too many coffees. Upon returning to the front seat, a customer stood in the office talking to the employee. Alarm bells went off in Austin's head, and he scrambled for the binos.

The Wyoming cop leaned on the counter, and the woman was all smiles as she handed him a piece of paper.

The agent tapped the comms unit. "Noland. We have company."

"Thank God. I'm bored." Dylan sounded excited.

"It's Noah Hunter. Apparently, he missed the flight."

"Should we move in?"

Gordon wanted to but had a better idea. "He's here for a reason. I'll keep eyes on him. Wait one."

When Noah Hunter left the office, he didn't go far and waited for the employee to lock up. Once clear, Hunter then walked the perimeter of the facility and disappeared.

"Hunter's on foot, approaching your direction. Do you have a visual?"

Thirty seconds later, his partner confirmed. "He climbed the fence and is searching the units."

Austin started the vehicle. "Find out which one, then meet me at the gate. We're going in."

"Roger."

A pass card was swiped at the main gate, and the barrier rolled to the side. Austin pulled out his pistol and chambered a round. Seconds later, his partner arrived, and they navigated the maze of storage lockers. When Dylan parked and angled his vehicle toward a locker, Austin mirrored the maneuver. Two cars were parked on either side, with the headlights shining on the door.

Dylan Noland held a short-barreled 12-gauge shotgun and flicked the safety switch off, then turned on the tactical light under the barrel. He took position to the side and nodded to his partner.

94

Austin stood beside the lock, held the Sig Sauer in his left hand, and counted down. "Three, two ..."

On *one,* the metal door was flung upward, and nothing but an empty locker was revealed.

"Fuck!" Austin kicked the wall in frustration. The steel rang like a bell.

They frantically searched the unit but didn't find anything.

"He couldn't have gone far." Noland flicked the safety on the shotgun.

Austin's eyes widened. "Hunter's car. He parked just down the street."

Both men sprinted for their vehicles and raced to the exit. Slowly the gate retracted, and the tires squealed once there was enough room to make it through. Austin's fist pounded the steering wheel when he pulled into the small plaza parking lot.

Noah Hunter's car was gone.

*****

Leslie tucked the pistol into her waistband and slipped her arms through the straps of the backpack while she whispered. "Grab the bag and follow me. Quickly."

She knelt and pulled two bolts out of the rear wall. The three-foot panel swung open, revealing a narrow passageway between the storage units, and ended at a maintenance door. The walls were lined with thick tubular beams and corrugated steel sheets with only a single light fixture above and a switch on the wall, just inside the door.

Surprised, Noah followed with the duffel bag, and she secured the panel behind him. As they filed outside, the sound of the door rolling up reached his ears.

"My car isn't far. Let's go."

They darted along the length of the next building, and as he turned the corner, the front gate rattled as it closed along the tracks.

The bag over his shoulder was too heavy and slowed him down. However, Leslie didn't have any problems with sprinting ahead. Twelve inches before it closed, she ran in front of the sensor, and it stopped.

"Just across the street. Next plaza." The adrenaline levels made the blood pound in his ears as they crossed the road, and he dug out the car keys. When they reached the rental, the trunk was already opened, and the doors unlocked.

Seconds later, Noah glanced in the rearview mirror as the storage facility disappeared from sight. For now, they were ahead of whoever had found them.

"Okay, it's time to talk."

Leslie nodded and took a deep breath.

Chapter 19

"I grew up in Yaroslavl, Soviet Union. Fair-sized city northeast of Moscow. I was born in 1970, and by the time I was nine, both my parents were dead." Leslie stared out of the passenger window as Noah randomly drove with no destination in mind. He just wanted to cover as much distance as possible.

"They called the orphanage Baby House No. 1, and it was the cruelest place you could ever imagine. They didn't consider children as human." Leslie paused to run a hand through her hair and shrugged. "There was a standard to maintain. If you did not meet the standard, you were separated from the others and denied food, clothing, even personal contact. So, when the state chose me for further education before I turned twelve, I leaped at the chance. For the next ten years, the SVR trained me at the Institute in Moscow."

Noah followed the flow of traffic and merged onto the I65 North. Any direction was good.

"Long story short, I was flown to America and eventually became Leslie Taylor."

"How did you meet Joe?"

She gave out a sharp bark of laughter. "It was arranged. After twenty years together, I will say we became fond of each other, but that was it. However, we periodically slept together in a moment of weakness or a mutual sense of need. So, naturally, our handlers weren't pleased, and we prepared for the worst when they found out I was pregnant."

Leslie grew silent and stared out the passenger window. Noah didn't need for her to elaborate on 'the worst.' He guessed the bodies would never have been found.

"What was your mission?"

She sighed and met his gaze. "I was a spy and sent information back to the Soviet Union. At least, I think that's where it ended up. I was never told."

Leslie studied him for a reaction. Noah's mind spun in circles. He was currently aiding and abetting a foreign agent on American soil. That was enough to classify him as a traitor and be charged with espionage as a co-conspirator. The sinking feeling boiled in his stomach.

"Where do you work?"

Leslie folded her hands on her lap and cleared her throat first before answering. "The White House."

Noah's foot came off the accelerator and hovered above the brake pedal. The vehicle slowed as he processed the information. The decision to stop the car and kick her out was hard to overcome, but he did. A thumb clicked the cruise control, and they resumed speed.

"Who took your daughter?"

"I never found out. I was told any attempt to learn where Angela went—they would kill her."

Noah held back a groan as the conflict warred inside. Logic fought against emotion.

Leslie added. "Joe never told me, but I think he knew what happened. We were both too fearful of what they would do to our daughter."

"Where did he work?"

For a moment, she did not answer as the miles slowly passed. "He officially never said, but I put the clues together year after year. I think he worked for the FBI or the CIA."

Chapter 20

Adam Clay tipped the large bucket with deft control on the joystick. The forty-five-ton excavator's boom extended, and the resulting sound from the hydraulic cylinder was audible in the cab. The definite ticking noise made him wince. He would have to check the fluid levels in the morning. Thick fingers tapped the controller once again, and the bucket smoothed the surface until it looked like it was hand-groomed with a rake.

Finished, he turned off the machine and wiped his forehead with a white cloth from his overalls. The fifty-five-year-old man climbed down and used a flashlight to scan the area. His steps were quiet on the freshly turned dirt as he bent to pick up a brass casing.

"You're an old one."

He vaguely recalled shooting at coyotes in this area a few years ago. The .308 made short work of them. You only had to kill one before the others got the message and disappeared—usually.

He tossed the casing out into the darkness and headed back to the farmhouse. Bugs were attracted to the bobbing flashlight as he crossed the acreage. Fields of corn swayed in the gentle night breeze as bats swooped low and feasted on the insects. Adam chuckled as one came within a few feet of his head before it veered off.

He took off his boots and left them on the porch before heading inside. The office used to be a sitting room off the front hallway that he converted decades ago. He lived alone, and he was never much for lounging, let alone watching television.

Once behind the desk, the large man pecked away at a keyboard with two fingers.

Order completed. Balance of payment due.

Before pressing send, Adam scratched his thick beard and glanced at the time, 12:09 a.m. He deleted the sender information and typed in a different recipient. He always followed protocol. Satisfied, he sent the email and was about to go to bed when a chime sounded.

New message.

Excited, he quickly scrolled through the information and let out a whistle.

The order was already pre-paid.

As he read the file, Adam pulled up the maps. Almost a twenty-two-hour drive from Kansas to Washington D.C. There was no way he would make it in time. Besides, he was still recovering from the last assignment.

He replied to the email.

Order will be fulfilled, but additional expenses may occur.

When the response came back, he smiled and picked up the phone.

On the second ring, a woman mumbled. "Hello?"

"Rise and shine. I'll be there in fifteen minutes. We have work to do."

"Ugh. Roger that."

Adam went upstairs to change and grabbed his go-bag. He couldn't help but whistle as he prepared. The money wasn't important, but he would take it. It was the job that got the blood pumping and made him feel alive.

His property held many secrets, and with almost twelve hundred acres and an excavator, there was plenty of room—time to fulfill another order.

Chapter 21

"There are political appointments to the White House, but I'm in a permanent staff position as the procurement manager. I ensure that the groceries are ordered to throw pillows, repairs, you name it, for over five administrations now."

Noah sipped a coffee as they sat outside a truck stop as he digested the information. Leslie had tea and picked at a biscuit while she talked. They had pulled into a strip mall outside downtown Washington. Finally, at three o'clock in the morning, the after-bar crowd dispersed, and they had the parking lot to themselves.

"What did you report and how?"

"Nothing I would have considered important. Advanced ordering for functions and any major repairs that had to be approved against the budget. I was more in the background and didn't interact with the president or his staff. My small office was in the basement."

Hunter cracked the window for some fresh air, then asked. "What did Joe do with the information?"

"Once a week, a car would pick him up, and they would be gone for twelve hours. It was a four-hour drive there and the same back."

Noah pulled out the burner phone and looked at the map. A four-hour drive would cover a few states, and they could have gone anywhere. "Anything more specific?"

Leslie closed her eyes for a moment. "He always said it was time for another rocky drive before laughing. It was his private joke."

As he scrolled through various maps and established the distance, Noah shrugged. "The possible area is too large. No idea."

She placed her cup in the holder and half turned in her seat. "Tell me what you can about Angela. I need to know about my daughter."

"Just a second." Noah quickly made a call to Dickinson. He wasn't surprised when she answered on the second ring and placed the call on speaker.

"Only a few people know my personal cell number." Angie sounded wide awake despite the early hour.

"It's Hunter. Are you at the station?"

"I'm patrol Nanny tonight. Driving around and checking the guys. What's going on?"

"Too much, unfortunately. Can you search for a location, a four-hour drive from Leslie Taylor's home? Target unknown. The only possible clue is a rocky road."

Her deep-throated chuckle made Noah grin. "You aren't asking for much. I'll see what I can do. Call me back in a few hours."

After saying their goodbyes, he reached into the backseat and pulled a sheet of paper out of his bag. When he passed it over to Leslie, she looked confused. "What's this?"

"A form used by the FBI for background checks. Standard throughout the country."

The light from the coffee shop was enough to see. "The name and other information are blacked out."

"Yes, but the data we needed wasn't." Noah pointed to the swirls and loops inside the small boxes. "These are a positive match to your daughter. These prints are definitive proof she is alive. We just don't know where. Yet."

She ran her finger over the paper as her eyes filled with tears. Then, a grin slowly spread across her face as hope made her glow. "Thank you."

"This was sent to me in Arrow Point. Someone knew about your daughter and my relationship with the case. I want to—" When the cell phone rang, Noah raised his eyebrows at the display number, then answered. "Are you a miracle worker?"

Dickinson laughed. "I'm at the gas station near the interstate. I used an old-fashioned map with the scale, and Rocky Mount, North Carolina, was the only thing that leaped out at me.

Just under a four-hour drive. Do you need me, Hunter? I can catch a flight and be there by noon."

Noah closed his eyes and leaned back against the headrest. Having a partner for the next stage would help, but he wanted to keep Angie as distant as possible from what he had planned.

"I appreciate the help. I'll keep in touch."

Leslie looked up when he plugged the phone in to charge. "Is everything okay?"

"Possible lead. Are you up for a road trip? No guarantees."

She looked at the fingerprints and wiped the tears from her eyes. "I've nothing to lose and everything to gain. I'm in."

Noah winked, and soon they were back on the interstate driving south. As to what they were headed toward, he didn't know—hopefully, some answers.

Chapter 22

When Steve Hutchings stepped off the plane in Cheyenne, Wyoming, he knew the shit was about to hit the fan. The area was well lit as the last flight of the night disembarked. Four men in suits by the terminal doors one hundred feet away were easily spotted.

Hutchings tried to blend in with the small group. Head down and carry-on bag in his left hand, he shuffled along. He still wore his dark brown suit and tie, though they were slightly rumpled from the long day.

He tried not to make eye contact, but it didn't work. The four men repositioned when he reached the doors and blocked his path.

Fuck it. Let's get this over with.

"Steven Hutchings, if you could come with us." The first man was five foot six and had a medium build, dark hair, and mid-forties.

"Why the hell would I want to do that, kid?"

"We would like to ask you a few questions." Two men flanked him, and one stood behind at an arm's reach.

"Identification."

The man in front glanced at his companions. "Don't make this difficult."

Hutchings had enough. *Punk-assed kids.* He pulled out his wallet and flicked the badge open. "Sergeant Hutchings, Arrow Point Police Department. Identify yourself, or get the fuck out of my way."

Several people stood behind as the doors were blocked, and they couldn't leave or step around them. Steve had no doubt cell phones were out and recording. Everyone wanted to be famous for a viral video. He counted on it.

The man's eyes flicked from Hutchings to the crowd of people behind him and back to his companions. Then, to the police officer's surprise, an ID was produced.

"Special Agent Louden, FBI. Come with us, please."

Hutchings tried to smile, but it came out more as a grimace. "See? Was that so hard? I'll cooperate once I have verified your identification. Unfortunately, I was recently attacked by someone claiming to be from the bureau. So, you can understand my hesitation."

Steve tucked his wallet away and reached for his cell phone, but a strong hand clamped down on his wrist, and the large man behind him whispered in his ear. "You can walk out of here, or we can carry you. Decide now."

Hutchings's arm twitched, and there was no give. It felt like he was trapped in a vise. Maybe if he were younger, but those days were gone.

"Ya, ya. Call off the goon. Quit wasting time, and let's get this over with. It's been a long day, kid, and I'm tired."

With a nod to his companion, Louden led Hutchings away. The small crowd was disappointed when nothing happened.

Steve hoped Hunter was having better luck. Their small advantage was over, and the feds were in the game.

Instead of heading inside, Hutchings was surprised when they did an about-turn, and he was escorted out onto the tarmac.

*****

The report from Gordon on the near-miss with Noah Hunter and possibly Leslie Taylor filtered through certain channels and landed on a stainless-steel desk. Three hours later, another statement by Special Agent Louden was printed out and placed on top.

Sean Cameron made a decision several steps above his paygrade.

He stepped out of his glass-enclosed office and into an operational cell. Six desks lined three walls of the large room with four or five monitors per station. The fourth wall had a series of monitors and a large screen in the middle.

Angled out from the corner, the polished oak podium had a small screen and keyboard on the flat surface.

When Sean stood behind the podium, he adjusted his glasses and buttoned his blue suit jacket before tapping on the edge with a pen. He stood an inch over six feet and had a stocky build that made the suit appear tight.

"Attention. I need everyone's attention here."

The sound of fingers striking keyboards halted as the six technicians swiveled in their chairs.

"We have an Alpha One target scenario. Location only." When the monitor closest to his shoulder flickered to life as a timer, a few couldn't hold back a groan. Sean nodded. "We are mandated to have three practice runs per quarter. I'm just following orders. Subject's name is Noah Hunter, last seen boarding a plane at Washington Dulles International Airport."

A Wyoming driver's license appeared on the large screen. Another picture was presented. It showed a man with a close-cropped goatee and short dark hair in a suit as he stepped out of a dark-colored SUV next to an older gentleman with short white hair.

"Mr. Hunter never arrived at his destination, and it's believed he never boarded the plane. So, let's try and beat last month's practice. The clock starts now. Any questions?"

The timer started on the monitor.

A woman in the corner shot her hand in the air. "Any known aliases?"

Sean Cameron shook his head. "None."

"Profession? Skills?" The young man on his left grinned at the challenge.

"Police officer, former military. Skills unknown. He has a thirteen-hour head start."

Three months ago, they had conducted a similar exercise with a former Navy pilot gone rogue, last seen in Dubai. Again, each training objective was fulfilled with real people on the ground. Far as they knew, it was planned ahead of time. What they didn't know wouldn't hurt them.

"I got financials."

"Transportation."

"Airport surveillance."

"Cell phone pinged in Washington, then in Wyoming at 23:26 hours yesterday." The man beside him worked his station like a virtuoso. Two keyboards were used simultaneously as a flurry of data streamed across the monitors.

"Have him!" The woman in the corner mirrored her screen on the large monitor. Noah Hunter left the airport and climbed into a dark gray taxi in clear detail.

"Running the taxi medallion." A large man in his late fifties sitting on the edge of his chair called it out. This team had been working together for over two years like a well-oiled machine. "Flyer's Taxi Service system breached. Route for 5K11 on screen."

A map of Washington DC overlaid the GPS coordinates of the taxi in question.

When the vehicle halted on screen, the location was identified. "CVS drugstore on Connecticut Avenue northeast."

"You are doing good, folks. Keep it up." Cameron gripped the sides of the podium as he watched the experts track down the cop like a bloodhound on a scent. He couldn't help but grin at the excitement. He had been doing this for over thirty years, and it never got dull.

"Inside the store?" the woman called out.

"Blind." There were no cameras inside. "Checking ATM across the street."

Twelve seconds later, a video of Noah Hunter leaving the drug store appeared on the large screen. It wasn't perfect with the camera angle, but they all could see him open a package and toss the plastic wrapper in the garbage out front.

"He has a burner phone. We'll have him in four minutes."

Sean glanced at the timer on the wall.

They were about to set a new record. It was a shame this wasn't sanctioned.

Three minutes and twenty seconds later, Sean's eyes grew wide when the final location of Noah Hunter appeared on the screen. "Well done. *Very* well done. Fill in the blanks."

Despite the sinking feeling, he smiled and darted from the room back to his office. Sean had a flight to redirect and to update the others. A tapestry woven with skill decades ago was slowly unraveling. He couldn't let that happen.

Chapter 23

Noah drove two hours, then switched places with Leslie for the same duration. A little bit of sleep was better than nothing. To his surprise, he was out within moments of closing his eyes.

Rocky Mount, North Carolina, was slightly larger than half the size of Arrow Point, with fifty-nine thousand people. They crossed the bridge over the winding Tar River as the sun crested the horizon. Despite the name, the water was a deep blue and sparkled with the morning light.

"I don't know about you, but I could use a coffee shop." Noah adjusted the passenger seat and rubbed the sleep from his eyes.

Leslie looked tired and agreed. "Coffee does sound good. What's the game plan? How do we narrow the search?"

Noah unplugged the burner phone. It was fully charged. Within seconds he showed her a list of buildings. "Government properties in Rocky Mount are public knowledge. We should be able to spot a place without going in. They would have a security system with controlled access."

She nodded and turned west off the interstate. There wasn't any need to look for signs. A small plaza with a gas station and diner was visible from the off-ramp.

"I would imagine the government would want some privacy for the location as well. I'm not sure what branch of government, though. CIA? FBI?" Leslie shrugged.

"I didn't think the CIA was able to act on US soil. It could be the FBI, Homeland Security, or any other agency."

The morning sun felt good on his face when he got out of the parked car and stretched. Despite the early hour, the diner was busy with truckers and travelers.

A blue minivan screeched to a halt on the road behind them, and Noah's hand automatically moved to his right hip. When two teenagers jumped out, Noah relaxed. They pounded wooden stakes into the lawn. A large red sign, Re-elect Andre Knight, Ward 1, was strategically placed in front of a blue placard. Seconds later, the minivan moved down the road.

Noah wasn't the only one who was jumpy. Leslie chuckled in relief. "Let's go inside."

The waitress didn't even ask. After one look at the couple, she poured them a coffee each and left the pot. Noah opened the map and checked each location. "The buildings are all downtown. City inspections, water department, and so on. The one that interested me is here."

He turned the phone around and slid it across the table. Leslie frowned as she zoomed in. "City zoning and planning?"

Noah nodded. "Why would they be four miles from the city center?"

Noah wasn't sure what to expect. Google Street View showed it to be a one-story building surrounded by fencing and in the middle of a field. They could barely make out the details, but there wasn't a satellite dish or antenna array on the roof. A dirt road led to the gate, and the surrounding countryside was mainly forested.

When their food arrived, Noah dug in. His mind was already working on a shopping list of items they would need.

"Going in blind would be the same as waving a flag and announcing ourselves." Noah topped off their mugs with more coffee. "We will need to observe the location and monitor any traffic in and out until a pattern is established."

"How long? They'll be searching for both of us."

Noah had spent weeks undercover watching a subject. The longer the assignment, the more information they could gather. "It's Friday, and I would guess the best time to go inside would be in two days. Assuming no one is working on the weekend. We will see."

After breakfast, the larger box stores had opened, and Noah bought a few essential things. Leslie looked at the items in the backseat and nodded. "Perfect."

The three-person turkey blind had enough room for a cot and chair, and one could rest while the other kept watch. The

Bushnell binoculars were a woodland camouflage pattern and good for low-light conditions. The large plastic bag held various backpacking instant meals, which Noah hoped were better than the MREs he had in the military.

They studied the maps, and the closest they could get driving was a quarter-mile. A dirt road off the interstate led to a hydro clear-cut, and the small rental car barely made it. It bottomed out a few times, and the undercarriage scraped against the uneven ground. Noah winced, but they made it.

The surrounding area was mostly wooded except on the far side, where a meadow was cleared around the building. Noah would have a hundred and thirty yards of an unobstructed view of the eastern side and a partial view of the front gate from the distant tree line.

Noah had backed in between two large spruce trees and unloaded the car. Midafternoon wasn't the time to set up in full view, but they could have a staging area. Once it got dark, they could set up.

"Let's go and recce out the position."

He shouldered a small backpack and carried the binos and hunting blind while Leslie followed the hydro cut. After ten minutes, they dropped the larger items before stepping into the trees.

Noah wished for a game trail to follow as dry branches cracked underfoot and threatened to poke out his eyes if he wasn't careful. Instead, they were forced to repeatedly crawl under and over fallen trees and move slowly in the dense wood to maintain direction.

The ground sloped in the direction of the building, and the return uphill walk would be more taxing. However, one thing Noah was grateful for—the lack of bugs. Except for the occasional bird call in the distance, there were no other signs of life.

Noah paused to pull out two water bottles from the pack and handed one to Leslie. "How are you doing?"

She had a fresh scratch on her left cheek from a branch. "I'll be fine."

He gestured to the bottom of a ten-foot drop. It led to a massive tree. Under the branches of the large spruce, Noah would have a good vantage point. "I'll be right back. Just going to check it out."

He left the backpack and climbed down the slope. A few small rocks and dirt slid down the incline when the heels of his hiking boots dug in.

Noah crawled on his stomach the last few feet and dug his elbows into the soft ground for purchase. He flipped the caps off the ends of the binos and scanned the area.

The building was two-hundred-feet long and a single story. The dark brown walls were broken up with several windows along the north side. Each window was covered in a metal cage for security, and the tint didn't allow inside viewing. At the corners of the building, Noah noted the dark glass bubbles installed under the eaves. Security cameras.

From the elevated safety of the spruce tree, he saw the flat, gravel-covered roof and antenna array with a small satellite dish reflect a heat shimmer from the afternoon sun.

He studied the structure for five minutes, but there wasn't anything remotely interesting. When a flock of Canadian geese flew overhead, Noah lowered the binoculars. He needed a better angle to view the building's front.

He was about to stand when his head snapped to the far eastern edge of the woods. A flash of light reflected off an object.

Lifting the binos, he focused two hundred yards across the clearing.

At the base of a similar tree, the shadows shifted. When the barrel of a long rifle swung in Noah's direction, he froze.

Movement could give a position away just as easily as sound or color—a lesson drilled into him on tour.

"Is everything okay?" Leslie slid down the slope carrying the backpack.

Noah ducked behind the thick tree trunk as the shot rang out.

Chapter 24

Hutchings could not take any more and let out a belly laugh at the two men. The handcuffs rattled against the steel bar bolted to the metal table as his shoulders shook.

"You guys are fuckin' hilarious. You should really take that act on the road. Rookies, both of you."

After the short flight to Denver, the staff sergeant was escorted to an FBI safehouse downtown. They removed his jacket, and he was thrust into a metal chair bolted to the floor. Handcuffs were wrapped around a steel bar on the table. Wearing a dress shirt and tie, he waited in the interrogation room for two hours until the men arrived.

The first man reminded Hutchings of a football player, with a nose that had been broken too many times. The other was slightly smaller, but his chest still stretched out the stock G-man blue suit. Steve just stared them down and asked his own questions with every question they asked. Neither man would respond. The file folder on the table was an inch thick, and after ten hours of flipping the pages, they started over at the beginning.

Steve remained awake throughout the night as they grilled him with trick questions and blatant lies to get him to talk. They wanted to know the full history of Noah Hunter and his involvement with Leslie Taylor. Past cases were brought up, and a detailed account of Noah's arrest record was questioned.

"Tell us about Noah Hunter's ex-fiancée. How well did you know her?"

Hutchings knew more about what happened than he ever told Noah. It was not his first rodeo. But if the sun were shining, he would not give these goons a weather update. However, if they did not know the full story of Megan Brooks, then sure as shit, he was not going to mention anything. *Over my dead body.*

"Do you guys have a license? Sorry, but I just have to ask."

Broken Nose glanced at his partner and frowned. They had an equally long night, and both were just as tired as Hutchings. Finally, he sighed. "I give up. A license for what?"

"For this horrible fishing expedition." Hutching shook his head and grinned. "You guys should really consider a career change. Seriously."

The cuffs rattled again as his shoulders shook.

The second man tapped a thick finger on the paperwork and sighed. "Let's start over at—"

After a quick knock at the door, a woman stepped inside. She carried Steve's suit jacket over one arm. "We're done. Send him home."

Hutchings did not know what happened, but he sure as shit wanted to find out. "I'm starting to like it here. How about you fill me in?"

The broken nose guy stood. "I'll take you back to Arrow Point."

The other suit collected the paperwork and reached into a pocket for his keys.

Hutchings stood and placed his right hand over the left wrist, and the handcuff fell onto the steel table, and after a bit of fumbling, the other shackle was removed. He adjusted his tie and reached out for his jacket.

"You guys are fucking rookies. Seriously." At the shocked expression on their faces, he shook his head. "You don't know how to shim a set of cuffs? What the hell are they teaching you nowadays? Next time, make sure to remove a suspect's tie clip."

The two-inch clip had a small APPD badge on the front, but the thin prongs on the back easily slipped inside the mechanism. As to how they could overlook it, he had no idea. Lack of training, most likely.

"Now, you are going to have to help me out. I've been sitting too long, and my hip is sore. If I fall, you're fuckin' going down with me. You look nice and soft."

With a final look at the cuffs on the table, the smaller man with the deep chest gave up. "Fine. Let's go, pops."

As they filed out of the small room, Hutchings turned as a large hand gently guided him by the elbow. Two steps later, he let out a sharp cry of pain and stumbled. A strong hand steadied and escorted him outside to a waiting car. No one noticed as broken nose's wallet slipped into Hutchings's suit jacket.

Fuckin' rookies.

*****

A fragment of bark tore from the trunk, inches from Noah's head. The jagged piece jutted out like an accusing finger. Leslie dropped beside him as the shot echoed across the clearing.

"*Jesus.*" Her fingers dug into his shoulder as she gasped for breath.

"Go straight up the hill from my position. Keep this tree behind you. Run!" Noah's hand twitched for a weapon but only grasped dried needles and pinecones at his feet. There would be no point in firing the pistol. The distance was too far.

Leslie didn't hesitate and flew back up the slope. Dirt cascaded down with her efforts. The tree vibrated from the impact with a dull thud when a second shot rang out. The echo was lost among the trees and wouldn't have carried far.

Noah didn't waste time looking for the shooter. The adrenaline helped propel him up the incline in three long strides. "I should have brought a rifle."

Leslie ran like a deer through the woods, and Noah had trouble keeping up.

A thousand dry cedar branches snapped as he held an arm up to guard his eyes and head. Now wasn't the time to be subtle.

When they burst out of the woods, the car was parked a hundred yards south of their position.

"Hold for a second. Listen." Noah froze in the tall grass. At first, he could only hear the distant sound of birds and the hum from the hydro wires above. The familiar retort of sticks snapping grew steadily louder. The shooter was running and sounded like a bear charging through the woods.

"Shit." Leslie took a step toward the vehicle.

Noah shook his head. "That's where he will emerge. We have to go the other way."

She winced. "Any chance it's a mistaken hunter?"

The third shot sounded closer. "I don't believe in coincidences. Let's go."

Noah turned north along the hydro cut and darted for the far side. Leslie stayed close behind. He tried to stay positive, but he couldn't shake a feeling of dread. Options were few and far between. The maps had shown nothing but wilderness for fifty miles north of this part of North Carolina. Eighteen miles south were more built-up areas. The best bet was to change direction and make it back to the car. After they left the interstate, it was a forty-minute drive. The only thing Noah recalled passing was an abandoned gas station.

"Damn." Noah glanced back over his shoulder and shook his head. The grass was bent along their trail. A blind man could follow them. "We need to make some distance."

However, soon as they left the hydro cut and entered the woods, Noah swore to himself again. The cedar and spruce trees grew close together, and he doubted they could make it through without alerting the countryside.

"If we have problems getting through here, anyone following us will as well." Noah dropped to his hands and knees. "Try to keep low, but more importantly, silent."

He wasn't sure how much of a lead they had, maybe ninety seconds. It would have to be enough. Leslie shook her head. "I have a different idea if you are up for it."

The sound of breaking branches grew closer, and Noah could not think of another option. Time was ticking. "What did you have in mind?"

Chapter 25

Being rushed into a situation was *not* how Adam liked to operate, and he knew it could cost him the kill. After last-minute orders, he had less than three minutes to prepare his position ahead of the target.

The camouflage suit had the new knee and elbow pads sewn in. The shooting pad was set up under the spruce with a water bottle and paper and pencil ready. Ideally, Adam would have created a range card, but there was no time. If he had the information available the day before, he would have had a chance to scout the area and be on his way home with two more notches in his belt.

When the targets unexpectedly approached from the north, it took a moment to readjust.

"Bloody hell."

The .30-60 Springfield swung around, and he managed to fire three rounds as they ran uphill. Unfortunately, a large spruce blocked his view, and the bolt-action rifle was slow. He dropped the magazine and reloaded. The gun had one in the chamber and five in the magazine. Although he had a Glock in reserve, ideally, it would not be used. For Adam, it was all about the distance shot.

He took two steps toward the target and paused.

The situation did not seem right, which was usually enough to call off an operation. But Adam pushed those thoughts aside and charged. His first shot nearly connected. It only missed by a few inches.

He slung the rifle over his shoulder and brought an arm across his face. The dry cedar branches made him sound like a charging bear.

He recalled the map and angled to the side toward the hydro cut. Hunter must have parked and walked in. After running for a minute, Adam paused. It was hard to gauge the distance, but someone was also crashing through the woods.

Good. When people ran, they were fearful and tended to make mistakes. It made his job easier.

Once he found the opening and vehicle, Adam used the roof as a firing position. Through the scope, he scanned for any movement.

Nothing.

However, a fresh trail in the grass led down the open area.

"Fuck, ya."

Adam came around the car and was on the trail within seconds. There was no time to waste. Carrying the rifle in both hands, he ran over two hundred yards. The bent waist-height grass pointed like an arrow to the northern edge of the woods. There were other signs of passage, but he ignored them.

High above, the wires hummed with contained energy. The distant hydro tower would have made a perfect sniper position, but a different weapon and optics would have been required.

The silence confirmed what he suspected. The targets had stopped running.

He brought the walnut stock up, seated it into his shoulder, and scanned the edge of the woods to either side. It was then he saw it.

At one hundred and twenty yards, a bush of a different color stood out to his experienced eye. A few broken branches tried to conceal the structure, but it did not disguise the pattern. The mossy oak stood out like a banner waving in a breeze.

A hunter's blind.

Quietly, he moved to a better angle and adjusted the range. He dropped on his right knee and wrapped his left forearm through the carry strap before settling into the kneeling position.

As Adam's breathing slowed, he calmly squeezed the trigger. Automatically, his right hand drew the bolt back, and the empty casing went flying. A second round was twelve inches lower and pierced the camo fabric. The third round was insurance, and the fourth was for fun.

When the last echo died away, Adam chuckled. He would be home by midnight.

Chapter 26

Noah stood thirty yards away and calmly maintained a two-handed grip on the Glock. Leslie had given him the pistol along with a spare magazine. The man dressed in the hunter's outfit had knelt and deliberately fired into the blind. Any lingering doubts vanished. They were his targets.

He brought the pistol up to shoulder height and took aim but didn't pull the trigger. Shooting someone in the back, unaware, was not something he could do. It was also hard to get information out of a dead man.

"If you move or turn around, you are dead. Drop the rifle and place your hands in the air." Noah's finger applied pressure to the trigger.

The man never moved, but his sigh said it all.

"Drop the rifle!"

"I can't do that."

Noah didn't need a crystal ball to predict what would happen. As the man turned, the rifle came up.

Without hesitation, the trigger was pulled, and the Glock fired. He aimed at the center of visible mass, but the adrenaline rush caused him to stray. The first 9mm round punctured the right kidney, and the second went into the man's side. The hunter fell as if hit by a truck.

The rifle went flying, and it was quite painful by all accounts. His screams carried for a mile, but Noah had no remorse.

There was no time to debate or second guess. Leslie mentioned she had a plan, and he had to trust her. She had run to the staging area and brought back the turkey blind. While she was setting it up, Noah circled to the opposite side and waited.

The blind was set up much like an umbrella, and once you popped out the sides, it was complete. Leslie had no difficulties. They had a full minute of silence until the sniper approached. Noah was worried about the pistol range, but the man moved close to fire on the blind.

"Leslie? Are you okay?" Noah shouted from the safety of a mature silver maple.

The screaming stopped, and a burst of horrific laughter came from the man. "You're a dead man, Hunter."

Noah kept the Glock ready as he walked forward through the grass. The man lay on his stomach with the rifle flung before him—inches from his fingers. The pattern on the jacket did little to hide a bloom of blood as it soaked the fabric and stained the grass. He would not last much longer.

"Who sent you? How did you know I was coming here?" Up until he called out his name, Noah was not one-hundred percent sure whether the encounter was random or not. It reaffirmed his mindset about coincidences.

The man coughed, and when his head turned to the side, blood trickled out his mouth. He whispered, "I was the quiet option. Now that's off the table. You better run, boy."

An uneasy feeling grew stronger as Noah scanned the woods. With a hiking boot, he flicked the rifle away. Leslie should have been here by now.

Noah took two steps toward the blind.

Nothing.

A muffled groan came from behind, and he spun about. Noah fired two rounds to the head in reflex as the man struggled to bring up a pistol. The echo of the small arms fire faded, and he dismissed the man to focus on the living. He had his chance.

"Leslie? It's okay."

Noah ran across the field and noticed three holes had perforated the fabric. Inside was empty. However, a flash of blue fifty yards farther under the cedars sent a chill across his soul.

~

According to the GPS route, the closest emergency hospital was twenty minutes away, but he made it in fifteen. Noah pulled up to the emergency doors behind an empty ambulance and ran around to the passenger door. With an arm under her legs, he gingerly lifted Leslie and held her against his chest. The make-shift bandage on her chest shifted, and more blood saturated his front.

The doors automatically opened as he yelled. "I need help. Now!"

The Nash General Hospital staff worked in a flurry of professionalism and competence. A tall thin man in blue scrubs and a colorful headscarf rushed over with a stretcher.

"What happened?"

"Gunshot wound to the chest."

"When?" Two nurses came to assist.

"Twenty minutes ago. No longer." Noah had time to apply a bandage and tape it on three sides to act as a valve. The shot went through her right lung. Nearly two decades of first aid and training came into play, and one minute out from the hospital, Leslie still had a pulse but was unconscious. Noah kept up the litany of we are almost there throughout the drive. *Hold on.*

A young intern guided Noah to a cubicle to get cleaned up so the medical staff could work. He had to reassure the young man that he was not hurt and that the blood was not his. There was no saving his clothes.

"I'll be right back. I have to move the car." Noah stepped outside and into the welcoming breeze. The cloying smell of dried blood was making him feel nauseous.

132

After he moved the vehicle to the far end of the parking lot, he stripped off the shirt and dug around in his supplies. Noah had an impromptu shower with a large bottle of water and a towel. He stripped down and dressed in clean clothes, not caring if anyone watched. The bloody shirt, pants, and towel were tossed in a garbage can as he made his way back inside. Dressed in jeans and a T-shirt, Noah walked back through the emergency doors.

A nurse stepped forward with a clipboard and took him aside. "What happened?"

Noah had thought of various responses but stuck with the truth. Mostly. "Random shot from a hunter. I just happened to be nearby and did what I could."

"Was anyone else hurt?"

Noah shook his head. "No. Is the woman going to make it?"

He had reasons to keep her identity secret. Soon as her name went into the system, Big Brother would know. They may know already, but he had to give Leslie a chance.

"We'll do our best," the nurse paused from her writing. "With a gunshot wound, we have to notify the police."

Noah nodded as he pulled out his wallet and showed the golden detective badge. "I was off duty."

Rocky Mount did not have a police force, but the county sheriff was on speed dial and would be notified soon. Noah was left with few options. He could have dumped Leslie off and ran to remain anonymous. But regardless of the situation, he was not

133

wired that way. Integrity was a constant struggle, but he knew the difference between black and white. The choice was made easier with the knowledge that someone knew where he would be and laid an ambush. That narrowed the playing field dramatically.

As the nurse asked a few more details, Noah could not help but look over his shoulder. He had been in one place too long and had to keep moving.

Noah agreed to wait on the sheriff for a statement and stepped outside. After ten minutes, the same nurse returned. By the remorseful look of sympathy on her face, he knew what she would say.

"I'm so sorry, but—"

When Noah's burner phone rang, the timing was near perfect. He knew who it would be. "Just a second, sorry."

Chapter 27

"Ah, Mr. Hunter. I'm sure you've heard the news by now. My condolences. I'm not sure how close you were to Leslie Taylor, but I'm sure she appreciated your efforts."

Noah remained silent, but he was impressed at the speed of information. The nurse held up two fingers. She would be back. He mouthed *thank you* and closed his eyes to lean against the building.

As the silence grew, the older man on the other end chuckled. "I applaud your efforts, and far as I'm concerned, this is now over. Don't worry about the sheriff. I've taken care of that. Enjoy Rocky Mount before you head home. There's a diner down the street that serves an excellent meatloaf."

Without warning, the call was disconnected, and Noah brought a hand up to smash the burner on the ground. With a slow breath, he regained control and looked out across the parking lot but did not focus on anything in particular. His thoughts were spinning a million miles a minute, and a slight grin spread across his face.

~

 While small, Rocky Mount, North Carolina, had the same rental car company. Noah ended up paying a premium for the interior cleaning. The blood on the passenger seat would be hard to get out and made the young man wince upon inspection. Cash seemed to work, and within half an hour, Noah drove away in a new brown Toyota Sienna minivan. He transferred all the items over, except one thing—the burner cell phone. The heel of his hiking boot made short work of it, and he threw the pieces into the trash bin. While in Wyoming, Noah would have chosen a pickup truck to blend in with the demographic. However, in North Carolina, the minivan seemed to be the vehicle of choice.

Back in the hospital parking lot, Noah parked on the far side with an eastern view of the entrance, and the only access from Parkland Drive was covered. On the passenger seat was Leslie's green backpack. He debated going through her things as he waited but didn't want to be distracted.

As the sun set, he nibbled on a protein bar and drank sparingly from a water bottle. The tide of cars ebbed and flowed from the parking lot as the staff changed and visitors or patients came and went.

At ten o'clock, his patience was rewarded when an unmarked ambulance pulled up to the emergency doors. A black

Chevy Tahoe with dark tinted windows followed. Two men got out of the ambulance, dressed in blue EMT outfits, and a man and woman dressed in suits got out of the SUV.

Noah parked near the exit and waited. Twenty minutes later, the two paramedics guided the stretcher out of the emergency doors and into the back of the ambulance. A nurse followed, an IV pole with two bags of clear fluid connected to the patient.

"Born at night, but not last night." Noah chuckled. His spirits were buoyed when his hunch was confirmed.

When the man and woman walked outside, a tall man in scrubs joined them. They talked for a few minutes as he referred to different pages in a folder. Noah could tell the doctor wasn't happy with the situation even a hundred feet away. He gestured toward the patient, vigorously tapped the paperwork before handing it over, and stood back with arms crossed. The woman shrugged, then abruptly turned her back to him and got into the car as the man got behind the wheel.

Noah slid low on his seat as they drove past, but his worries were unfounded. The woman remained glued to a phone, and the others never glanced in his direction.

Over the years, especially when doing undercover work, Noah had quite a bit of experience following a suspect vehicle. Two or three-person teams worked great. However, the latest technology slowly replaced the tried and tested methods. Quad-drones can be carried and launched with a given target to follow, or GPS trackers contained within a small dart can be fired from a chase car. Most importantly, such new methods didn't place officers' lives in danger, and they were fairly reliable.

Right now, he would love to have some air support or another set of eyes, but he would have to make do.

Noah waited thirty seconds before following.

The hunt was on.

Chapter 28

Noah followed the procession on the interstate toward Rocky Mount. When the SUV pulled off at the exit, he expected them to head to the federal building. But, instead of turning east, they went north. The lack of streetlights made Noah uneasy, and the minivan's headlights couldn't be turned off. If they were paying attention, they would know someone followed with the lack of heavy traffic. Fortunately, they were not the only people on the road. Large transport trailers and the occasional car were heading south. However, as he slowly increased the distance, he realized it also worked in his favor. Half a mile back, Noah followed the red lights through long stretches of open country road surrounded by farmland.

Ahead lay a small community called Enfield, but the SUV turned west on Highway 481, three miles before downtown. Noah passed a few homes and a small school for the rural town, but they quickly gave way to farms and large tracks of woods. At eleven o'clock, the streets were empty, and most lights were off. In the small farming community, most were up early.

After ten minutes, the vehicles turned north, and Noah pulled over on the shoulder and turned off the minivan.

Despite the cloud cover, the quarter moon was bright enough to turn the farmer's field into a blanket of shifting grays and shadows. Noah didn't know what the crop was, but he could see over it when he stood beside the driver's seat.

Five hundred yards across the field, lights came on in the farmhouse as the SUV and ambulance pulled up. It was too far away to see what was going on, but Noah didn't have to imagine. They were bringing Leslie Taylor inside.

Whatever agency involved that tracked him through the cell phone had enough time to lay an ambush. Right now, Noah doubted the small federal building was the place where Joe Taylor had gone. *This* place, however, fit the bill quite nicely—a farmhouse in the middle of nowhere. They would have an unobstructed view of anyone approaching for miles during daylight hours. The driveway was over three hundred yards long, and no doubt was monitored by cameras.

Noah made a fist and knocked on the Toyota's roof. There would be no going back. There had been times when he placed his career on the line, but this situation was different. He wasn't going up against a killer or mafia goon. He wasn't sure which branch of the government was operating behind the scenes, but they had anticipated his moves. Unless there was a satellite tracking him, he was off the radar. The rental van was a base model without the upgraded GPS and navigation systems.

Eighteen years ago, a little girl went missing, and after seventy-two hours, the worst was assumed. And after all that time, answers were within reach. He couldn't walk away. Some things were more important.

As to how far he was willing to go, Noah was about to find out.

It took seconds to turn the vehicle around and find a dirt laneway down the road. Noah backed into the tree line, rummaged through the equipment, and stuffed a small backpack. The dark nylon jacket and jeans blended into the night as he climbed over the waist-height fence. The Glock was thrust into a zippered pocket and two spare magazines in another.

The fall weather had a crisp, refreshing chill to the air once the sun had set and small plumes of breath were visible. He was glad of the jacket as Noah found himself walking through a field filled with corn stalks. The dried plants were knee to waist height or fallen over and crunched underfoot. He slowed the pace and tried to walk between the rows. Thankfully, the soil was also dried out, and while uneven, he wasn't sinking into any mud.

The farmhouse lights acted as a beacon. He didn't head toward it. Instead he turned north. He needed to get closer, but Noah didn't want to chance being seen with the county road as a backdrop. The approach from the fields felt safer with the night as a cloak.

Noah pulled out the binoculars and studied the property two hundred yards north of the farmhouse. While not perfect, enough details came into focus that he had to adjust his plan.

The two-story home, at first glance, appeared normal—an eighty-year-old farmhouse. However, the interior lights on the main floor revealed bars across the windows. There was movement near the front door, but the posts blocked his line of sight, so he moved twenty feet away on an angle. Noah waited when the lights in the front yard and porch turned off. A glowing red dot flared, then arced out into the yard. A bald man rose from a chair, and the front porch light came back on before going inside. The lights stayed on for ten minutes before shutting off— a security motion sensor.

Blinds were drawn on the main-floor windows, but enough light escaped around the edges to show the bars. The immediate area around the house was devoid of trees or shrubs. However, across the driveway were three forty-two-foot shipping containers.

Noah slowly lowered to the ground when the porch light came to life again and wasn't worried about being spotted. One of the paramedics came out and got in the ambulance. After a three-point turn, he backed the vehicle between two shipping containers, out of sight.

Once the slim man entered the home, Noah stowed the binoculars away as he glanced at his watch. When the light turned off, he nodded. Nine minutes.

Noah had the plan, and soon it would be time to pull the trigger. Answers lay within that farmhouse, and before the sun rose in the east, he *would* have answers. One way or another.

Chapter 29

Throughout the drive from Denver to Arrow Point, Hutchings sat in the back of the Chevy Tahoe as the agent drove. After a night of interrogation, he gladly tilted his head back and slept the four hours. There was no point in small talk.

When they pulled off the interstate, Hutchings sat up and gave directions to the police station. "I'll get a ride home from there. I don't need you near my house."

The man with the broken nose chuckled. "Trust me. I'm glad to see the last of you."

Hutchings picked up his carry-on bag and stepped out into the APPD rear parking lot. At dawn, the sky was overcast, but a warm breeze carried a hint of rain. Glad to be home.

He leaned down and made eye contact. "Look, kid. I know you think you're doing your job, but there is a huge difference between knowing what's right and wrong. A badge does not automatically place you on the winning side. You have a lot to learn, Agent Noland, but I wish you all the best. For a fuckin' rookie, you seem all right."

Noland was about to say something, then changed his mind. He just nodded and placed the SUV in gear as Hutchings slammed the rear door. As the Tahoe drove off, he watched it leave and then entered the station. Constable Glen Luttrell got up from his desk as Steve dropped the bag onto the floor.

"I'm only here for a bit. Go take a break, and come back in fifteen."

"No problem, Sarge."

After Glen left, he wrote down a few notes and picked up the phone. Hutchings did not have to look at the list on the wall. He knew the number by heart after all these years.

"Hi Linda, it's Hutchings from Arrow Point. I have a possible 10-99 that needs to be followed up outside our jurisdiction."

*****

Dylan Noland flipped through the radio channels to find something to help keep him awake. The last twenty-four hours have been non-stop, and he preferred returning to Denver before sleeping. He made one stop in Casper for two large black coffees and a sandwich. An hour later, he felt better as he headed south on Highway 287 and merged onto Interstate 80 West.

The traffic was light, and despite the fresh air, the secret service agent had trouble focusing, and his thoughts wandered. As he hit cruise control, he frowned when a detail came to mind.

How did Steve Hutchings know my name?

At no point did anyone, including Austin, mention it since they walked into the interrogation room. Procedures were followed, especially for that part of the operation. Maybe he imagined it. After being awake for a full day, he could have misremembered.

When Noland glanced in the rearview mirror, it took a few seconds to register that the Wyoming Highway Patrol was pulling him over.

"Goddammit." *Let's get this over with. I need some sleep.*

He pulled over, turned off the Tahoe, and waited. Two state troopers got out of the cruiser and approached on either side. The larger cop had one hand on his pistol, and as he passed the back end, he placed a thumb on the taillight.

"How can I help you?"

"License and registration."

Noland frowned. "I'm working. Secret service, on duty."

"Identification."

The trooper's partner tried to see into the backseat of the Tahoe, but the tint was too dark.

"No problem." Dylan reached into his jacket pocket but couldn't find the wallet. His back pocket was empty as well. He was about to check the glovebox when the action started.

"Gun!"

The second trooper pulled out his pistol and aimed at the passenger window. He had spotted his Sig Sauer P226 in the shoulder holster. "I told you, I'm on duty and——"

When he looked out of the driver's window, he stared straight down the barrel of the highway patrol service pistol.

"You are going to place the weapon on the dashboard. Then you will get out of the vehicle and get face down on the ground. Move slowly."

Noland glanced at the nametag, then into Trooper Gaston's eyes, and nodded. He looked ready to pull the trigger. As he followed the instructions, he held back a grin when it all fell into place.

Bravo, old man.

Chapter 30

At four o'clock in the morning, the siren from the ambulance wailed to life. The sound carried for miles across the countryside. The flashing red strobe lights made the shadows dance and leap between the long storage containers and were visible for a mile. Four seconds later, the lights came on in the front room of the farmhouse.

At first, there was no response from inside, but the front door opened shortly. The barrel of a long rifle led the way as it swept the yard. A large white man with a crew-cut, T-shirt, track pants, and running shoes stepped outside, and a flashlight came to life under the barrel. Over 1500 Lumens focused on the ambulance to reveal an empty cab.

His partner came out in an undershirt and boxer shorts with a 12-gauge shotgun at the ready. She moved to the side and shouted over the siren. "Anything?"

"No." The flashlight illuminated under the ambulance and the tops of the storage containers. "Tell the doctor to come out and shut the damn thing off."

The woman relayed the order through the open door, and two slim men stepped outside and crossed the yard. The first man with the rifle escorted them to the ambulance.

"The driver's window is down, and there's mud everywhere."

One man opened the door, and seconds later, the siren turned off, then the lights. "There's mud all over the cab and dashboard. Racoon?"

"Maybe." The man stepped behind the ambulance and scanned the fields. "Lopez, come here for a second."

The woman joined him and squinted. Three hundred yards across the field, a dim light moved in a small cluster of trees that separated the neighbor's property.

"Pretty sure a raccoon doesn't carry a flashlight."

The other two men continued to check out the ambulance for damages while Lopez and another brought their weapons up and proceeded through the corn stalks. The flashlight under the rifle turned off, and the setting moon gave enough light for them to move safely.

"Carlson, look to your two o'clock."

The man glanced right, and another flashlight bobbed in the distance, nearly four hundred yards out. "Let's check this one out first. Did you bring a radio or phone?"

Lopez shook her head and glanced back at the farmhouse. The two men opened the rear of the ambulance to check it out. "No. Do you want to head back?"

"They'll be fine. We need to clear the area. We'll be back in fifteen minutes. Probably local kids playing a prank."

"Hurry up. I'm not dressed for the cold."

They crossed the field to find an LED puck light duct-taped to a sapling. The light breeze made it sway back and forth.

"What the hell is this?" Lopez used the shotgun, batted the puck-light to the ground, and crushed it with a heel.

*****

Noah waited until the two paramedics were occupied with the ambulance, then rolled out from under the Tahoe. Dressed in dark clothing and a balaclava pulled down to hide his face, he came up between the vehicle and the farmhouse. The light sensor was already tripped, and the door was left wide open.

After stepping inside, he quietly closed the door behind him. The door was heavy and constructed from thick metal, with inch-and-a-half bolts that sunk into the steel frame. It would be easier to cut the window's bars than attempt entry through the door.

Noah stood in a small foyer with a converted bedroom on the right, where the dining room would have been. Three beds were against the walls, and a TV was in the corner. A set of stairs went to the second floor from the foyer, with an old dark oak railing. The pine floors looked original but were well maintained. A glance at the ceiling didn't reveal any cameras, but he knew they could be hidden.

A dimly lit kitchen was visible through an arched open doorway at the end of the hall. The door on his immediate left was closed, and he tried to control the adrenaline that coursed through his body. He reached out a gloved hand and slowly turned the handle. The door swung inward with a slight protest of the hinges. A familiar disinfectant scent announced what lay beyond as he stepped inside.

An array of modern hospital equipment ringed the bed. Leslie Taylor rested under clean white sheets while hooked into various devices. Noah only recognized the blood pressure monitor, and to all appearances, she was doing fine. Unfortunately, there was nothing he could do for her. Despite being captured, she was receiving good care—more than he could provide.

Noah took two steps inside the room, pulled the sheet up, and tucked it in around her. He whispered. "I'm doing what I can and not giving up on your daughter. Rest up."

Noah quietly backed out of the room and closed the door.

When he got a whiff of stale cigarettes, instinct made him spin around. Instead of taking the baseball bat to the back of his head, it struck his left shoulder and upper chest. He was hurled into the door as a stocky bald man grunted, and the bat swung again.

Chapter 31

Noah had served many arrest warrants in nearly nineteen years on the police force. They were usually executed in the early morning hours, which had a few purposes, but most importantly, the law enforcement officer's safety. Most people were asleep at four o'clock in the morning, and the intrusion made them disorientated and confused. When in such a state, people were more complacent, and the police suffered fewer injuries as a result—it gave them an edge.

Noah knew that was the only reason he wasn't unconscious on the floor from the first swing. The bald man appeared to be shaking off a deep sleep, and he easily side-stepped the man's telegraphed overhead blow. Noah rushed in with a burst of adrenaline before the man could swing the bat a third time. They crashed into the staircase railing, then to the floor. The man retained the grip on the baseball bat and struggled to drive it under his chin. Noah dropped his weight on the man's chest.

Fear shone in the man's eyes as the wind was knocked out of his lungs, and he struggled to breathe. As the man groaned and began to roll to the side, Noah brought a gloved fist around and clipped him behind the ear. Dazed, the man started to call out as Noah's arm snaked around his neck. *Were there others in the house? Was he calling for help inside?*

Noah clasped hands, placed an inner elbow against the throat, then squeezed like a vise-grip. The sleeper hold, when applied properly, had a victim out in fifteen seconds. It wasn't the lack of air but the restricted blood flow to the brain which knocked them out.

The man made a feeble attempt at a forward roll to escape, but Noah shot a leg out to the side to drop his weight and squeezed tighter. His opponent tried to gouge his eyes and drove an elbow back into his ribs, but it was too late. When the man became limp, he held the choke a few seconds longer to make sure the man wasn't faking.

Noah slid the backpack off and pulled out some plastic zip ties. Noah gasped for breath once the man's wrists were secured to the banister. The adrenaline surge had his hands shaking and muscles twitching.

"Sorry, buddy."

Noah flicked the Louisville Slugger down the hall with a foot as he went into the kitchen. The design was forty years out of date with avocado green appliances and seafoam tiles, but it was spotless. To the right was a small den with a brown love seat and TV, and on the other end was an office. The television volume was very low, with an Afghan blanket thrown to the side. The bald guy must have fallen asleep watching a show.

Darting into the office, Noah sat behind the desk and knocked the mouse. The two monitors flickered to life but asked for a password. Noah looked under the keyboard, but there were no notes. Not even attempting to guess a password, he went through the drawers. The top center drawer held stationery. The bottom right drawer was mostly empty, except for a small box with dozens of USB keys, each one with a unique number, letter combination—*456665-YYZ, 23332-01SAA.* Noah opened the backpack and dumped them in, unsure of what they were. There was nothing else of note.

There didn't appear to be a basement, so Noah made his way up the stairs. The man was still breathing and out. Hopefully, for a few minutes longer.

The second floor had a narrow hallway with four closed doors. The first room on the right had a steel table in the middle with bench seating on either side. Everything was bolted to the ground. From the doorway, Noah spotted video cameras in each corner of the ceiling. He had been in similar rooms many times.

"That would mean there's a control room."

The next door opened into an office. It reminded Noah of the computer room at the police station. Two server racks filled the back wall, and a U-shaped desk sat in the middle with an array of computer screens. A five-foot-tall filing cabinet stood beside the desk. A thick lock secured the top drawer.

Frustrated, Noah slammed a fist on top, and the hollow boom sounded like a drum. He came into the farmhouse to get answers, but so far, there was nothing but, most likely, useless USB keys. The risk wasn't paying off.

A moral war raged within, and he knew the man downstairs would have answers. But torturing someone to justify another crime wasn't a line he wanted to cross. He only had a few minutes before the distraction was over, and there was no time.

Noah would need a grinder and half-an-hour to get through the lock, and he quickly gave that up. The servers looked new; however, he did not know enough to recognize a hard drive storage nor remove it.

Sitting at the desk, he went through each drawer, but there wasn't much besides stationery and blank paper. The bottom right was locked, and it gave him hope.

He pulled out a Leatherman multi-tool and slid the blade in the crack above the lock, then worked it back and forth. After a few seconds, the knife snapped. "Fuck!"

He had enough of subtly and flicked open the slim screwdriver. Once the tip slid into the lock, Noah slammed the end with an open palm, driving it deep inside. Then, with a quick twist, the drawer popped open.

The only item was a small black binder. *Procedures and Contacts* were handwritten on the first page, and on the second page was a list of four names and numbers. The remaining pages were filled with notes.

"Bingo."

It would be enough to move forward. Hopefully.

However, as Noah placed everything in the backpack, his heart froze. Someone was pounding on the front door, and he could hear yelling from outside. He ran to the window and pulled back the blind just enough to see the front yard. The two EMTs leaned against the Chevy as the man with the rifle yelled again at the house. It must be the woman who pounded on the door.

Noah had run out of time. He was trapped.

Chapter 32

Noah darted downstairs to look for a back door. The man he had knocked out was groaning and starting to move. Time to leave—if he can.

The front bedroom faced the driveway, so he ruled that out. The kitchen had a small window above the sink, but there were bars on the window, same for the den.

There wasn't a basement, so he made his way to Leslie's room. The pounding on the door grew more frantic. As Noah passed the bald man, he awoke.

"No time for this."

Wide-eyed, the man struggled to gain his feet. Noah brought up a boot and slammed the heel into the side of his head. The man slumped to the floor, dazed but not unconscious. Leslie hadn't moved inside the hospital room, and the windows also opened up to the front yard. Even if the bars were not there, it wouldn't be a good choice.

That left the upstairs.

There were no windows in the interrogation or control rooms—they may have been sealed over.

The third room was set up as a minimal bedroom that had seen little or no use. The mattress was rolled up at the bottom of a metal frame with a folded gray blanket on top. The single nightstand was empty. The dark curtains concealed a window, but there was no opening, just a sheet of glass. That explained why there were no bars. They would have to break the glass to get in.

The last door at the end of the hall was a bathroom. The lime-green tiles matched the tub, and the sink was a light blue. Noah wasn't sure what decade created the style, but he ignored it as he flung the shower curtain to the side.

The single window opened with a hand crank, and it was wide enough that he could fit sideways, but most importantly, there were no bars.

The pounding on the front door grew frantic, and the sound of wood splintering echoed throughout the home. It was the banister spindles being snapped. The man was breaking free.

Noah quietly closed the bathroom door and locked it. It may buy him precious seconds. Once he stood in the tub and turned the handle, the window swung open. He pushed the screen out and dropped the backpack to the ground. He had to jump and twist to get his shoulders through the narrow opening. As he squirmed through, the noise in the house grew louder. Noah held onto the edge and flipped around.

After taking a deep breath and grinding his teeth, he dropped.

The landing was enough to send a flash of pain through his knees and ankles before he rolled to the side.

"Come on, Spiderman. Run."

He scooped up the backpack and sprinted for the field. Noah knew enough not to head directly back to the vehicle. Instead, he turned north. Sweat soaked into the balaclava, and he struggled to gain control of his breathing. Noah swore to do more cardio in the future as he kept the pace across the field.

He turned east after five hundred yards and made a beeline to the minivan. When Noah glanced at his watch, he realized only ten minutes had passed since he sounded the sirens on the ambulance, but it felt longer. His adrenaline levels dropped, and the aches and pains became obvious. His shoulder ached from the baseball bat—no doubt it would bruise. Luckily, nothing was broken.

Two hundred yards from the car, the sound of engines echoed across the countryside. Two ATVs roared to life, and one headed west and the other east. Directly toward his location.

Noah didn't want to fire the Glock, but there may be little choice. The familiar weight was reassuring regardless. With a glance over his shoulder at the approaching headlight, he realized there wasn't a chance of making it to the car in time. Time for plan B—whatever that was.

*****

To say Special Agent Andrea Lopez was pissed would have been an understatement. After fifteen years in the FBI and five years on the task force, she had fallen for a distraction. With more seniority than Carlson, it would hit her first when the shit rolled downhill. Hoping to avoid a transfer to Alaska, she wasn't ready to give up.

Still wearing an undershirt and boxers, she grabbed a Glock 22 to back up the shotgun. Once the storage container opened, she ordered Carlson to search west, then north. Once Troy had broken free, they entered and cleared the safehouse. They missed the intruder by seconds.

As the ATV flew across the field, she kept the shotgun tucked under the front storage rack with a bungee cord and the pistol in her left hand. Her head constantly swiveled, looking for a target, but the bright headlight destroyed her night vision.

When the flash of light and sharp retort from small arms fire came from the side, she wasn't prepared when the front tire blew out. The ATV tilted, and the handlebars were wrenched to the side. Within a split second, Lopez found herself flying through the air.

She heard the crack as her collarbone snapped, and pain spread like a forest fire as she landed face-first in the field. It took a moment to realize she was alive and not dead, although it felt like it. When the ATV tipped, the engine shut off, and the area was plunged into darkness. Lopez could only lie in pain as she ground her teeth together. Her pistol was missing, and she expected another round to be fired, but she wouldn't hear this one. *Hopefully, it will be quick.*

When someone approached, she closed her eyes to wait for death.

Two fingers felt her carotid artery. After four seconds, she felt a gentle pat on her head. Instead of a gun firing, Andrea heard someone running away through the field. The crunching of plants faded, then a vehicle engine roared to life. Tires tore up the gravel and dirt before driving out on the county road.

Lopez opened her eyes and struggled to sit. Maybe Alaska will not be that bad—if she was lucky.

Chapter 33

Walter Scott.

Sean Cameron.

Miriam Glenn Davis.

Dennis McCallister.

Noah wasn't sure if the names were in order of importance or not. Old phone numbers beside each had been crossed out and updated. Nothing in the rest of the book may have revealed a location or organization—just documentation and recording procedures. The USB keys Noah tossed out the window as he drove away. Malware could be activated once it was plugged into a system, and he didn't have the knowledge to break encryptions.

With the speed at which he was tracked from the burner phone, Noah was hesitant to get another. However, there were more old-fashioned methods.

It took two hours to drive to Richmond, Virginia, and by seven o'clock, Noah sat in Millie's, a diner downtown, eating a large breakfast. The lack of sleep, coupled with a few injuries, had given him a headache, and the bright lights and background noise didn't help.

Noah needed to rest. A bottle of aspirin, an ice pack, and a soak in a hot tub would not hurt either. He added bourbon to the list.

"Excuse me. Can you recommend a good hotel nearby?"

The waitress had tucked the bill under his orange juice.

"My sister-in-law works at The Berkeley Hotel on East Cary Street. Although, it's a little pricey. There's a Holiday Inn a few blocks farther down."

"Thank you." Noah left an extra twenty dollars on the table before heading outside.

It was time for John Visser to earn his living.

Before heading to The Berkeley Hotel, Noah bought a tablet. It would have to be connected to a Wi-Fi signal to be of any use, and with five floors and over one-hundred-and-fifty rooms, it would be almost impossible to pinpoint. Besides, he was just using the email client, which no one else knew. He used the credit card from the bank to book a suite for the week. It wasn't in his name, and the electronic trail back would be a dead end.

Once he showered and sent the request to his lawyer, Noah was asleep before his head hit the pillow.

When he awoke seven hours later, his shoulder was sore and stiff when he tried to move it. He would have a colorful bruise in a few days, but nothing was broken. After ordering room service, he read the report.

The lawyer must have a good team working for him, and Noah knew he would be billed accordingly.

Walter T. Scott joined the Air Force in 1959 and left in 1971 at the rank of major. He worked at the Pentagon for five years as an analyst, then moved into the CIA. Current administrative position—unknown. The only other information on Scott was a photo opportunity with President Ronald Reagan in 1988, outside Nevada, at a military test range. Despite the thirty-two years which have passed, Noah easily recognized him. It was the same man that escorted Hutchings and himself to the airport.

Sean Cameron had the title of Information Assurance Director (IAD) at the National Security Agency since 1992. There wasn't any information on what task the IAD cell performed, but Noah could guess. If Cameron had the capabilities of the NSA and worked with Walter Scott, following Noah from the airport and tracing a cell phone would have been fairly easy. Before joining the IAD, there wasn't any background or picture available.

Miriam Davis had the most publicly available background. From 1976 to 1992, she rose to Executive Assistant

Director of the Counterintelligence Division. She spent eleven years working with the CIA in the Directorate of Operations. In 2003, Davis moved into Homeland Security after helping the administration push the Homeland Security Act as a response to the 9/11 attacks. Her current Disaster Prevention and Management Director title made Noah's brow furrow. The position did not make sense with her past experience, but he didn't know what it entailed. Over the last few decades, there were several pictures of the woman, and she reminded Noah of Diane Keaton, the actress.

Dennis McCallister was the Deputy Special Agent in charge of the FBI based out of Jacksonville, Florida. After forty years of bouncing around the country in various positions, it seems he had settled down in the Sunshine state. There were several reports on his administrative actions and accomplishments, but he flew under the radar. The picture of Dennis posing in front of the American flag would have been taken for the bureau. He had a rather large nose and a receding hairline with dark circles under his eyes. However, the half-grin didn't reach his eyes, and it gave him a sinister look. Noah figured him for a hard ass. It was just a hunch, but he had seen that same look many times before.

Four different branches of the government, and as to why their names were written in the book, Noah had no idea. They had the answers, and that left him little choice. He promised to do his best to find Leslie's daughter, and he would do so.

When room service arrived, Noah groaned as he got off the bed. Everything was stiff and sore. He would be going nowhere for a few days, and that would also give him time to rest before heading east.

The scope of the investigation seemed daunting, and despite the dangers that awaited, Noah would see this through.

It was time to pay one of the four a visit, but first, there were a few things to do.

Chapter 34

Sergeant Angie Dickinson shook her head as the tow truck pulled the golf cart out of the ditch. The blue and white Coleman cooler shifted, and broken beer bottles fell onto the seat, along with a half-eaten pizza slice. The fifteen- and seventeen-year-old brothers were bruised, and one had a broken left wrist. Their parents have been called and were on the way. The EMTs cleaned the cuts and told them they were lucky they were not killed.

The boys spent the night drinking and stole the golf cart from a neighbor. After narrowly missing a car, they went down a fifteen-foot embankment before crashing. At one o'clock in the morning, the police were called by another driver that witnessed the accident.

"Sarge, what do you want to do with this?"

Constable Robertson held up a starter pistol that he found hidden in the dash of the cart. Jesus Christ.

Angie knew how her father would have dealt with this fifty years ago. March the kids home, broken wrist and all, and let the father discipline them—after paying for the damages. Times were different, and she had no choice.

"Clear it and log the pistol as evidence. Add weapon charges to impaired driving, theft under, and underage drinking. They should be lucky that they weren't over eighteen."

Chief Birch had a zero-tolerance for underage drinking, and the golf cart counted as a vehicle. Hopefully, they would learn from the lesson. As minors, the drinking infractions would count as a misdemeanor. Probation or a small fine would most likely be the result.

Dickinson slowly let out a deep breath and sighed as she turned back to her cruiser. Maybe she did have a choice.

"Robinson, wait."

She turned around and held out a hand for the starter pistol. Robinson nodded and passed it over. They both knew the charges would have been elevated well beyond just a fine. Neither of the boys had any priors.

"This is the only break I'm willing to give. I'll hand it over to the father."

He nodded. "Understood. I'll keep it out of my notes."

Angie grinned. "Go put the fear of God into them on how bad this could have been."

With a wink, Robertson put on his "tough cop" face and went to the back of the ambulance. The large man had a deep voice, and he never had to speak loudly to get the point across.

No one here had to know about a tea party with his little girls before his shift. That would ruin his reputation. Angie loved his kids, and he had shown her the pictures back at the station. They had gone through the law enforcement academy in Douglas together five years ago and remained good friends.

Dickinson began to fill out the reports and wait for the kids' parents to arrive back in the cruiser. When her personal cell phone chimed with an email notification, she had a glance then deleted it as spam.

It took twenty minutes to finish the paperwork, and by then, the kid's father arrived in an old Ford pickup truck, still in his pajamas. Robertson took him aside. Angie was about to join them when her phone dinged. It was another junk email about a hunter course in Washington, D.C.

She took a few steps toward the ambulance when the phone was suddenly in her hands once again. The email was an invitation to attend a hunter course experience, including paid flights and hotel stay. Dickinson chuckled when she read the senders name:

Threezeroseven.4417@gmail.com.

Wyoming's area code is 307, and 4417 was Noah Hunter's badge number. Dress was casual with semi-formal appearances, and attendance was voluntary. However, she had to confirm by email, not by phone. That detail set alarm bells off, and a finger hovered over the reply button.

Noah wasn't just her partner but a friend and colleague. He had saved her life many times, and she would do the same for

169

him without hesitation. After talking with Staff Sergeant Hutchings there was no doubt the government was involved. As to what extent they were monitoring, Angie wasn't sure. She would have to show identification to get on a plane, and at that point, if she were being watched, the government would know within seconds.

It would come down to how well they monitored every aspect of Hunter's life. Her finger pressed reply. The risk was worth the reward and any trade-off. Besides, it had to be more exciting than what was going on in Arrow Point.

When the oldest kid leaned over and puked in the ditch, Angie was ready to pack a bag and leave right then.

Chapter 35

"Thanks for the fun, but it's not you. It's me."

Noah patted the minivan on the hood and transferred the items into the black Lincoln Navigator. After another solid eight hours of sleep, he awoke feeling better. As predicted, a deep bruise started on his shoulder and across the chest. It was tender to the touch and stiff to move, but nothing was broken. In a few days, it would turn almost black, then varying shades of orange and yellow. At least he didn't add to the scars that decorated his torso.

Dressed in the charcoal gray suit and light blue shirt and tie, Noah took the holster for Leslie's Glock and tucked it on his belt in plain sight. He kept the two spare magazines inside the jacket pocket. The tint on the Navigator's windows was dark enough so others couldn't look inside, and Noah looked at his reflection. The beard was gone, and he was clean-shaven. When he ran a hand over the smooth skin, he couldn't help but grin. It made him look years younger but, most importantly, changed his image.

Noah had called down to the concierge at the hotel to ask about rental companies and changing out his minivan. It took thirty minutes, and they came right to the parking lot for the exchange. Outstanding service.

A driver pulled up in the Lincoln and performed an inspection on both vehicles and waited while Noah finished loading.

"Thank you. This will do nicely."

He shook the young man's hand and slipped him a good tip before climbing behind the wheel. Noah ran his hand over the hand-stitched leather steering wheel and examined the interior. The vehicle had to be the same price as his house. The driver's seat had a heating and cooling option, and it was easily the most comfortable he ever had been behind the wheel. Hands down.

"I could get used to this."

He punched in the address on the GPS, and the large screen turned into a map with directions. Before heading to Ronald Reagan Airport, he drove by a small subdivision called Virginia Square.

Even on a Saturday morning, the roads were difficult with volume. It took ninety minutes with traffic before he cruised through the quaint neighborhood. Kids were playing baseball in the park, and vehicles lined both sides of the street.

A beautiful two-story Victorian home overlooked the park on a normal day. An unmarked step-van with a parabolic dish on the roof parked at the end of the driveway blocked the view. A bright orange extension cord snaked out of the back and up the driveway. Two Ford Interceptors were parked on either side.

Two men sat in the first car, and Noah figured they must have been there all night. Suit jackets were off, and both were slumped low. The man in the passenger seat may have been sleeping or looking at a cell phone in his lap. The driver leaned back with sunglasses on. Both men were in their forties and had a thin build, with holstered pistols in shoulder harnesses. The passenger had a long mustache that curled at the ends. Otherwise, they were unremarkable.

Noah pulled over, and his fingers drummed on the steering wheel as an idea formed. Luck favors the bold. He pulled into a driveway and turned around, and double-parked across the street before he could second guess.

When he got out of the Lincoln and headed toward the Ford, the driver sat up straight and nudged his partner. The driver's window lowered as the sunglasses were placed on the dash. Noah buttoned up his jacket, but he knew they would have seen the weapon.

"Sorry guys, I'm going to be a bit late. My partner is landing in thirty minutes."

The men briefly glanced at each other, then stared at Noah.

"Who are you with?" The driver had a southern accent he couldn't place.

173

"Investigations. I just found out a few hours ago about this assignment. I'm supposed to relieve you at nine."

"ID?" The driver didn't look worried, but he was fully awake.

Noah chuckled. "Nope. I'm not supposed to be working since this isn't happening."

Silence.

The men glanced at each other again, then the passenger grinned and spoke, "We aren't here either."

Noah winked at the conspiracy. "Can I pick up some coffees on the way back? Bagels?"

"I won't say no to that." The driver grinned at the offer of breakfast and his shift ending.

"Sorry, again. I'll be back soon." Noah climbed back in the Navigator with a little wave and drove straight to the airport. Despite the cool morning breeze, a trickle of sweat ran down his back. It took five minutes for his heart rate to return to acceptable levels.

Chapter 36

An encrypted email arrived at a carpeted office at seven o'clock on a Saturday morning. The message normally would not have been read until Sunday or at the least Monday morning, but Walter Scott had forgotten his new putter behind the desk. A tee-off time was booked, and the driver waited outside the Langley main entrance.

Walter had intended to check his messages and be on his way within minutes, but a cell phone appeared in his hands after he scanned the screen.

"I'm going to have to cancel the golf game, and I'll be here a while. I'll call you if needed." Geoff, his driver, was used to such last-minute changes over the years.

"Yes, sir."

As he settled behind the desk, he re-read the lengthy recommendation—Walter came to the same conclusion. It was a shame, really, but essential to keep the status quo.

There was only one option to guarantee success, and despite the cost, it would be worth it. He transferred the money with a series of keystrokes then leaned back in the chair. He placed the satellite phone on top of the desk from the middle drawer and waited.

Two minutes later, it rang.

Walter placed it on speaker and leaned back. "That was rather quick."

A woman with a British accent replied. "A deposit that large gets my attention. Details?"

"Sending now." With a few clicks of the mouse, the file transferred halfway around the world. The STARTTLS (Transport Layer Security) encryption system was two-fold. A file could only be sent if the receiving computer knew it was incoming. Coupled with the DMARC program, it not only validates the sender but the recipient as well. Even if someone were to intercept the transmission, they would need possession of the other half of the encryption to decode.

"Receiving."

After a minute, the woman spoke. "This seems rather … mundane for our services."

Walter cleared his throat. She was correct, but too many bridges were burned, and those that were left pointed in a direction that made him uncomfortable. "Due to conflicts, we need to keep this at arm's length."

"No problem." He could hear the woman tapping away at a keyboard as she scanned the file. "Method and collateral damage?"

Walter had made many such decisions over the years, and sometimes the innocent had to be sacrificed for the greater good. It was unfortunate. Hunter appeared to be a good man. Had things been different, Noah may have been working for him.

"Accidental and minimal, unless no other choice. Also, if possible, play the Tecumseh Scenario."

"Roger that. Is there an early completion bonus like Syrian rebel operation?"

Walter winced. It would cut into his budget, but he needed to wrap this up. "Not that significant, but it will be substantial."

The excitement in the woman's voice made the English accent thicken. "Talk to you soon, dear."

*****

Noah stood inside Ronald Reagan at the arrival concourse with time to spare. He was still apprehensive about what had just happened. When he was training in Georgina, he had a glimpse of the multitude of different law enforcement agencies out there. In the United States, there were over 17,000 various groups with policing powers. When he mentioned investigations, the terminology was broad enough to have referenced almost anything. Technically, he hadn't lied. Noah was an investigator, but with Arrow Point Police Department.

The other thing he had counted on was the "law-enforcement" radar. Within a few seconds, Noah could tell if someone was a police officer or not. Sometimes, military personnel gave off the same aura of command, but after any discussion, he could usually guess correctly on their background. Noah had counted on those men in the car to recognize and read him as he read others. Coupled with the fact that no one willingly volunteered for watch duty sealed the deal.

When the large double doors opened, Noah immediately forgot what he was thinking as he recognized his partner. It seems Dickinson had taken his formal attire note seriously, and he barely recognized her.

Dressed in a short gray skirt, white blouse, and matching blazer Angie pulled her carry-on luggage behind as her heels clicked on the tiled floor. Her long brown hair fell to one side when she noticed him leaning against the pillar. In the dress shoes, she must have stood six-foot-two, and Noah struggled to tear his eyes away from her legs and a brief glimpse of a toned thigh.

Of course, my partner had legs—now focus.

"You shaved."

Noah ran a hand over his smooth cheeks and realized they were also warm. He tried not to groan with embarrassment. "Had to change up my image. Before I say anything, I need you to realize what I'm doing isn't sanctioned and could be dangerous. There can, and most likely will be repercussions. Are you sure you want to help?"

Dickinson let out a throaty chuckle, and her dimples made an appearance. "Damn right, I'm in."

Noah nodded as the seriousness set in. "Okay, but if I order you out, I need you to listen. We good?" He held out a hand, and it hung in the air for a moment.

She firmly shook his hand. "I promise to listen. Now, where do we start?"

First, I have to get my head out of the gutter. "We have to stop by a Starbucks. I'll explain on the way."

~

Noah pulled in behind the rear Ford unmarked cruiser shortly after ten o'clock. Angie balanced a cardboard cup holder in one hand and a white bag of bagels and pastries in another.

"Ready? It isn't too late to change your mind."

Angie didn't bother to answer but instead rolled her eyes. She passed him the coffees and stepped out of the Navigator carrying the food. The two men got out of the car and slipped on their suit jackets.

"Hope you like it black." Noah passed over the drinks.

"Thanks. We aren't used to being treated like this. Hope it's habit-forming." The man with the mustache accepted the bag of food and checked out Dickinson when he thought no one was looking. Dirtbag.

Noah winked. "We shall see. Are you relieving us tomorrow morning or tonight?"

The driver shrugged. "We've been here for over twenty-four hours. We don't know the schedule yet, or how much longer till they shut this down."

Noah nodded. "We haven't been told of a rotation yet. Hopefully, that will come down today. Do you have a logbook?"

He had been on countless surveillance operations throughout his career. Surveillance was broken down into three different types: premises, vehicles, or persons. Each type demanded a different observation post. With the lack of disguise and parked out of the residence, they must be here only for the premises. There were also many rules to follow, such as no littering, contingency plans, and knowing the shift schedule. One thing consistent across different law enforcement agents—a handwritten journal.

"Just a second." The driver leaned down, pulled a black notebook from between the two front seats, and held it up. "Here you go."

Angie asked, "Bathroom?"

The man with the curly mustache gestured toward the home. "The front door's unlocked."

"That's a lot better than a pop bottle." Noah wryly added.

The men chuckled, and Dickinson shrugged. "You gotta go, you gotta go."

When the men separated and both vehicles drove away, Noah pulled the Lincoln forward to park behind the truck. With a wave goodbye, he turned off the engine and settled in.

"Holy fuck. How the hell did that just work?" Angie turned to face him, stunned.

Noah let out a nervous laugh. "The more secretive an organization, the more information is restricted to a few. I guessed that the worker bees were not told the big picture."

"You *guessed*?" Angie's eyebrows rose in disbelief.

"For now, let's finish our coffees, then see if we can find out what happened with Miriam Davis. Because up until now, I wasn't sure she was even missing."

Chapter 37

Noah flipped through the surveillance log, and the entries started six days ago. There were four different types of handwriting, along with comments and observations. The first day filled several pages with details of vehicles and plates and descriptions of anyone who passed the home more than once. But the problem became apparent. The neighborhood and park generated a lot of foot and vehicular traffic.

On Tuesday, the notes were barely a page long. Wednesday at 19:30, the computer technician arrived and parked the van at the end of the driveway. After connecting to the server, he left at 21:00 in his assistant's vehicle. The Virginia plates were recorded. The remainder of the week had nothing of note except for Saturday morning. Noah read the last entry, and it had his description and plates for the Navigator—*after almost thirty hours, our relief finally arrived.*

"There is no mention of what they were on the lookout for or whom to contact in an emergency." Noah passed the book to Dickinson and finished his coffee.

Angie quickly read the pages before tossing them on the dash. "What's the call, boss?"

Noah opened the armrest and pulled out two walkie-talkies. "These aren't the greatest, but they work. One of us searches the home for anything we could use, while the other stands guard."

Angie turned them on, and a faint baby cry came through the speaker. "Switching to channel four."

"Do you want to rest? You must be tired after working late."

She grinned. "I got three hours last night and a few more on the flight. I'm good. But I wouldn't mind changing out of this outfit into something more comfortable."

"Go ahead. Keep me updated. I'll take first watch."

*****

Angie pulled out a change of clothes from her suitcase before going inside the home. The hardwood floors looked original, and the wainscotting and floral wallpaper made the house look like the cover of a decorating magazine. The orange cord from the van went down the hall and into the first room on the right.

Originally, it would have been a parlor or sitting room, but it was converted into an office. An antique desk dominated

183

one end with two Victorian wingback chairs facing it. The far wall had floor-to-ceiling bookshelves. The remaining walls were filled with framed pictures of a lady posing with various presidents and heads of state going back nearly five decades.

Miriam seemed to have a prominent career and had aged well. A current picture of the president and herself stood in a gold frame on a small table under the front window.

Angie ignored the near-celebrity status of the subject and followed the orange cord to a buffet cabinet behind the desk. The front had been removed, and a series of computer components on server racks were inside—the cable connected to a small stainless-steel hub, and from there, various wires connected to the system.

"If a tech can't access the computers, I doubt I can. Time to work."

After changing into jeans and running shoes, Angie went upstairs and started with the bedroom. While the place wasn't trashed, it was apparent the home had been searched thoroughly. Dresser drawers were still open as each was examined and the clothing dumped back inside. Someone had emptied the closet and placed Miriam's wardrobe on the bed. Dress shoes were scattered across the carpet and under the bed.

In her recent training with the marshals, she learned about the Spiral Method. Start at a fixed point and methodically work your way outward. Paying attention to objects that could be modified, like the depth of a drawer not going fully to the back or the dimensions of a room that seem off—hidden rooms or spaces could lay in between.

"Radio check. All good?"

Angie was startled but quickly recovered. "All good. Home has already been searched."

"Give it a once over, and then we'll switch. Two sets of eyes are better than one."

"10-4."

Dickinson clipped the handset to her belt and started in the closet.

Chapter 38

At 16:52 EDT, a flight from London, England, landed at
Washington Dulles International Airport thirty minutes early due
to favorable conditions. The lineup for customs, while long,
moved quickly. Having multiple flights land simultaneously
from around the world was a regular occurrence and not an issue.
Agents were used to processing millions of people annually.

A middle-aged couple, husband and wife, were visiting
from Sweden, and after a few questions, a customs agent barely
looked up at them before he called the next person to step
forward.

Five minutes later, a woman from the airline pushed an
older gentleman through the crowd in a wheelchair. A pair of
crutches were tucked into his side, and a small bag rested on his
lap. The man was brought to the customs agent on the end, who
helped those with special needs. He was whisked through

without incident, and the woman brought him to the luggage area, where his nephew was allowed to help.

On the opposite end, a customs agent's finger caressed the red button under the counter, and twice, he almost pushed it. Something about the man in front of him made him nervous.

There wasn't anything remarkable about him—forty-five years of age, short dark hair, and casually dressed in a gray sweatshirt and khakis. The Irish passport held a new picture, and there was no doubt of the resemblance. Maybe it was the total lack of emotion on his features or the way he seemed to glide as he walked, but the button was nearly pressed a third time. He wrote R-45 on the CBP Traveler Entry form with a blue marker and allowed him through.

After collecting his luggage, the man showed the paperwork to the departing agent. He was led to a secondary inspection, where detailed questions were asked and a thorough search, including a body scan, was conducted. Every piece of clothing and luggage went through the X-ray. Swabs were taken and run through the "puffer" machine as it looked for trace detection of explosives.

The man was polite and did not hinder the agents. After a dog handler brought a black Labrador retriever through to sniff his possessions, he was free to go.

At 18:12, a blue airport panel van with tinted windows pulled away from the authorized short-term parking. The set of crutches left by the wheelchair would eventually end up in the lost and found and remain unclaimed for sixty days before being donated.

*****

After two hours, Noah used the handset. "Anything?"

"Nothing. Even if we were to bust walls, I think the place is clean." Angie sounded tired.

"Come on out, and we can switch. I need a break."

"Roger. Out in two."

Noah grew bored after countless hours of sitting in a vehicle and watching a target. He found his mind drifting as to Miriam's involvement. The information kept adding up to a foreign government being involved, long past Leslie and Joe Taylor's involvement. Revenge against the US government agencies for discovering their spies? That line of thought didn't make sense. Any actions taken would be done covertly and not in a public kidnapping.

Dickinson came out of the house, and he could tell she carried something wrapped in her skirt. She passed him a Smith and Wesson MP&9 pistol at the driver's door. The 9mm gun was much smaller than the Glock, and it would be easier to conceal.

"Whoever searched the place left it unloaded on the bed. It wasn't what they were looking for or just didn't care." She showed him the extra magazine.

"Keep it for now, but tucked away." After flashing the Glock to the agents, he had placed it in the armrest storage. It would court trouble and shift attention where he didn't want it. "What section of the house is left?"

Angie opened the door, and he stepped outside. She knew enough that the vehicle should always be ready to drive away if needed. "Kitchen, office, and exterior."

Noah grabbed the handset and made his way up the walkway. He had no doubt Dickinson was methodical in her search, so he didn't waste time double-checking. Before he began a systematic examination, Noah stood in the middle of the office and did nothing.

If something is out of place or odd, your attention will be drawn to it. So, to start, do nothing but take it in. Hutchings gave that advice to him eighteen years ago, and he couldn't help but hope Hutch was staying out of trouble.

After three minutes, Noah found one thing missing. The lack of any security systems or cameras throughout the home. He stepped out on the front porch to confirm. Nothing. A woman in her position should have *something*—even a false outdoor camera as a deterrent. Why? Only one answer came to mind— there was nothing of any real value within the home.

As he turned around and saw the pictures, a grin spread across his face. He removed a small five-by-eight frame to examine the photo.

"It looks like we're going on a road trip."

Noah tucked the picture inside his jacket when the flashing lights came through the front window. They had company.

Chapter 39

The Alexandria City Police Department cruiser parked behind the Navigator and blocked it in. A lone officer stepped out of the vehicle and approached the driver's door.

"Are you good?" Noah whispered into the handset.

Angie toggled the PTT button once. Affirmative.

He pulled back the curtain just enough to see what was happening. Dickinson must have wedged the radio between the seat and console. The toggle was continually broadcasting.

"Good afternoon, Officer. How can I help you?"

"We've had reports of suspicious vehicles parked out front of this residence. Can I see your driver's license and proof of registration, please?"

"I'm legally parked. Are you accusing me of a crime?" Noah could hear the incredulous tone in her voice. He knew right away where this conversation was headed. He had pulled many people over, and it usually started the same way.

"I'm just following up on complaints. Driver's license and registration, please." The officer appeared to be young, mid-twenties, and was built like a football player—all shoulders and chest. Noah's view was obstructed, but he could see the cop step backward toward the hood and rested a hand on his holstered Taser.

Angie chuckled. "Unless you are accusing me of a crime, I am *not* required to show identification. I have no doubt you've learned the fourth amendment in your training."

"I have complaints of suspicious activity on this street, and I'm asking you to show identification." Noah could see the officer's face turn red with embarrassment from forty feet away.

"What's your name and badge number?" There was an edge to Dickinson's voice he hadn't heard before.

The officer remained silent. He was trapped with trying to have his original order followed. "Last chance. Produce your identification."

Noah was ready to step outside.

"Listen here, Constable Clarke. First, you have yet to identify yourself as a police officer. Secondly, I can be suspicious all I want. That's not a crime. *You* are being suspicious by being unreasonable and demanding documentation outside of your legislation to do so. You do not have any reasonable or can articulate suspicion of any criminal involvement. Feel free to call your supervisor as confirmation, or you will be at risk of litigation, as well as your department."

"I could place you under arrest." Clarke stepped forward and pointed the finger at Angie.

"Sure. Go ahead. In order to detain me, you have to prove a crime has been committed. What's the crime? Come on. I'm waiting."

The officer was flustered.

"Just as I thought. Have a good day." Noah heard Angie raise the window and turn on the radio. He was dismissed.

Officer Clarke's hand gripped the yellow-bodied Taser. He stood there for a few seconds, eyes wide in disbelief. Then he went back to the cruiser, and Noah could see him on the radio as he called it in. The officer whipped his hat into the car as he got behind the wheel.

Five minutes passed before the flashing lights were turned off, and he backed up and used the neighbor's driveway to turn around.

"What an asshole. Are you okay?" Dickinson held the radio in her hands and turned toward the home. Noah pulled back the curtain to give her a thumbs-up.

"I'm good. I'll be out in a minute. Keep an eye out for any neighbors that may have called this in. No doubt we attracted some attention."

Noah felt the knot of tension fade. She handled herself well, probably better than he would have. He turned to the one thing that had to be addressed—the computer behind the desk.

The orange cord had over a dozen smaller cables inside, and they connected to the back of the system. Noah had thought it was an extension cord. Twelve separate lines snaked around to the back of the electronics. The low hum from various internal fans was barely audible.

"I would imagine a woman with her experience would have one hell of a system." There wasn't one piece of equipment Noah recognized. He had trouble with laptops and could barely handle email, let alone a complicated system. Was someone looking for Miriam Davis and attempting to break into her computer? It was only a guess, but it felt right. Noah realized the answers could be inside as he followed the cord back out the front door to the step-van.

After scanning the park and surrounding homes, Angie figured out what he was doing, then nodded. He tried the handle and sliding rear door, but they were locked.

Dickinson rummaged in her luggage and stepped out of the rental. She had an eighteen-inch collapsible baton and passed it over.

"Thanks."

Noah stepped to the side, with his back against the truck. With a sharp flick of his wrist, he extended the baton. Contrary to popular belief, a vehicle's windows are designed to be stronger in the middle—where a collision or impact is more likely. Along the perimeter is the weakest point. The rounded steel rod went through the bottom with little effort. The window shattered with a muffled pop, and the tempered glass exploded inward across the passenger seat. Noah used the shaft to outline the opening to clear the clinging fragments.

Angie stepped forward and reached inside to unlock, then opened the sliding rear door. The orange wire went in through the bottom of the truck and into a computer bank built into the driver's side. It looked like a mini-office, including two chairs against a small desk.

"Anything?" Noah kept a lookout while Angie went inside.

"There's a laptop and three cell phones connected to the system."

"Those could be traced if we took them. Right now, I believe we are under their radar. I'd like to keep it that way."

"Roger that." She reached inside and showed Noah a small black case the size of a tissue box. A black wire and plug hung from the back. "I do know what this is. An external hard drive."

"Can it give away our position?"

Angie shook her head. "There may be software that will connect to the internet and broadcast a signal, but until that happens, no."

"Take it. We've pressed our luck too far. Time to go."

"Where next?" Angie got back in the Navigator as Noah patted his pocket. "Road trip. Just a second."

Noah grabbed two large bottles of water out of the backseat and went back to the van. He emptied both onto every piece of computer equipment inside. At first, nothing happened, but then everything shut down after a series of pops and crackling. A think trickle of smoke rose from the server bank along with a sharp smell of burned electronics.

Now, he was ready to hit the road.

Chapter 40

The miles passed on the I-95 South throughout the afternoon as Noah increased the distance between themselves and Miriam's house.

"How did you get this information?" Dickinson had quickly caught up on the background of the four names. She held the book from the farmhouse and turned off the tablet after reading the lawyer's report.

When Noah finished the story of how he obtained the book, Angie remained silent and stared out the passenger window. One finger tapped on the armrest. It was a lot of information to digest, and most importantly, all true.

"Did you kill anyone?"

Noah shook his head. "No. I won't do that unless there is absolutely no choice and only in self-defense."

"How did you find out about the four subjects? The data came from a law firm."

Trust. Trust balanced the equation, but Noah didn't know how far to push. Dickinson knew about the cash he had stashed away in the woods at his cabin. She had stumbled across it when Noah went missing. He did not lie to her, but again, he hadn't told her the full story either. How do you explain that your former fiancée stole the money from her uncle, an organized crime boss, stashed it in various accounts, then gifted it to him? Despite several dozen anonymous donations, the property investment corporation he used to move the money continued to grow at an alarming rate. The real-estate market was hot. CD Consulting was now worth over one-hundred-million dollars. How would Angie react? Only one way to find out.

"I have a law firm that works for me, almost exclusively. They handle mainly real estate deals for a company I own. Their research team is top-notch, and they compiled the report."

"Okay." Dickinson looked over to see if he was joking. "How is this possible?"

With all the risks she was taking, Angie deserved to know. "Do you remember when my house exploded? That was just the start …."

It took almost forty-five minutes to tell her everything. Absolutely everything. Not only was Dickinson his partner, but they had saved each other's lives, which created a bond not shared by just friends. Noah found that once he started, he felt relieved as he unburdened and spilled his guts. He hadn't told anyone the full story before. Only Megan (Rachel) knew everything, but they hadn't talked or seen each other since the shootout with the FBI.

Once finished, Noah was prepared for anything. If Dickinson wanted out, he would drive her to the nearest airport. Should she wish to report everything to the feds, he wouldn't stop her. Noah respected her too much. He would cross that bridge, should he come to it.

For now, they drove in silence as they headed south.

"So, not only do you have untold millions stashed away, you are still working as a cop?"

"The money doesn't change who I am. I've given away twelve million dollars to charities and organizations. However, the investments seem to be doing rather well."

Angie cleared her throat. "This will take a while to process." She glanced at him, then back out the front window. "But, I'm still in. However, I have one condition."

Noah raised an eyebrow but nodded. "Go ahead."

"If I lose my job, you will support me until retirement."

He grinned. "Done."

"Also, it's possible we'll need good lawyers. You'll have to cover that. I don't make enough." Her dimples made a brief appearance. "I'm also partial to weekly manicures and massages. We can negotiate on that one."

Noah couldn't explain the relief as the knot of tension fled. He couldn't help but chuckle. "I'll buy you a salon."

"I also get to listen to my music for the next two hours."

They talked about inconsequential things as they drove through

Virginia toward North Carolina. Neither heard the electronic chime as the GPS on Angie's cell phone turned on and began to broadcast their location.

*****

"A cop? Seriously?" Emma tossed her handbag on the table and took a seat around the edge of the control room. "We wacked a president in Chad last spring, and now we are chasing a police officer?"

The woman was of average height, with long brown hair. The scattering of freckles across her nose made her look younger than thirty-eight years old. When she glanced at her bare forearms, she pulled the sleeves down to hide the multitude of scars.

"He'll come to a sticky end, don't worry. From what we're being paid for this one, consider it a working vacation. Iain, how are you doing?" Eric closed the blinds on the living room window and sat in the only armchair. The safe house had not been used in almost two years, and puffs of dust rose in the air.

Eric had been at the game longer than anyone else in the room, and he was looking for an easy score. Just a few more, and he would get out of the game and retire. That's what he kept telling himself anyways. Men like him never retired.

"Good. I remembered the power supply adapter this time." Iain Caldwell held the item in the air and plugged it into

199

the wall. His luggage was mostly electronic items, with three laptops taking up the main bulk. The thin man was used to Emma's outbursts and ignored them. He had posed as her husband so often that it felt like a marriage of sorts.

"Get crackin'. I'd like to be home before we get used to the time zone." Emma pulled a water bottle out of her purse and tapped a foot on the hardwood floor.

"We all would, dear. Now quit your fuckin' whining."

They could hear a sledgehammer from the cellar as it pounded the concrete flooring. Oliver knew where to look, and he always seemed to enjoy getting his frustrations out. After hearing the story, Eric had no doubt the visual of a customs agent overlaying the floor.

Within a few minutes, Iain had the system up and running. He plugged in the high-speed modem and was online.

"Checking connections." He switched to the middle laptop and logged into a server. The pounding in the basement stopped. "We have access."

For five minutes, each screen had a black background and white typing as he entered a string of command code. Then on the third screen, an image of Noah Hunter was pulled up, and Eric studied the man's face. He didn't look special, just your average law-enforcement officer. "Can you check if he's ever been charged?"

Back on the first screen, Iain called up the database search engine. "Nothing."

"Current location?" Eric was curious about the charges but not that curious. He didn't need to know, and none of his business. He didn't give a rat's ass what the cop did as long as he got paid. Let God sort it out.

"His cell phone is online and operational. Pinging in Arrow Point, Wyoming."

"He's probably ditched it. It conflicts with the latest intel. Can you pull up his known associates?"

The third screen flashed, then reset with the APPD logo in the top right-hand corner. Iain's fingers flew over the keyboard, and then with a series of clicks, a woman's picture came on screen. She stood in a police dress uniform in front of a blue background with the American flag at her side. A hat was tucked under her right arm.

"Sergeant Angela Dickinson. She's his partner."

"Start there. Women are usually involved if you want things done right." Emma smirked and ignored the look Eric gave her.

"She is on a leave of absence from the station. I can pull up their payroll records if you like? Checking her cell phone."

Oliver thumped up the stairs carrying a green sports bag in each hand. He dropped them on the dining room table and proceeded to empty both bags. Stone dust covered his hoodie and jeans, but he didn't care. An array of weapons soon filled the table. Pistols, rifles, knives, and two shotguns were examined. A function test was performed on each, and then he began to field strip and clean a select few.

Eric kept an eye on Olley, but he wasn't worried. There were zero reasons to doubt the man for the last three years they worked together.

He had his quirks, but then again, they all did. Mother recommended him, and after a trial operation, the merger was finalized.

"Here we go. Sergeant Dickinson is currently heading south on I-95. From the cell tower switch-over, she just entered North Carolina."

Eric stood, and his knees cracked. One more thing to ignore. "Can you activate the Hound Program?"

"It's already done." Iain stood. "I think this will be a quick one as well."

"About bloody time." Emma walked over to the table and picked up a Glock 17, and hefted a silencer in the other hand. Everyone soon joined her as they chose a weapon. What they didn't pick up, Oliver placed back into the bags and left them by the door.

Iain prepared to leave. Before the laptop was shut down, a circular logo flashed on the screen. The left-facing eagle clutched a key with a shield on its chest and blue background— National Security Agency ringed the design. It confirmed that the user wished to log off, and Iain clicked yes.

Eric chuckled. It was all about who you knew.

Chapter 41

Noah pulled off the interstate in Richmond Hill, south of Savannah, Georgia, at ten o'clock at night. "There are still five hours left until we arrive in Tampa. Did you want to push on or spend the night here and leave early?"

Angie held back a yawn. She had been fighting to stay awake for the last two hours. "I didn't sleep much last night, and it's been a long day. I would rather be rested for whatever awaits us than be half asleep."

"Sounds good to me." Noah followed the signs for the hotels from the ramp and pulled into the Homewood Suites. The parking lot seemed half full, so there should be rooms available.

They had driven for eight hours and only stopped for food and to fill up the Navigator's tank. The chill had left the air, and Georgia was almost humid by comparison. Another reason for a night's rest was the fog covering the countryside. After a herd of deer suddenly appeared on the shoulder of the road, Noah dropped his speed significantly. The last thing they needed was an accident.

Deer and elk were a common occurrence near Arrow Point, and throughout his life, he had seen the results of a collision. When possible, he liked to avoid pushing his luck.

Noah booked two rooms on the third floor and left a wake-up call for seven o'clock in the morning. That would still place them in Tampa by noon or shortly thereafter. As to what would happen from there, too much depended on the only address the lawyer could find.

He kicked off his shoes and hung the suit in the closet. The time for dressing up was over, and Noah was glad to shed the formal wear. Three seconds after hitting the pillow, he was sleeping.

~

The complimentary continental breakfast had the basics, and Noah lingered over a third cup of coffee as he read the newspaper. He had been unable to sleep late and was wide awake by five o'clock, and, after a hot shower, he dressed in jeans and a light-blue collared shirt. He tucked a note in Dickinson's door before going to the lobby.

"You should have woken me up." Angie walked in behind a family of four and joined him at the small table. The large room was filling up as the promise of a complimentary breakfast drew them downstairs.

"If you weren't up by eight, I would have knocked."
Noah grinned. She had a long day and needed the rest, so he had
canceled the wake-up calls. However, it was six-thirty in the
morning, and they had lots of time.

"Be right back." Angie grabbed some fruit and coffee as
he folded the newspaper and pulled out the tablet. Her hair was
still wet from the shower, and she had dressed similarly—jeans
and a pin-striped black and white collared dress shirt.

Noah removed the picture from the frame in his room and
brought it to the table. The photograph was older, and he
couldn't say the age. The man and woman wore football jerseys
as they leaned toward each other on a backyard patio. They were
clinking beer mugs and having a good time. Miriam Davis
grinned with a glass of beer next to Dennis McCallister.

While he had never been there, the home of the Tampa
Bay Buccaneers, the Raymond Jay Stadium, was a familiar
backdrop. With Google Earth, Noah zoomed in close enough to
see the neighborhood and found the backyard deck and home.
The lawyer could not locate a home address for Dennis, but the
picture helped. Noah could not find out if he lived there or
visited a friend, but it was a place to start. He wanted
Dickinson's opinion on the location. She was the one to show
him the online tool, and he had spent hours snooping around the
planet for the last month.

"What do you think?" He spun the picture and tablet
around when she sat. Dickinson closed the application and pulled
up another image. After a few adjustments, she grinned.

"Google Street View. I would say that's definitely the location in the picture."

Noah studied the image and compared it. A few trees were different, and one was missing entirely from the online photo. Things had changed since the picture was taken, but there was no doubt. It was the same angle as the stadium.

Dickinson finished her coffee and brought the apple and banana with her. "See how I didn't say anything about an old dog and new tricks?"

Noah winked. "Appreciated, young pup. Ready?"

"Just need to grab my bag."

Five minutes later, Noah handed in the room keys and checked out. There were no problems with the Chase credit card. He still did not want to use his in case the accounts were being monitored.

"Can we go to the Starbucks before we hit the interstate? As good as it was here ..." Angie preferred a strong dark roast.

"It's on the way. I'll have another as well."

After they turned north on Ocean Highway toward the I-95, Noah passed the Taco Bell and Wendy's and braked for the red light ahead.

Across the street, a gray Chrysler minivan pulled out of the Sunoco gas station and collided with a pickup truck going south. The collision sounded like an explosion as glass shattered and metal crumpled.

"Jesus Christ."

The minivan spun in a half-circle, then the rear tires caught on the median barrier and flipped onto its side. It rocked on the grass but didn't tip over. Noah was on the other side of the intersection, less than sixty feet away.

He placed the rental in park, and Dickinson reached for her seatbelt. "Just a second." He held up a hand. He had seen something wrong.

A man struggled to climb out of the driver's window, and it was then the shotgun came into full view. The man began screaming at the woman in the truck and brought the weapon up to his shoulder. The man wore track pants and a blue T-shirt with a red baseball cap. His left arm was bleeding from a long cut.

Angie opened the glove box for the MP&9 as Noah pulled the Glock out of the armrest. He performed a quick press-check to confirm a round was seated. As Noah opened the car door and stepped outside, he could hear the woman's screams from inside the truck.

"Okay, you stay at least ten yards from me and—"

Noah paused when a familiar flashing of lights and siren sounded from the McDonald's parking lot. The gray and black cruiser of the Virginia State Police pulled into the intersection and blocked the oncoming traffic.

As soon as the two officers stepped out of the car, everything went to hell.

Chapter 42

The first state police officer ran out from behind the driver's door and drew his sidearm. He screamed. "Put down the gun!"

His partner yelled into his shoulder handset and held his pistol with one hand. He remained behind the passenger door.

The man with the shotgun didn't hesitate. The stock rested in his shoulder as the muzzle swung toward the new target. The roar of the gun carried for a quarter-mile and echoed off the buildings. The officer had turned, but it was too late. His feet left the ground at twenty feet as his upper torso and throat were shredded. A vest wouldn't have saved him.

The man calmly turned and cycled another round into the chamber, and the red cartridge went flying off to the side.

"Holy fuck!" Angie had ducked down in front of the Navigator next to him.

The second officer crouched as the shotgun fired again. The pellets bounced from the passenger door. The man threw down the gun and, from under his T-shirt, pulled out a handgun.

"I just can't sit back. I'm going in. I want you to stay here and cover me." Noah's adrenaline levels spiked, and he gasped for breath as the situation developed. Then the training kicked in. Cool and calm, no time to panic. Look for collateral damage. Were there any civilians in the line of fire or beyond? Was there an opportunity for a covered approach? How many rounds were fired?

Dickinson nodded and moved so the engine block would lay between them. It wasn't the ideal range for the Smith and Wesson at sixty feet, but it wasn't horrible. She was a good shot.

As the man fired 9mm rounds into the cruiser door, Noah ran around to place the minivan between them and sprinted across the road and grass-covered median. With his back against the Chrysler, he had a quick peek around the corner. The shooter stood at the rear of the truck. There was only a partial target.

The woman stopped screaming and lay flat under the dash as rounds continued to fire into the cruiser. When Noah heard an empty magazine clatter on the road, he darted forward twenty feet to the green Chevy's damaged hood and front end. Traffic had stopped on the main road, keeping well back.

There was a moment of silence, and Noah heard the distinct sound of a pistol being loaded. There was no return fire from the cop, and Noah counted him out of the fight.

When he turkey-peeked around the driver's side, the man wasn't there. *Fuck.*

While on his knees, he pivoted and looked around the passenger side. Nothing, although he could see dozens of people pressed up against the glass window at the McDonald's.

Noah slowly lowered his head to look under the vehicle. He could see the second officer lying in a growing pool of blood and a running shoe briefly as the shooter climbed into the bed of the truck.

Nowhere to go. Dammit! Think.

*****

Oliver shook off the impact and ignored the blood trickling down his left arm. He had been trained decades ago to ignore the pain and carry on with the mission. Today was no exception.

The voice in his earpiece was calm. "Trap sprung, and the bait is taken."

Climbing out of the driver's shattered window, he dropped to the ground and began to scream at the truck's driver.

"Bloody hell, we have company." The voice in his ear was no longer calm. "Shit's about to hit the fan."

When the cruiser appeared, and a cop jumped out screaming, Oliver grinned as he pulled the trigger. The second bugger hid behind the door, and the shotgun would never go through it—time for the backup. The Sig was his favorite anyways.

After twenty-one rounds through the door, the cop wasn't getting up again. With the money from this job, *and* he got to kill some pigs—life was good. Wankers, all of them.

"Target is at the front of the truck. All clear." Eric sounded almost happy after he dealt with the police. He usually did when an assignment was almost over. What a sick fuck. Oliver laughed to himself as he gingerly climbed into the back of the truck. The fully loaded pistol was steady as he swept the sides.

Without rocking the vehicle, he stepped onto the back of the bed and onto the roof. The pistol moved up as he closed the angle. When he stepped onto the windshield and hood, his jaw dropped.

"Where the bloody hell is he?"

Detective Noah Hunter was gone.

Chapter 43

Oliver looked over to the gas station parking lot. Eric sat in the front seat of the window van with Iain behind the wheel. The old man shrugged. "I can't see him from my angle."

"He has to be under the truck, asshole," Emma swore and turned the ignition over. The comms link was on permanent broadcast. They found over the years that it saved time and their necks.

The Chevy roared to life, and the sharp whine from under the hood sounded like someone had stabbed a cat. Oliver stood on top of the cab and bent his knees for balance. When the truck dropped in gear and slowly moved forward, he looked for Hunter. After driving the length of the vehicle, there was still no sign of the target.

The sharp retort of small arms made Oliver spin around. Behind the minivan was movement. It was Hunter's partner. She was tall enough to hide behind the vehicle and pop up and take a shot. He fired two rounds into the hood to keep her down. Bitch.

"I'm getting in the truck bed. If Hunter is underneath, let's take 'em for a ride."

"Hold on to something." Emma didn't wait and stepped on the accelerator. A belt squealed as the truck leaped forward, and Oliver jumped down into the back. His left hand clutched the tailgate. When they drove past the minivan, the woman popped up and fired. He wasn't worried. They would be warning shots. If her partner were underneath, she wouldn't chance it.

It was then Oliver grinned. He did not have to wait for Hunter to show himself. He turned toward the middle of the truck bed and fired through the thin metal.

*****

Noah stuck the Glock down the front of his jeans. The choice was to use both hands and have the possibility of maneuvering or have the pistol in one hand with limitations. There was barely enough clearance for him to slide under the Chevy, but soon enough, he felt the heat from the engine on the side of his face. Luckily, no fluids leaked after the collision.

The truck subtly rocked as the man moved forward, and Noah gripped the transfer box skid plate to move toward the rear. There wouldn't be any choices if the truck weren't raised for off-road except a shoot-out. Too many civilians were around for that option. The sound of the cab roof popping under the man's weight gave away his position, and Noah froze.

When the truck squealed to life, Noah's heart leaped, and he came close to wetting his jeans. *What was the woman doing? Trying to get away?* There was no time to figure it out when he felt the truck dropped into gear.

Under the truck, four skid plates protected the transfer case, front and rear differentials, and the fuel tank. While holding onto the front plate, Noah pressed his running shoes against the rear crossbar as the truck shot forward. His body lifted from the ground in time, but only inches were between him and the asphalt.

Within seconds, the burning of his fingers and shoulders almost caused him to drop. When they hit a slight bump in the road, his right foot slipped. As the heel hit the ground, the running shoe was torn off in a split second. It bounced off the spare tire and spun away.

Fuckfuckfuckfuck!

Noah knew if he let go, he would be dragged beneath the truck and bounced around before spitting out the back end as a pile of dog meat. His toes curled around the edge as he hung on for life.

He could barely hear the retort of a pistol over the road noise and engine. The cop-killer fired at him through the truck bed, and the round hit the driveshaft and ricocheted to the sidewall. Noah didn't have a choice.

He had to drop and risk it.

As the truck slowed and began a wide turn, a second round passed to his right—inches from his chest. He could hear the man screaming above. When the truck was at the slowest speed, he let go.

At fifteen miles per hour, Noah didn't have much of a chance to escape injury. Both arms were spread to absorb the impact and prevent bounce as he hit the ground. The back of his head hit the same time the rear passenger tire ran over his left wrist and hand. An explosion of pain knocked the air from his lungs, and Noah's eyes rolled back as he stifled a scream.

He had enough presence to roll once the truck passed overhead, and he was clear. Noah ignored the burning sensation that covered his upper back as his right hand fumbled for the Glock.

As the brake lights came on and the truck stopped, Noah realized the pistol was gone.

Chapter 44

Angie didn't feel she had a chance to hit the target with an unfamiliar weapon at that range. The MP&9 only had an eight-round magazine, and the backup only had seven. As Noah left the minivan, she ran around the Navigator and took her partner's former position.

Dickinson used the fender to brace her forearms. With one eye closed and teeth clenched, she waited until the truck moved forward so the possibilities of hitting a civilian were lowered, then squeezed off two shots. The shots went high and missed. There were too many businesses in the background, rattling her nerves.

But the shooter did not have that same problem. When he turned, she ducked. Two rounds crumped through the hood, and the engine stopped them from going through.

Angie looked at the fallen police officers and the fleeing truck. Worry about the living. In seconds, her long legs and arms were pumping as she bolted down Ocean Highway in pursuit. The truck drove a hundred yards before it slowed to turn, and a dark shadow detached from the underside.

The congestion built, and the oncoming traffic began to slow, but the southbound lane was clear. The truck stopped after another ten yards, and Dickinson dove into the prone position to present less of a target.

Angie's hands were rock steady as she fired despite the adrenaline coursing through her body. The first round hit left of the target and shattered the truck's rear window. A woman screamed from within. The man ducked as a second and third round impacted into the tailgate.

Seconds later, out of ammunition, she dropped the magazine and loaded the remaining seven rounds. Noah had staggered to his feet and ran to the side, well clear of the line of fire.

The man's head rose, and he fired in Noah's direction, but Angie slowly squeezed the trigger, and the 9mm bullet went through the tailgate. The man fell from sight. It looked like a hit, but it was hard to tell.

The Chevy truck straightened out on the road heading south and made the first left turn. It was gone, but a new issue materialized.

Sirens were approaching.

Dickinson unloaded the pistol, placed it on the ground, and stepped away. She produced her badge and identification from her back pocket before her hands rose in the air.

*****

"Jesus Christ! The bitch fuckin' hit me."

"Abort. Cops are on their way." Iain was running the police scanner and made the call. "We'll meet you at Blue Location."

"It can't be that bad if you're whining. Heading to Blue." Emma pushed the damaged truck along the country road as Oliver rode in the back.

As Eric started the panel van, he dialed a number from memory. "Update."

"Go ahead." The woman's voice echoed as if down a deep well.

"Unable to fulfill the contract with the original ending." Eric joined the line of cars and drove around the police cruiser. Many leaned out of their cars to take pictures of the fallen officers lying in pools of blood. Savages.

"How much longer?"

"Within two days. No longer."

"Try not to make a mess, dear, but wrap it up. I have another job waiting." Mother disconnected the call.

Iain had heard everything. "What's plan B?"

Eric double-tapped a finger along the side of his nose and winked.

Chapter 45

Noah winced as he slipped his arms through a new shirt. The nurse fitted the brace over his left wrist and snugged it tight with the straps. They had to wait for the swelling to recede before a permanent cast. That was something Noah wanted to avoid if possible. The brace stabilized the wrist and could be removed for showering—eight to ten weeks to heal. It could have been worse. He'd take a broken wrist and road rash. The goose egg on the back of his head went down with an icepack but left a headache.

The Virginia State Police swarmed the area and originally had him facedown in the dirt and handcuffed Dickinson until they could sort out the scene. Once they had verified the police badge and identification for them both, the cuffs were removed. They had over thirty witnesses with dozens of angles of video. A trooper rode in the back of the ambulance with Noah to the urgent care center—a four-minute drive.

The care center was the size of an Arrow Point clinic, but inside they had everything a hospital had, from X-rays and ultrasounds to a surgical room. Long as you had approved insurance, or the ability to pay, you could receive the best care without waiting.

Noah avoided the awkward questions and handed over the credit card. "Fix me up."

Noah gave his statement as the nurse picked stones and dirt out of his upper back. He was traveling north with his partner when they saw the accident. They were about to help when the man produced a shotgun and killed the police officers. He tried to apprehend the shooter, but things had taken a turn for the worse.

The young officer nodded. "I've known those men for my entire career. Even trying to help is appreciated."

"Sorry, I couldn't have gotten there sooner."

"Your weapons have been processed. Once you are done here, come by the station and pick them up. My sergeant wants you to go over the witness timeline if you can."

Noah knew firsthand about the timelines. If you get twenty people to report what happened, you will have almost twenty different versions. Having an official accounting from a police officer or two would make a difference. Off duty or not, Noah would help.

"Not a problem."

Dickinson gave her statement on scene and had driven to the care center once released. She handed the nurse a new shirt for Noah and his missing shoe. The officer left, and the nurse finished with his back and applied bandages.

She fitted a black cloth sling over his head and gave him instructions. "Keep the arm elevated, and apply a cold compress. Over the next day, the swelling will go down, and make sure to tighten the straps."

His wrist had doubled in size, and while he could move the fingers, it was painful. There was a distal radius fracture, lengthwise along the bone. The nurse handed him a small white paper bag with pain medication and something to help him sleep, along with an ointment for his back.

Noah saw concern in Angie's eye when he walked into the lobby. "Are you okay?"

"I'll be good in six weeks or so. It could have been worse. Thank you for saving me."

She looked at the sling and winced. "I didn't do too good of a job."

"I'm breathing. Far as I'm concerned, that's a good thing." From the accident to the police arriving after the truck had left, it was less than three minutes. Giving statements and the hospital visit was three hours, and Noah was exhausted. "We have to stop by the detachment to pick up the pistols and to verify the timeline of actions."

"I'm driving. Don't even think of it." Dickinson stepped outside and opened the passenger door for him.

Once he buckled in, Angie climbed behind the wheel and turned to face him. "I didn't want to say anything inside, but what do you think about the accident and shootout?"

Noah took a deep breath and slowly let it out. "It's been bothering me. The woman ended up helping the shooter. It doesn't make any sense."

Angie nodded. "I've thought about it, and it seems the woman was working with him. The moves were coordinated."

"Then why the accident in the first place?"

She nodded toward the glovebox, and Noah opened it. Her cell phone was inside with the battery removed. "What do you say about coincidences?"

Noah leaned back against the headrest and went through the day and each event. "I have nothing that can track me. If they were tracking you, that would make the whole accident a trap. What about the state troopers?"

Dickinson started the Navigator and buckled in. "Wrong place, wrong time."

Before she could place the vehicle in gear, Noah asked, "Do you still want to go on? I wouldn't blame you for wanting out at this point."

Angie rolled her eyes. "Haven't you figured it out yet? We're partners. Let's get this over with and get out of here. I'm starting to hate this town."

Chapter 46

The Virginia state police shared the building with the Richmond Hill Police Department, less than ten minutes from the hotel and interstate. As the budget for law enforcement was slashed across the state, various agencies had to make do, and merging facilities saved money.

The building was typical of the area and resembled a sprawling bungalow with a double-peaked roof above the entrance. Ringing the parking lots were small shrubs and silver maple trees. Civilian cars filled the front and the side with a couple of cruisers in the rear. All hands were on deck with the officer deaths, regardless of the agency—a nightmare for any department.

Dickinson pulled into the parking lot at twelve-thirty as Noah finished a protein bar and bottle of water. His stomach didn't care what was happening around him. He needed to eat. Despite the throbbing pain in his wrist and headache, he wanted to avoid the painkillers. Three Advil were swallowed with the last of his water.

"Okay. Ready."

The front of the station could have decorated the cover of a landscaping magazine. Two maple trees acted as columns to either side of the walkway, and a bronze plaque showed the building was built in 1977. The short grass and garden beds were immaculate, and the American flag was already at half-staff for the fallen officers.

The lobby was almost the same as APPD, with a public access counter and a wall of forms and pamphlets. Richmond PD did not have a receptionist, but the staff sergeant and a rookie officer had a desk on the other side of the ballistic glass.

"Detective Noah Hunter and Sergeant Angie Dickinson. We're here to sign our statements and verify the witness timeline, if we can, for the accident."

There was no need to clarify *which* accident. They were still reeling from the loss. Sergeant Russo's uniform was dark blue and almost the same as Arrow Point's. The man was in his fifties and a few inches shorter than Noah with a premature short white beard.

"I'll buzz you through."

Russo led them down the hall, past a series of offices, and into the station's briefing room. The rows of desks and seating inside were for the morning roll call that each station conducts. Officers would get their daily assignments and any be-on-the-lookout (BOLO) alerts that may have changed or updated since their last shift. Sometimes there would be uniform inspections—they would be random as not to be expected.

"The conference room is being used. If you guys don't mind waiting here, I'll get Sergeant Chandler." Russo gestured to the first-row seating and left the door open.

"A little nicer than ours." Angie looked at the white screen and projector connected to a computer on the podium. There was a section on the wall for the FBI's most wanted pictures and a large chart for the football pool.

Sergeant Chandler was of average height and stocky, with short dark hair going gray at the temples. He wore a dark blue uniform with a black tie. His prominent chin and sideburns made Noah think of an Irishman, but the accent was pure Boston when he spoke.

"Mark. Sorry to meet you under these circumstances." He shook their hands as they introduced themselves. He nodded toward the sling and brace. "How are you doing?"

"They want to stick a cast on me in a few days, but we shall see. Sorry, I couldn't have been more helpful."

"We found the truck. It was torched a few miles away. We have a team already checking it out. Pictures of the suspects are out. Some of the videos were good enough, and there's full media coverage. Right now, we have to hurry up and wait."

Chandler asked them to follow him to his desk. The small office was near the rear of the station, nestled next to a storeroom and a small kitchenette. He didn't ask but led them over to the coffee machine and poured them each a cup. The office was small, with barely enough room for a desk and two chairs. Two floating shelves above the desk were packed with training and procedural manuals.

Once they sat, Sergeant Chandler pulled out Noah's Glock and the MP&9 from the top desk drawer and passed them over, along with the magazines. Angie's was empty, while his was full. Noah never got a chance to fire. "They've been processed and recorded."

"Do you have any information on the suspect's vehicles?" Angie confirmed the pistol was unloaded and left it on the desk.

Mark sipped the coffee and then shook his head. "Both were reported stolen early this morning."

"That confirms it. They were working together." Noah placed the coffee down and picked up the Glock with only one hand.

"Just a second." Chandler rummaged around in the bottom drawer and pulled out two clip-on holsters. "Neither of you have a conceal permit for Virginia. No issues with open carry, though."

"Thanks." Angie loaded Noah's pistol, and he slid it on his belt. At least his right hand was fine. Things could have been worse.

"Do either of you have any further information about that clusterfuck?" His thick finger tapped the top of the coffee mug while staring them down.

Noah shook his head. "Never seen them before, but I'm sure they were working together. Things were just—"

All three jumped when the detonation shook the building.

Chapter 47

Immediately after the explosion, three muffled *pop pop pop* noises came from the rear of the station. The Richmond Hill Police Department was under attack.

"Fuck!" Sergeant Chandler pulled out a box of 9mm ammunition from the lower drawer and tossed it to Dickinson as he drew his service pistol. "You both stay here. Hide if you can."

Angie wasn't wasting time and began to load the magazines as Chandler looked up and down the hallway. As the sound of a rifle firing echoed through the building, he darted away.

The office window was too small for either of them. "You good?"

Angie fumbled, and a handful of loose ammo spilled on the floor. "Working on it."

Small arms fire, mixed with a weapon on full auto, made Noah's heart leap. He quickly stood, quietly closed the office door, and turned off the lights. Screams and shouts were cut short as another burst of rapid-fire drew closer.

Noah didn't recall doing it, but the coffee mug was on the desk, and the pistol was in his right hand. "Same as the scenario we did for the work-up training with the marshals, but in reverse. Make our way back to reception and out the front door."

"Roger." Dickinson stood at his shoulder and tucked the Glock's spare magazine into the pocket of his jeans. "Ready."

Noah cursed his left wrist as his partner opened the door. He glanced around the corner. "Clear. Covering."

"Moving."

Angie darted down the hallway and took a position behind the kitchen counter. "Covering."

"Moving." The next position wasn't ideal, and he had to cross her line of fire, but it worked. The next office door was locked, and Noah knelt in the hallway. "Covering."

Dickinson leap-frogged past Noah as a figure looked around the corner at the end of the hallway. The man wore a tactical black Kevlar helmet and gas mask. The M4A1 carbine rifle swung up, and Noah fired.

The first round hit the wall above his head, and the second went through the door to his right. "Target!"

The man ducked back. Angie kicked open the next office door and used it for partial coverage. "Covering."

As Noah turned to run back, a small round object with yellow lettering was thrown around the corner and landed ten feet away. "Grenade!"

Instead of darting down the hallway, Angie grabbed his shoulder and swung him into the office where they both tumbled to the floor. Two seconds later, the explosion left him momentarily deaf as doors, walls, and ceiling pieces were shredded. Smoke shot out, filled the hall, and rose to the top of the office. Despite landing on his right side, the pain made Noah's eyes water, and he ground his teeth as he struggled to his knees.

There wasn't a moment of respite. Full auto fire followed the grenade and flashed past the open doorway. One round hit the frame, and the wood splintered with a sharp crack.

Forward wasn't an option. The small office had a large filing cabinet inside the door next to a full coatrack, a large desk, and a bookcase to the side. Most importantly was the large window.

"Cover the doorway."

Noah didn't wait for a response as Angie swore.

He fired four rounds at the window in each corner. "Dickinson, need your help."

Noah stepped forward and ripped the blinds down. A series of cracks turned the window opaque. Angie picked up the desk chair and threw it. The firing in the hallway stopped as the window exploded out, and the chair fell four feet onto the grass.

He stood with his back to the window and brought the Glock up toward the doorway. "Go. Covering. Get to the car and don't stop."

Angie gave him a funny look but easily leaped out the window and darted away. But Noah didn't follow.

*****

Oliver placed the shaped charges at the rear door of the station and stepped to the side. He had a limp after the bullet was removed from his thigh. Plans to make the bitch pay were foremost in his thoughts. After a quick final check of his gear, the red button was pressed.

"Breaching."

Despite being alone, he still called it out. Years of habit. He had left the comms unit with Eric. This was a solo mission and one he had done many times. The others would get in his way.

After the hinges and handle were blown off, Oliver kicked the door down and threw the flashbangs. One second after they exploded, he stepped inside. The rifle smoothly came up to his shoulder. He stood in a processing area, and officers rushed forward, pistols drawn.

Oliver killed the first with a double-tap to the head, and before the body hit the floor, another died across her desk. A bullet glanced off his body armor, and as he turned, his left thumb flicked a switch to full auto. A tall, dark man in a suit died as he walked farther into the building.

A woman in a red dress screamed and died, clutching a file folder, three wounds to her back. The smoke rose to the

231

ceiling as Oliver killed ten people in total. The officers tried to rush his position, but he mowed them down. Civilian workers tried to bolt to safety, but he didn't discriminate. They all died as he chuckled.

Speed and violence have their own rewards.

When a man charged from a side hall, another round glanced off his chest piece, and he staggered back a step. The carbine spat five rounds in a fraction of a second, and the officer with the tie flew twelve feet back. The smell of gunpowder filled the air along with blood and excrement as they died.

The rifle's bolt stopped in the rear position. Oliver's left thumb pressed the release. The empty magazine clattered at his feet as a fresh one was inserted. Slow is smooth, smooth is fast. He had picked up on the American saying, and it couldn't have been truer. Those actions were performed countless times under pressure and the mantra echoed in his thoughts.

After a quick peek around the corner, a wide grin spread under his gas mask. "Target acquired."

The time for playing was over. Oliver opened the pouch and pulled out an L109A1 HE (high explosive) fragmentation grenade. His left index finger slipped through the ring, and he gave a sharp pullback. *Always confirm the pin is separated and in which hand.* As his right arm whipped the one-pound grenade around the corner, he ducked low.

Three, two, one.

The concussive wave was felt in his chest and ears as the steel shell sent fragments out at a high velocity. But there was no time to think. Oliver stepped around the corner and fired a full thirty-round magazine into the smoke. After a quick reload, he was disappointed that Hunter wasn't lying in bloody chunks in the hall.

Fear made him curse when the sound of glass shattering echoed from one of the small rooms. There was no danger to himself, but he knew Noah was getting away.

After darting down the hall, the carbine rifle swept the office, but he only had eyes for the smashed-out window.

Oliver glanced outside and saw the office chair on the grass. When he noticed a movement out of the corner of his eye, he turned. An arm extended from the mass of jackets on the coat rack.

Bravo, Hunter.

The former SAS officer barely had time for a sense of appreciation when seven 9mm rounds ended his life.

Chapter 48

This time Noah didn't get to keep the Glock as Special Agent
Christopher Carnes confiscated it. Thirteen people were shot, and
only one had a chance of surviving. He worked with Dickinson
to check each person, and only one had a pulse. They focused on
saving the man's life as the minutes felt like hours. Eventually,
paramedics took over before the feds, and every other law
enforcement agency descended on the scene.

Noah took charge and directed the stunned personnel for
the first fifteen minutes. Shock hit the seasoned officers as they
discovered the carnage. Protecting the scene was foremost in his
thoughts as he restricted access and allowed the EMTs and a
select few inside.

The tall man in a blue suit and tie eventually guided Noah
to a waiting ambulance to get checked out. In all the chaos,
someone had the presence of mind to call out on the radio about

the assault. Carnes was at the accident scene and followed the state police to the station.

In any incident involving a firearm, the officer was relieved of his weapon until special investigations cleared them of any wrongdoing. Noah wasn't worried about being accused of anything. Since 9/11, security was upgraded at many police stations, including interior surveillance. Various cameras mounted in the ceiling had recorded the man's arrival in the rear parking lot and how he gained entry.

Dickinson was quiet, and Noah could tell the incident bothered her. She had held up admirably, and it wasn't until later that the shock hit. They sat on the rear step of the ambulance, wrapped in gray wool blankets. Noah's right arm went over her shoulders as she shook. Truth be told, he drew strength from the comfort as well.

Agent Carnes returned and took Noah aside for his statement, as another agent stayed with Dickinson. He started with the vehicle accident and ended it with killing the man in the body armor.

"Do you believe they were connected?"

Noah was not one-hundred percent positive, but the answer felt right. "Yes, but I'm not sure how. Yet."

Carnes rested a comforting hand on his shoulder. "We got it from here, Detective. Be proud of your actions today."

"I owe it to my partner. Without her, I wouldn't be here."

Half an hour later, Noah's vehicle was released from the scene, and Dickinson sat in the passenger seat. She was doing better but felt emotionally numb. The harrowing experience would take a long time to digest, and there were bound to be repercussions. He knew Angie would be up for the task. She was stronger than she knew.

"Ready to get the hell out of this town?"

"Damn right." A small smile tugged at the corner of her lips.

They drove through the original accident scene, and the southbound lane was closed. Traffic was being redirected as a tow truck flipped over the Chrysler minivan. Yellow barricade tape surrounded the patrol car as details were recorded and analyzed.

After twenty minutes of steady driving on Interstate-95 South, Angie blurted out. "I need to shower and change."

Noah mentally kicked himself. He didn't want to push too hard, and he should have thought of that first. "Next stop is in two miles. There's another hotel. I think we've done enough for today."

He booked two rooms on the first floor and ordered pizza. Noah asked the driver to pick up a few six-packs of beer as well. They sat on his bed and watched the news channels cover the shooting as they ate. Neither Noah nor Angie's names were mentioned on air. That was one item he insisted on to Carnes.

After Dickinson left, Noah wrapped his left arm in a garbage bag to keep it dry and had the hottest shower he could stand. He tried to let the stress and worry of the day wash down the drain, but he knew only time would help. Images of the bodies and all the blood were still vivid when his eyes closed. The echoes of screams and gunfire rang in his ears, and despite changing his clothes and a shower, Noah could still smell the stench of death.

Regardless of how seasoned a police officer he was, today's events struck a chord.

By nine o'clock at night, he was drifting off to sleep when a gentle knock sounded on the door. Angie stood in the hall, hair still wet from the shower, dressed in a long T-shirt.

Without a word, Noah held the door open as she walked inside.

Chapter 49

Eric sent the update to Mother, and he wasn't surprised at the reply. "Finish the assignment, or you're done." Other teams wouldn't blink before taking them out. He had done two such assignments in the past—money talks. Failure wasn't an option in this line of work.

"Well?" Emma leaned against the van. The country air carried a hint of rain, and a flock of sparrows settled into neighboring blue spruce. They drove ten miles and were surrounded by trees in the middle of nowhere.

"We keep going." Eric turned off the sat phone and handed it to Iain. "I need you to get back into the system and arrange a meeting with the client."

"You fuckin' nuts? That's Mother's job. We're supposed to be hands-free." Emma's mouth dropped open, and she took a step back.

Even Iain knew this wasn't a good idea. "Either we finish this job, or we're done. I'll arrange the meeting."

Eric got back into the van as Iain followed orders.

*****

The Raymond James Stadium was known to the locals as Ray Jay or even The New Sombrero. One look at the design, and the latter seemed to fit. Noah had watched many Buccaneer games, and the pirate ship overlooking the endzone was a sight to behold. The ship's bell would ring when the Bucs got a touchdown, and the cannons fired. Even though he was a Bears fan, he had to hand it to the marketing team. Noah would love to watch a game while on the ship rather than sitting on the fifty-yard line.

Early Monday morning, the vast parking lots were empty, and Noah drove thoughts of football from his mind. Dickinson wasn't a fan, but she had driven to the main doors for him. He flicked through the screen-shot images on the tablet and orientated his position to the ground.

"South-east."

Although they had driven through the neighborhood and verified through the terrain map, Noah insisted on checking the angle in person. Not that he didn't trust computers, but he wanted to be thorough.

From the far corner of the parking lot, they walked one hundred yards to the home. Originally, the house was a bungalow, but it had undergone some renovations, and a peaked second story was added. The light blue siding made the red front door stand out. The yard was in a state of disrepair. The overgrown gardens and bushes were in dire need of help, and the lawn was almost ten inches tall. The interior California shutters were closed, and it appeared no one was home.

"Do you want to check around back?" Dickinson wore her usual jeans and hiking boots but opted for a matching blue T-shirt with the warmer Florida weather. Noah's left arm remained in the sling, and he added the Velcro strap around his torso to hold it in place over the gray hoodie. The swelling had receded, but a spectacular array of red and purple bruising started to develop.

The home sat on the corner, and he couldn't see over the hedges along the side. "Lead on." Noah did not want any surprises. However, if this did not pan out, he would have no choice but to head back to Washington D.C.

The wide driveway was empty past the seven-foot hedges, but vehicles could be in the double garage. The gate into the backyard was low, and Noah could see lawn furniture stacked next to a large barbecue. The rear sliding doors had a heavy curtain drawn.

"Nothing left to do except knock. Ready?"

Angie looked up and down the street. No cars were parked nearby, nor were any pedestrians out for a walk— Suburbia at its finest.

The events of yesterday, while never forgotten, were easier to deal with in the light of a new day. If you could not handle the stress of the job and everything it entitles, law enforcement might not be for you. It had taken a while, but you eventually learn how to partition your mind and deal with the bad days at a later date.

"Lead on, boss." With a brief grin, she gestured for him to go first.

Noah knocked on the front door before stepping back and slightly to the side. Habit. After a couple of minutes, he was about to use the brass knocker when the door opened.

"Yes? How can I help you?"

The woman inside wore a white sweater with straight gray hair and glasses. Her left arm was in a sling similar to Noah's, but her right arm was hidden behind her back.

"I'm Detective Noah Hunter, and this is Sergeant Angie Dickinson from Arrow Point Police Department. Can we have a moment of your time, Mrs. Davis?"

Chapter 50

Instead of being startled, Miriam's eyes narrowed as she studied the officers. "How did you find me?"

Noah pulled out the photograph from her office from his sling and held it out. Her right arm twitched, but she didn't reach for it. "This may look familiar."

"Congratulations, young man. What can I do for you?"

"Jesus Christ, invite them in. If they tracked you down, they deserve a few minutes." A man's voice rumbled from inside, followed by a hacking cough.

Noah felt like he was under a microscope as she studied them both, head to toe. After a lengthy pause, she stepped back and held the door wide for them to enter.

The interior had been remodeled, and the open floor plan made the house look huge. The kitchen was toward the back with a large island, and it opened into a sitting room. A sectional couch was pushed to the side, and in the middle sat a hospital bed. Dennis sat in the chair next to an oxygen machine with tubes connected under his nose. To say he was gaunt would be an understatement. Dark circles under his eyes and yellowish skin color were not good.

"Don't worry about catching anything. Come in and sit down." Despite his frail appearance, his voice was deep and strong. He waved an arm connected to an IV bag and blood pressure monitor toward the sofa.

As Noah took it all in, Miriam went to the kitchen and laid a Glock 19 down on the counter. "Coffee?"

"Can I help?" Angie offered.

"I can manage." Miriam paused. "But thank you, dear."

Before they sat next to a large screen TV, Noah could not help but notice the framed number twelve signed jersey on the wall and the football in an enclosed glass next to it on the floating shelf. There was a framed picture of Dennis in a dark coat standing beside a player on the field after the win. Tom Brady made him look small, but they both had big grins as Dennis was being handed a football.

"Are you kidding me?" Noah's jaw dropped as he took in the memorabilia.

"It's not the game-winner. This was a ball from the first quarter." Dennis let out a little cough, but Noah could hear the pride in his voice. "That's Brady's game jersey, though. Buccaneers are the first team in the NFL to win the Super Bowl at home."

Noah ran his fingers over the glass case and grinned before turning to shake Dennis's hand. "Didn't like the Chiefs much anyways."

He joined Dickinson on the couch as Dennis looked fondly at the picture before turning his attention to them. "It seems like you both have a story to tell us, but please be brief. I tire easily now. Last month it was stage four cancer. I'm probably at five and a half by now." His chuckle turned into a wet cough, and he pulled out a handkerchief to clean up the mucus. Everyone ignored the splotches of bright red blood on the white linen before it was tucked away.

"Eighteen years ago, I joined the Arrow Point Police Department in Wyoming …"

As Noah told the story, Dennis leaned back in the chair with his eyes closed. Miriam held onto the kitchen island with one hand while she bowed her head. They had his full attention. But he had a problem. How much information to tell them? As far as Noah knew, Miriam was still with Homeland Security and Dennis with the FBI. What he didn't know was their roles in what had happened. So, after he mentioned the form with the fingerprints arriving at the station, he stopped talking.

Miriam kept her eyes down as she brought two mugs over for each and sat on the edge of the bed. Noah thought Dennis was asleep, but after a minute, his eyes opened. "Let me guess. You've had nothing but trouble since you reopened the case? Ordered not to investigate, and when you didn't listen, your life has been in danger?"

Noah grunted. "That puts it mildly, to say the least."

"Mr. McCallister, can you tell us what's going on?" Dickinson sat on the edge of the couch, cupping the mug with both hands.

Dennis turned in the chair slightly and stared at Miriam until she looked up. "Your choice. I won't be around to deal with the after-effects."

Miriam Davis sat up straight and adjusted her glasses before nodding. She looked into their eyes and asked. "I'll tell you some things, but you have to finish what happened to you." Once Noah nodded, she continued. "What do you know of President Truman and UFOs?"

Chapter 51

"In 1945, almost to the day after World War Two ended, the United States government had a problem. There was a dramatic rise in UFO sightings by fighter pilots during the war, and they continued back at home. The next year, the Army Air Forces announced a captured flying saucer at Roswell, New Mexico."

Noah nodded, but he wasn't sure how this was connected. If they both believed in green aliens, he would quietly leave and not bother them again. He wasn't ready to assume the Fox Mulder role.

"A few hours later, they changed the story to a weather balloon, but it was too late by then. The news story of a UFO being captured by the government had spread worldwide. The threat of the public being scared and revolting was real, as panic quickly spread. President Truman signed an executive order creating an agency that operated outside the government autocracy to handle the situation. Initially, a council of twelve was formed to deal with rumors and reports. They were called Majestic 12, or MJ-12."

Miriam shrugged. "Even today, we don't know if real UFOs or aliens were covered up and hidden, but the narrative was certainly changed. Rumors were squashed, sometimes forcefully. However, Truman had made a mistake. The order he signed not only created a group of powerful individuals but a second executive branch. A council that wasn't accountable to the American public and operated from the shadows for the country's benefit."

Angie whistled as the implications sunk in. "They didn't have to report to the house or senate?"

"Officially, neither of them knew about MJ-12, although some must have. That group of twelve men didn't have to report to any sub-committees or report to President Truman."

Noah nodded as it became clear. "So, the current administration doesn't know about the secondary executive branch."

Dennis let out a sharp bark of laughter. "Not a chance. They are politicians who only run the country for four or eight years. After that, they are just citizens. Such secrets can't be entrusted to them, not when hard decisions are being made."

"Which leads us to the term espionage and how you are both involved. Although, I can now guess." Dickinson sipped her coffee and nodded toward Dennis. Noah wasn't the only one to connect the dots.

Miriam shrugged. "We've worked for the council for over three decades, and I suspect you have come in contact or know about the First Chair. While we have an equal vote, some initiatives are undertaken in the name of national security without consulting everyone. Eighteen years ago, the CIA found two deep foreign agents reporting back to Russia, and we could not flip them. The First Chair made a decision, and for the last seventeen years, we've been feeding false information back through their channels."

A chill ran up Noah's back, and he whispered. "Oh my God. What was the cost?"

Miriam didn't blink. "A young girl was separated from her parents. Traitors and spies. While much worse has been done in the name of good, that was the first time we involved a child. However, she now has a normal life, and the Russians have been set back for decades because of bad data."

As a police officer, Noah never passed judgment on anyone. He was there to enforce the laws, and if there was any problem with legalities, that was for the courts to decide. He dealt with facts and rules. These people seemed to make up their own guidelines and operated outside the law. Listening to her speech made him sick to his stomach.

Dennis cleared his throat. "Not all of us were good with that decision."

Miriam's head snapped over to study her companion. "What did you do?"

He held a hand up to forestall a rising storm and shook his head. "What happened was wrong, no matter how good our intentions. Since she was adopted, I've been stuck in Florida monitoring the child out of choice. I sent the FD-258 fingerprint card to your station. In case my actions were monitored, I redacted some information and was discrete. Mostly, I wanted the child's mother to know her daughter was alive and well."

Another piece of the puzzle fell into place.

Miriam got up and paced the living room while Dennis sat back content. When she froze and turned to face Dennis, understanding crossed her face. "You were the one to have Adam send out the order verification and location."

The dying man remained silent, but he winked.

"At times, members of the council threatened to go public with what we do, and they were taken care of. When Walter ordered the hit on me, I had enough time to prepare."

Noah gestured to her sling. "Is that what happened?"

She nodded. "Synthetic Dyneema SB61-4 material prototype. The thin cloth was made into a suit that fits under clothing and has more stopping power than a bulletproof vest, while less than three mils. However, kinetic energy still packs a punch. Broken collarbone."

Dennis coughed and cleaned up again. "Time for my meds and to sleep." He pointed a shaking finger at Miriam. "Walter is cleaning house, so this won't come back on him. I'm trying to atone, and I suggest you do the same. Third chances don't come often."

Noah wanted to ask what he meant, but Miriam let out a large sigh and nodded. She understood what he wasn't saying and made a choice.

Beside the fridge, she picked up the phone and dialed a number from memory. "Hi, Donna. This is Miriam Davis. Can you have the president call me back when it's convenient at this number?"

With everything that was happening and a woman who could call the president, Noah knew this was above his paygrade—by several levels.

Chapter 52

Dennis grabbed the gray cord looped around the bed rail and pushed the red button on the end. An older woman in purple scrubs emerged from the back bedroom and was startled when she saw everyone gathered around the living room.

"You don't have to go home, but you can't stay here. Out. Mr. McCallister needs to rest."

The nurse turned the bed down and helped Dennis stand. Miriam opened the back porch door and waited until Noah and Angie stepped outside.

He pulled three chairs around the patio table, and they sat facing each other. The silence grew until Miriam sighed.

"The little girl wasn't harmed."

Angie had enough. There was disgust in her voice. "There's right and wrong. Despite your intentions, kidnapping a four-year-old went *well* beyond wrong."

Miriam's fingers tapped on the table, and her nails clicked on the glass top. Her face remained neutral. If Angie's statement bothered her, it didn't show. "Over the last eighty years, the council has made decisions that have toppled and created governments. Headed off disaster for the United States that would have taken years for congress to approve, let alone take action, countless times. Sometimes, horrible choices have to be made to benefit the greater good."

Dickinson was about to speak, and Noah could see her temper rising. He held up a hand. "Right now, my only concern is to find Angela Taylor and reunite her with her mother. I would also like to see her kidnappers brought to justice. Good intentions or not, kidnapping is a crime, and I can't imagine what she went through as a little girl, let alone her parents."

"Various law enforcement agencies all have members who work for the council in various functions. I don't know the particulars of what happened eighteen years ago, but I have no doubt federal agents were used to apprehend the girl. As to who planned the operation and threatened the foreign agents to comply, that would be Scott, the First Chair."

"You mean Walter Scott?"

The first sign of expression crossed her face. Eyebrows raised in surprise, she nodded. "I think it's time you told me what you know so far. Much of what happens next will depend on what you say, Detective Hunter."

Noah wasn't sure if that was a threat or an offer for help, and he glanced at Angie. She knew the whole story and what it

252

cost to get this far in pursuit of an old case. He couldn't read the look in his partner's eyes, but he had to gamble on Miriam's intentions. He wasn't sure if he was extending a hand into the lion's den or not.

Time to find out.

He started at the beginning and how Jessica Ross performed a genetic family trace on the DNA sample for the missing child. Miriam mumbled about new technology while he continued. When he relayed what happened in Richmond Hill, Miriam frowned. She had him go over the details of the accident and what happened at the police station twice.

"Did you hear either of them speak? Do you recall what the woman from the truck looked like?"

Noah shook his head. "She screamed, but I didn't hear her or the man speak."

"Was it the same man from the accident that came into the police station?"

"To be honest, I'm not sure. I fired seven rounds into his face. I couldn't tell." Noah shrugged.

"The council has many contacts throughout the world. At times there are operations where we hire out. If a team has been paid to kill you, they will not stop. If they are not successful, another will take their place."

Angie looked worried. "How do we stop them?"

"You pay the full contract fee upfront, with authorization, plus a cancellation bonus. That isn't likely to happen unless you have a hundred million dollars."

Noah smiled. "The money isn't a problem. Who do I send it to?"

For the second time, he shocked Miriam. "Apparently, I'm not the only one with secrets, Detective."

When the door opened, the nurse held the phone out. "Call for you, Mrs. Davis."

"I'll be right back."

Once they were alone, Dickinson had to ask. "Seriously? You would pay that much to end this?"

Noah nodded. "The money wasn't really mine to begin with."

Angie smiled, and the dimples appeared. "That's the only reason I agreed to help you after you told me everything. I would have turned you in if you had quit the force and disappeared with all that money. But you kept working as a cop. You actually care."

He chuckled. "Don't let that get around the station."

Miriam opened the door and joined them. "I have decided to accept an offer that was made two weeks ago. I'm now the deputy directorate of operations at the Central Intelligence Agency."

Noah and Angie must have looked confused because she continued. "I'm now Walter Scott's boss, and he reports to me. If you want to work together, I have an idea."

Noah had sworn to see this to the end, so he listened. If he had to thrust his hand into the lion's den to make it happen, he would. With reservation, he nodded and stood to shake her hand.

What Noah didn't mention were his thoughts on modifying the strategy.

Chapter 53

Amanda Rawlings blocked the hook with her left forearm and stepped into her opponent. Her right fist drove the wind out of the large man, and he struggled to breathe, bent over.

With a half-spin, she pivoted inside his guard and bent her knees. When she pulled down on his right arm, her left hand snaked around his back. Amanda's hip shot out to the side as she straightened her legs. It all came down to physics, and within a second-and-a-half, the man had lost.

Her opponent groaned as he was lifted, spun in a tight arc, and landed on the ground at her feet. The two-hundred-and-ten-pound man was stunned after being thrown by a woman five inches shorter and sixty pounds lighter.

Amanda placed two thumbs on the back of his right hand and turned him fully onto his stomach with a wrist-lock. Before he could roll, a handcuff encircled his wrist, and the blond woman used the links to hold him steady. A knee to the back drove the remaining air from his lungs as his left wrist was secured.

"You are under arrest. You have the right to remain silent—"

Her remaining words were drowned out as the class applauded and the instructor stepped in.

"Well done, Miss. Rawlings." Ernie Hammond waved his clipboard and gestured to the eighteen students lining the mats. "Reminder, tomorrow morning we have a test on accident scene management, zero-nine-hundred, sharp."

There were a few groans as they were dismissed. Amanda helped Brian stand and grinned. "Sorry if you landed too hard. I tried to pull up at the last second."

The large man resembled a boxer, with a nose flattened too many times and a heavy brow. But he smiled and turned so she could unlock the cuffs. "All good. How did you flip me so easily?"

Amanda laughed. "Judo. I had too much energy when I was young, and my parents enrolled me in classes."

Brian rubbed his wrists as she placed the cuffs back in the leather pouch. They both wore dark gray tracksuits and blue T-shirts with the Police Foundations across the back in white letters. Their utility belts had everything a real police officer would carry, except the pistol made of red rubber.

St. Petersburg College was a public college in Pinellas, Florida. There wasn't a student residence, but Amanda didn't mind. It was only a twenty-minute walk home. A few months into her second year for police foundations, she still loved it.

"Are you ready for the co-op placement in December?" Brian walked with her to the lockers. They had to stow their gear before leaving. Two second-year students were removed from the course when pictures were discovered online of them "playing" cop for friends at a party. Those who remained on course took that lesson to heart.

"I'm still waiting on the background check, but I hope to get into Orange County Sheriff's office."

Brian let out a deep baritone laugh which echoed off the walls. "You just want to work at Disney Land."

Amanda flicked her blond hair back over one shoulder and grinned at her friend. "Maybe."

"Good luck."

"Local is fine for me. My car isn't that great, and I don't want to push it." Once they reached the change rooms, he added. "However, it's running good now, if you want a ride home?"

Amanda raised her eyebrows. "That's the second offer this week, and it's only Tuesday."

"Just being friendly." His flushed cheeks said otherwise, and she thought it was cute.

"Can you give me five minutes?"

"Not a problem. I'll wait out front." Brian grinned and rushed off. She watched him until he turned the corner and found her own cheeks were warm.

Six minutes later, Amanda walked out the front door and found Brian not only had locked his things away but had run to the car and drove over. He was slightly out of breath as he held the passenger door to the green VW Beetle and gestured for her to enter.

"Your chariot, my lady."

"You're an idiot." Amanda laughed. "Thanks."

As they drove through the parking lot, neither noticed a brown minivan pull off the shoulder of the road and follow.

Chapter 54

Noah waited until seven o'clock Wednesday morning before he made the call.

"Staff Sergeant Hutchings. How can I help you?"

"How about you retire so that I could have a nice cushy job inside the station."

"Ha! You couldn't handle it, rookie. What's going on?"

"Wanted to give you an update. Dickinson and I have some new information, and we're heading back to the Washington D.C. area. I think we will be done soon."

"Is this line secure on your end? Where are you now?"

Hutchings tapped his pen on the desk. He did that when he worried. "Don't panic. We're just leaving Tampa. I got a new burner phone, and I'll ditch it after a few days."

"What do you need me to do?"

"Nothing. I'm just looking forward to you arranging another welcome home barbecue."

Hutchings paused, and Noah heard the blinds in the office pop as they were bent. "I guess I can do that, although the weather isn't as nice in Arrow Point as Tampa, but let me know when."

"How does this weekend sound? It should be in around ten-thirty or ten thirty-five. I'll call to confirm."

"Okay … take care, rookie."

"See you soon, Hutch."

Noah powered down the burner phone and threw it in the glove box. "Ready when you are."

Angie pulled out of the parking lot and merged onto the interstate with the rising sun ahead. Four days. It should be enough. "Do you think he caught it?"

Noah chuckled. "He doesn't miss much."

*****

"That kid has hit his head too many fuckin' times."

Hutchings pulled up the long-range weather forecast on the computer. Fifty-eight and raining. Damn, rookie wants a barbecue? Seriously?

"Wait. Was that ten-thirty at night or morning? Which day?"

He was about to call Noah back, but the display had unknown number. Confused, Hutchings went back to work.

However, a computer-generated program recorded the conversation seventeen hundred miles away after recognizing the

261

voice pattern matching the target. All known contacts of Noah Hunter were being monitored. The call was under a minute in duration, so they could not pinpoint the originating location. A flash email was usually sent to a level three agent to analyze the recording and verify the data. In this case, the parameters of the program notified only one person. Sean Cameron.

The information assurance director left a mid-morning meeting, citing an emergency. With the world's best computers at his fingertips, he sent the encrypted information to the First Chair.

Chapter 55

Noah and Angie had spent two nights and gone over the plans in great detail for most of Tuesday. The studio apartment over the garage hadn't been used in years, and they gladly accepted the hospitality.

Despite Dennis's failing health, his mind was still sharp. Noah truly believed he wished to leave this world with peace of mind and wanted to do some good. He still didn't trust Miriam Davis one-hundred percent, but soon as Walter Scott found her, she was as good as dead. Already, news of her acceptance for the position would be raising eyebrows as pieces on a chessboard were repositioned accordingly.

The drive from Tampa to St. Petersburg was only thirty minutes, and they easily followed the directions given to them by Dennis. When a distraught woman answered the door, Noah took a step back. The woman was in her fifties and just over five feet tall. Her eyes were red and puffy, and she appeared to have had little or no sleep last night. A handful of tissues was clutched in her left hand. She was still dressed in a flannel nightgown despite the late morning hour.

"I'm Detective Hunter, and this is Sergeant Dickinson. May we have a word with you?" Noah and Angie held out their badges and identification. They had agreed to be upfront and honest with what would happen next.

"Sarah Rawlings. I thought they were not going to send anyone?"

Noah looked at his partner, not understanding. "Who wasn't going to send someone? Not sure I'm following."

"You're not from the St. Petersburg Police Department? They said there is nothing they could do since she's an adult."

A chill ran down his back, and Noah tried not to wince. "Your daughter?"

"Yes. Amanda never came home from college yesterday, and she wasn't in class today. Nobody's seen her."

"Ma'am, may we come in and talk?"

Sarah held the door for them.

The living room had a large sectional couch filled with blankets and pillows. She opened the curtains and sat holding a cushion on her lap. "How bad is the news?"

Dickinson leaned forward. "We don't know what happened to your daughter. We are here for another reason, but it seems we may be too late."

Sarah whispered. "Too late?"

Noah cleared his throat. "We're here in regard to her birth mother."

"What do you mean?" Sarah's hands clasped as her eyes widened. "Should I call my husband, Connor? He's out driving around the college campus."

"We don't know what happened to Amanda. However, we came here to warn you of a possible danger, but we may have been too late." Before she could jump in, Noah held up a hand. "I can explain. What can you tell me about Amanda? Adoption?"

"My husband and I couldn't have children, and we placed our application. After six months, we got a call of an orphaned three-year-old girl. We were told her parents died in a car accident, and there was no family left."

"Amanda's mother was alive last I saw her. Her father passed away a few years ago from cancer."

"She's alive?" Sarah's voice was barely above a whisper.

"Yes, and she's—" Noah turned when the front door opened.

"Honey? Whose SUV is in the driveway?" Connor had come home.

Sarah stood. "In the living room. The police are here."

Noah and Angie stood as her husband walked down the hall and into the living room. Connor was a few inches taller than Dickinson, at six-foot-four-inches, bald with a salt-and-pepper goatee. He appeared to be in his mid-fifties and wore a dark blue windbreaker.

"Did you have any information …" He trailed off after looking the two officers up and down. He frowned when he studied Noah.

Connor drew a pistol from under the jacket and pointed it at Noah in the blink of an eye. Recognition made his eyes wide. "FBI. Get the fuck away from my wife."

"What are you doing?" Sarah screamed as Angie's hands rose in the air, and Noah left his at the side. One arm was in a sling, and he didn't see any point. There was nowhere to maneuver, and they had no weapons.

"Hands up! Move away from them, Sarah!"

"Calm down. We are here to talk about your daughter." Noah tried to keep his voice steady and soothing.

Connor adopted the Weaver stance, and the Sig Sauer P226 didn't shake. Noah was kept in his sights, and Sarah remained frozen.

"Connor Rawlings, explain what is going on!" Sarah stepped forward and shook her finger at her husband.

Angie moved a foot to the side, away from her partner, ready for anything. "Mrs. Rawlings, the question you should be asking is how does your husband know Detective Hunter?"

Connor's eyes flicked back and forth between Dickinson and Hunter as his face became flushed.

Noah found the man familiar, and his jaw dropped in disbelief when it dawned on him.

"I know you. You're the man from the hotel in Arrow Point—room nine. You were next to Leslie and Joe Taylor the day their daughter was kidnapped."

Sarah's sharp intake of breath drew Connor's attention, and she walked over to stand in front of her husband. The end of the pistol shifted to the ceiling instead of her chest. "Put the *fucking* gun away. You better start explaining, or there won't be anything left of you for the police to arrest."

A grin twitched across Dickinson's face at the woman's ferocity. The attention shifted, and the threat level dropped dramatically.

Connor looked like a cornered animal, and despite the height and weight difference, signs of panic began to show as Sarah put it together.

"Look. I can explain."

Noah stepped forward and growled. The inner rage made his muscles twitch. "You better start right now because if you don't shoot me, I will arrest you for kidnapping."

When the Sig Sauer was holstered, Sarah's finger poked her husband in the chest with each word. "What did you do?"

Chapter 56

"I had little to no choice. We were on an operation, and orders were followed." Connor rubbed a hand across his face as his wife stepped back in horror. "However, they wanted to place the little girl into the system. We had been trying for so long to have a baby and couldn't. We had talked about adopting, and a few strings were pulled."

"The FBI kidnapped a child from her parents, and you didn't think to tell me until eighteen years later?" Sarah backed up until her legs touched the coffee table. "I'm going to be sick."

Noah ground his teeth, and his right hand clenched into a fist. Despite the knowledge of who was playing puppet master behind the scenes, before him was the one who perpetrated the crime. Right. There.

Originally, Connor had longer shoulder-length hair and a beard, but that could have been part of the disguise.

"It all worked out." He gave a nervous look about the room but received zero sympathy from anyone.

"Amanda barely spoke for the first thirteen months and had nightmares for years." Sarah turned to Noah and Angie. "Can you give us a few minutes alone? I have some things to discuss. Trust me. He's going nowhere."

Despite the height difference, there was little doubt about who wore the pants in their relationship. "We'll be outside."

Sarah didn't wait for the front door to close before she started in on her husband.

"Strangely, that felt pretty good." Dickinson couldn't help but grin.

Noah agreed. "However, my intentions haven't changed. I'm still here to help Angela … now Amanda."

"How much do you want to tell the Rawlings?"

"I'm sure Connor must know more. At least minimal background on the Taylors. There would have been intel briefings as they ran through various scenarios as the team prepared." The inner fire wasn't extinguished but banked and smoldered within. Noah hardened the emotions into resolve.

"Where do you think they took Amanda? Do you think she's all right?" Angie looked worried.

"These types of people are worried about one thing. Retaining power. Amanda will be used as a bargaining chip or bait until this is all over. No doubt she will be treated well. They are after me, and with Miriam coming out of hiding, they should have a secondary target."

From inside the home, they could hear muted yelling. It appeared to be one-sided, and Sarah wasn't holding back. So far, there hadn't been the sound of dishes breaking or gunshots. Noah took that as a positive sign.

After five minutes, Sarah opened the door. She had changed into a blue T-shirt and track pants and appeared to be flushed. "Thank you. Come back in, please."

Noah and Angie sat back in the living room as Connor came down from upstairs. He carried some photographs. "I owe you both an apology."

"Here are a few recent pictures of Amanda." Sarah handed over the recently printed photos. The young woman had long blond hair, a straight nose, and high cheekbones. "Hopefully, they will help."

"I'm here to let you know that I'm going after the person responsible for orchestrating the abduction. I didn't know Amanda was missing until we arrived." Noah passed the pictures to his partner.

"What can we do to help? How do we get our daughter back?"

"For now, we need information. How were you contacted through the FBI for the assignment?"

Connor had problems meeting their eyes, and he stared at his hands. "Taskforce assignments are common, and they are a good opportunity for advancement, should you do well. I was chosen, and we monitored the subjects for two months. As the husband-and-wife team went on vacation, we received the orders. We managed to delay them in Cheyenne and got ahead of them to the motel."

When Noah was in the military, he could be ordered to charge a machinegun nest firing on his location, and he would have to comply. However, if he were ordered to shoot civilians, he would refuse. It came down to the type of order given—was the command lawful or not? Illegal orders can be rejected without repercussions. Noah had no idea if the FBI had such directives built into their chain of command, but common sense *should* prevail. However, in this case, it failed horribly. But now wasn't the time to fix past mistakes.

"Leslie Taylor was the mother, and Joe Taylor, the father. They named their little girl Angela. I'm not here to judge if what the FBI did was right or wrong, but I'm here to make sure she is safe and those that made those choices are held accountable." Noah stared at Connor, who finally looked up. "There is no doubt you will be called to testify on your actions. I would find a good lawyer."

"Connor has agreed to make amends if possible." Sarah elbowed her husband. "Didn't you, dear?"

"Yes."

"What else can we do?" Sarah perched on the edge of the couch. "Please. Anything. We love Amanda and have raised her as our own."

When Noah shifted on the couch, the missing weight on his hip gave him pause. "Well, there is one thing I could use ..."

Chapter 57

Angie placed the larger duffel bag into the back of the Navigator, and Noah threw the smaller bag into the backseat. Connor Rawlings had a small armory in the basement, and Sarah told Noah to help himself.

He had stuffed two ballistic vests into the bag after removing the FBI Velcroed lettering, along with a thigh holster for each of them. Connor had two *police* patches, and Noah grabbed them. He didn't have any Glocks, but Noah gladly helped himself to a Sig Sauer P226 and half a dozen magazines. Dickinson liked the feel of the Sig M18 P320 but also chose the P226. The pistols had upgraded optics, and the Red Dot installed. Dickinson placed four boxes of 9mm ammunition, extra magazines, and a speed loader in the small bag.

Noah didn't feel the slightest bit guilty for helping himself to the weapons. He wasn't sure if they would be needed or not, but it was one less thing he had to worry about.

"What do you think?" Noah asked Dickinson as she got behind the wheel and then made their way to the interstate.

She winced. "Assuming this ever goes to trial? There are a lot of moving parts right now. If one of them fails, the rest will as well."

"Everything depends on Miriam." Noah grabbed a bottle of water and a protein bar from the backseat before buckling in. "Guess we're ready. Back to Washington."

*****

Miriam Davis walked out the front door and into a waiting black Chevy Tahoe. Three men in dark suits, earpieces, and holstered weapons, confirmed the area was cleared, then escorted her from Dennis's home. A small travel suitcase was placed in the rear.

Instead of driving to the airport, they arrived at the Westshore Plaza Shopping Center within fifteen minutes. It was one of the largest malls in the area. Even on a Wednesday morning, the parking lots were full.

As the Tahoe cruised the aisles and passed vacant parking spaces, it passed under the walkway from the parking garage. Anyone watching from above wouldn't have noticed the Chevy momentarily stop. Two men and Miriam stepped outside, got into a waiting 1988 Pontiac Montana minivan, and drove away while the Tahoe continued. Eight seconds had passed. The rusted blue vehicle was unremarkable and blended into the landscape.

The dark tint on the windows prevented anyone from looking inside.

"Okay, Miriam. I'm not sure what strings you pulled, but this better be good." Daniel Edwards, her new boss at the CIA, held the position of Directorate of Operations (formerly known as Clandestine Services), and sat in the third-row seating. Next to him was Paul Adams, director of the CIA. "We were ordered to meet up with you and pulled off the golf course."

Both men wore light collared golf shirts and khaki pants. No one had to mention who could order them about.

Director Adams added. "We all know your work history and what you've done for the agency in the past. I doubt this is frivolous. What's going on?"

Miriam glanced at the two men in the front seat. They were also officers in the CIA and could be trusted. She hoped.

"Gentlemen. Before I begin, let me assure you everything I'm about to say is true." She waited until they both nodded before continuing. "What do you know about President Truman?"

Chapter 58

Noah and Angie drove for seven and a half hours until they entered South Carolina. Soon as they crossed the border, he powered the new burner phone back on.

"Ready?"

"How long until we get a response?" Angie pulled off Interstate-95 North into a rest area.

Noah shrugged and tried to gesture with his left hand. The pain made him grind his teeth. He forgot too easily, and while better, it would be a long road to recovery. The swelling had gone down, but a colorful bruise circled his wrist like a band. Angie had tightened the brace, and he had forgone the sling. "It could be within the hour, five minutes, or a full day. However, if the hit team has the resources, I would expect something soon."

With that, he dialed his home phone number and listened to the messages. The first had an offer of duct cleaning, and the second recording was a few seconds of silence before someone disconnected. The third recording, Noah placed on speaker.

"Detective Hunter, since you have dropped off the face of the earth, call back at this number, and arrangements can be made."

The voice wasn't familiar, and after dialing, they could hear a series of clicks and dead air before the call was picked up.

"Ah. Noah Hunter, I presume?"

"Who am I speaking to? I'm guessing this is Sean Cameron."

"For a simple police officer, you are well informed."

Noah had enough. "What's the deal? Where's Amanda Rawlings?"

"You are under the assumption I'm here to help you, and you couldn't be farther from the truth."

Angie's knuckles turned white as she gripped the steering wheel, and her left knee bounced.

"Fine. Spill it. I'm guessing there is some ultimate threat about to come down. I have things to do, so if you could hurry it up, that would be great."

Sean chuckled, but there was no humor in it. "No. I've just finished pinpointing your location. That was it. You'll be dead within the hour. Have a good day."

Dickinson lowered her phone and stopped recording when he disconnected. "What an asshole."

Noah threw the burner phone on the armrest. "We knew this was coming, and we have two choices. Somewhere remote or try and get some help."

Angie grinned, and the dimples made another appearance. With the sparkle in her eyes, Noah knew she had a third option. Game on.

~

Florence, South Carolina, was a quarter the size of Arrow Point with less than forty-thousand people. While it had a few large box stores and hotel chains, the small city felt quaint and had a comforting atmosphere. As the stores were closing downtown, many still lingered outside on the cobbled walkway. A group of kids rode their bikes down Main Street, and everyone gave them plenty of room. As a family left a restaurant, the two-lane traffic stopped as they were waved across the street, without a walkway.

"This is the kind of town where I would love to hit the thrift stores and explore." Dickinson had said that same thing for the last three towns they drove through.

Noah glanced at the clock and held back a chuckle. "We were supposed to have been killed an hour ago."

"I'm getting a little nervous. I don't want anyone else involved or hurt because of us."

He had those same misgivings. "Miriam Davis is doing her part, and we have to live to do ours. Before that happens, we have to survive what's coming."

Angie was about to reply, then thought better of it and simply nodded. They had gone over contingency plans during the drive. There was very little left to do except choose the location—home-field advantage would play an important factor.

By nine-thirty at night, Freedom Park was empty. Five baseball fields were laid out in a circle, with a pavilion in the middle. A line of trees separated the areas inside the fences. The floodlights on the standards were off, but there was enough light from the surrounding homes and streetlights to make out some of the details.

Dickinson found a place to park on Senior Way, away from the main road. The Navigator snuck in behind the blue Freedom Florence Recreational Complex sign. Neither were sure how much time remained or if it would work at all. Noah would know the answer soon.

Angie helped place and strap the ballistic vest on Noah and place fully loaded magazines into the pouches. He felt like a kid getting ready to go out and play in the snow as his mother dressed him. With one arm, it wasn't possible to get prepared. Noah knew he was a liability, which solidified a train of thought. If it came down to choosing, he wouldn't let Dickinson risk herself for him.

Lost in thought, Noah jumped when she buckled the thigh-holster onto his right leg. Angie chuckled. "Just making sure the straps aren't twisted."

The Sig Sauer pistol slid in with a click. "Right."

The melancholy disappeared.

Dickinson dressed, and the vest was a little too big, but it was better than nothing. Noah grabbed the items they had appropriated from Dennis's garage, then locked the Lincoln. "Guess that's it. Let's see how greedy they are."

Chapter 59

Eric hung up the phone and opened the tablet. He punched in the coordinates and showed Iain. "There's the signal."

Iain linked the tablet to the laptop, and his fingers flew over the keyboard. The screen linked the data to the overlay map, creating a route. "They are two hours north of our position."

"Can you insert the tracker?"

The progress upload bar was stuck at ninety-eight percent for a while, but soon it read one-hundred. "We're good."

Eric didn't wait but dropped the transmission in drive. The Jeep Cherokee's tires spun the gravel on the shoulder of the interstate as the load shifted in the back. Emma had her own assignment, and they had separated. Usually, Oliver would pair with Iain, but that wasn't an option.

Iain kept the screen active on the center console as he climbed into the backseat. He found the police scanner and opened the long case. He removed the rifle and a cleaning kit. A four-piece rod was assembled and inserted down the barrel. He attached a bore brush to one end and a T-handle on the other and pulled it through. Iain repeated the maneuver a few times, then switched to a swab with a few drops of CLP.

Iain slid on the tactical gloves with reinforced knuckles, then wiped down the entire rifle. A dry white cloth polished each bullet and casing. Afterward, he loaded the five-round magazine. Years ago, he had learned to minimize evidence left behind—that included prints, digital or physical. In the heat of the moment, a missing casing could spell disaster.

Forty-five minutes later, Iain had finished going through their gear and leaned back to close his eyes. Rest when you can.

It seemed only minutes had passed when Eric spoke. "They've stopped moving."

Eric had repositioned the laptop on the passenger seat and propped the tablet on the dashboard. Iain blinked away the fatigue and scanned the countryside. He had been out for three hours.

"ETA?" He slipped on a dark jacket and wool cap.

"Ten minutes. Small town, up ahead."

"Game plan?"

Iain handed over Eric's Browning 9mm and knife. The eight-inch fixed blade had seen more quiet work than most combat veterans. The recently sharpened knife slid into the sheath on the older man's left hip.

"I'll drop you a quarter-mile short of the target. Then I'll move once you are in position."

"Roger, that."

Iain removed the earpieces from the neoprene container and ensured the comms links were matched to the base unit. Another case revealed an older but functional NVD (night vision device) headset. The wool cap prevented the straps from digging into his forehead. After three tours in Iraq and one in Afghanistan, Iain grew to hate the Kevlar helmet. The day he quit the SAS, he kicked the helmet across the parade square and told the QM to keep it. Instead of making seventy-thousand pounds a year, he made one hundred times that.

At midnight, the small town was empty. The streetlights downtown flashed red and amber. "The signal has stopped for longer than a minute. They're stationary."

Eric slipped off his seatbelt and steered with his knees. A glance down confirmed a round was loaded. He turned north on Freedom Blvd and then west on Senior Way and pulled over.

Iain grabbed the rifle and small pack and slipped out of the back. He quietly closed the door. As Eric drove away, he flicked the switch at his belt. The throat microphone picked up the lightest whisper.

"Radio check."

"Loud and clear. Pulling off to the side up ahead. Let me know when you have eyes on the target."

"Roger. Out."

The last image on the screen placed Hunter's position across a field at a recreational park of some type. Iain darted across the ditch and lawn before he flipped the night vision down. On patrol, he would have waited the full twenty minutes for his eyes to adjust as he listened. However, waiting wouldn't improve his vision with the distant street lights and ambient light from the town.

"Almost in position." Iain climbed the four-foot fence and was in the outfield of a baseball field. "I have a visual of the target, but I don't think it's Hunter."

From the prone position, Iain did not need the scope to see the target. On the pitcher's mound, a long pole stuck in the dirt. A white flag hung perpendicular from the post without a breeze. An object on the ground and a piece of paper was fastened to the flag.

"Bloody hell," Eric whispered under his breath. "The road I'm on is a dead end. Turning around, and I'll check it out. Keep me covered. Any other movement, shoot to kill."

Iain settled down, flicked off the safety, and scanned the field to his front. He was too close, but there wasn't an elevated position that would be better. As always, ground dictated.

The headlights from the Jeep swung about, and within a minute, they shone toward home plate. Eric got out of the vehicle and approached the flagpole. He pulled down the note and quickly looked around the field.

Iain wasn't ready went the muzzle from a pistol was jammed into the base of his skull.

A woman whispered. "One move or sound, and I pull the trigger."

Chapter 60

The bleachers for each baseball field were on the other side of the short fence. They were constructed out of aluminum and had four rows. Underneath, there was enough room for Noah. It provided concealment and protection. Behind him offered an avenue of escape should things change.

He had trouble settling down, and his nerves threatened to blow his cover. Doubt trickled into his mind. *What am I doing? This should be the job of the FBI or someone more qualified.*

That was the juxtaposition. The country was filled with people who had the skills, but who did they really work for or report to? That was the problem.

After an hour of being in position, a vehicle drove along the dead-end road toward the recreational complex. Noah had time to scout the area and discovered the road went nowhere. They had tracked the burner phone, as predicted.

He patted the Sig Sauer in the thigh-holster and waited. Eventually, the headlights flicked over his position as they settled onto home plate. The car had driven along the access path toward the first baseball field and parked.

Dickinson had constructed the post and flag from scrap material found in Dennis's garage while Noah wrote the note. They had placed the burner phone on the ground leaning against the pole. A man dressed in dark pants and a thick green sweater held a pistol close to his right hip as he tentatively approached the pitcher's mound. From eighty-five feet away, Noah watched him tuck the gun in his jacket, pull down the note, and hold it up to the car's headlights to read.

Noah felt the vibration from Angie's cell in the chest pocket of the ballistic vest, and he answered on the second ring. "I'm buying out the contract with authorization."

The man spoke with a British accent, and he heard a strange echo delay across the field. "I don't think so, Hunter." He pulled out a small tactical flashlight from a pocket and flicked it along the fence line and into the trees.

"Keep looking all you want, but we have a transaction to finish." Noah remained still. When the flashlight beam swept over the bleachers, he closed his eyes, but that was it. Movement gave away a position more than obscured shapes, and he fought the temptation.

"I highly doubt a cop has that kind of money." The man dropped the note and walked toward second base. The flashlight scanned the outfield.

"Your opinion doesn't matter. I have a sixteen-digit code, and I can complete the transaction. Call it in."

*****

Eric swore and placed the call on mute.

"Iain, do you have a visual?"

Silence.

The feeling of unease grew as he looked around. Eric had walked into a trap, and even if the offer to cancel the contract were valid, it didn't ensure his safety.

Eric darted back to the car and turned off the headlights and engine. He pulled out a paper and pen. With a flick of a finger, he unmuted the call.

"You have one shot to get this code correct. Should it be wrong, there will be no second chance. Go."

Noah Hunter spoke slowly and enunciated each letter and number combination. Eric read it back.

"That's correct. Call me back." Hunter disconnected.

Eric had been on an operation in Australia several years ago when the hit had been called off moments before execution. While all teams knew it could happen, it rarely did. He dug the satellite phone out of the backpack, and Mother picked up on the second ring.

"Completed?"

Eric cleared his throat. "Not quite. Noah Hunter wishes to buy out the contract, plus penalty."

"Well … that's interesting. Relay the information."

He slowly read the sixteen-digit code and waited.

"The code is valid. Give me a number to contact Noah Hunter to finalize the transaction. Stand down." Mother sounded amused at the turn of events. Being paid in full without further risk was the ideal scenario. Replacing a team member was costly.

Eric checked the connection on the comms unit and tried to raise Iain, but nothing. He thought there was a click and grunt at one point, but he couldn't be sure.

Fifteen minutes later, Mother returned the call. "Transaction finished. This operation is now considered complete. Return home."

"We still have pieces in play and down a member."

"Update."

Eric mentioned what Emma had accomplished and her next steps.

"Take your partner and go to ground. Return home once the dust has settled. I'll take care of your darling daughter."

Eric chuckled. "Good luck with that."

After they hung up, he called Hunter back using the burner phone.

"Everything is good. Release my partner, and we're gone."

There was a long pause. "What assurance do I have for my safe conduct?"

"This is a business transaction and not personal. No offense, but we're leaving."

"Leave the phone on the ground, and in two minutes, you can pick up your partner by the road."

Eric was surprised to find he was relieved that the mission was over. He was looking forward to returning to Manchester and seeing Emma once again. Retirement never looked so good.

Chapter 61

Emma stared into the bathroom mirror and counted down.

"Three, two ..."

The heel of her right palm struck the side of her nose on *one* with a sharp blow. A sound reminiscent of a chicken wing snapping echoed in the small, tiled room. A groan quickly followed as her eyes rolled back in her head, and fresh blood dripped into the porcelain sink along with a few tears.

"Oh, fuck me. That hurts."

Though her eyes watered, she stared into the mirror and nodded. She held a damp hand towel filled with ice gingerly on her face and waited for the bleeding to stop. Despite the swelling and dark bruise, the nose was set. Her eyes would have dark circles in a few days, but it would be better than having a crooked nose.

The idea to take the young woman did not go quite as planned. Emma had thought the large man was the primary threat

289

and taken him down first. The bitch had fought like a caged mixed martial artist and managed to crack an elbow backward before the cuffs were on. When Emma drew a pistol and pointed it at her friend's head, Amanda finally relented.

If Amanda had a few more years of training, Emma doubted she would have been able to take her in a fair fight. *But life ain't fair, deary.*

She would have taken Amanda earlier, but she had to prep the safe house an hour north of Tampa, Florida. The small town didn't even have a name, just a black dot on the map. Most of the stores had closed in the "downtown" area, leaving a gas station and corner store. It had only taken ten minutes to find an abandoned farmhouse in the countryside. They were plentiful. No one had been inside for years, and the dirt-floored cellar was perfect. There were no windows or tools to use to escape, and the thick timber in the middle was strong enough to tie them to.

With a final look in the mirror, Emma returned to the kitchen and sat in the only wooden chair. The home had been emptied except for a few items—the wobbly chair was one of them. Back home, this farmhouse and property would sell for half a million pounds, but here it sat empty.

She was jarred when the satellite phone rang. Only two people had this number, Mother and her father, Eric.

"Go ahead."

"Your current assignment is now over. Go to ground and return home once it is safe to do so."

"They got the fucker? Good."

Mother chuckled. "No. Hunter bought out the contract."

"Seriously? Wad the fuck?" Her nose started to bleed again, and Emma held the towel underneath. She would have to go to the gas station again and buy more ice.

"Yes, dear. Noah coughed up the money. Although, there was one strange thing."

"Yeah?" Emma closed her eyes. All this for nothing and a headache. Oliver was gone, and no doubt the entire country would be looking for them. Hell of a mess for her cut.

She could hear Mother's fingernails click on the keyboard. "It seems our American friends may be having a power struggle. The authorization was valid, but it didn't come from the originator."

Emma hummed as she thought it over, then an idea struck. A way to make it worthwhile. "Does the originator know about the rescinded order?"

Mother laughed. "Are you thinking of double-dipping?"

"Being paid *not* to do the job, and being paid to do it, sounds like a win-win to me." Emma could hear the muffled screams from the cellar, and it lifted her spirits.

"Hunter can't complain that we didn't fulfill our end of the bargain if he's dead."

"Exactly."

Mother cleared her throat. "Do you want me to activate your father and Iain? Or is this something you can handle yourself?"

Emma stood and grinned. She ignored the blood that dripped off the end of her chin. "How about we don't mention this to anyone else, and we split the payout?"

"Tread carefully. There's no safety net on this. But if you can do it ..."

"I'm not worried. What do you want me to do with the kids?"

"They are no longer part of this operation. Have they seen your face?"

"No."

"Cut them free."

Emma laid a finger gently on her nose, making her eyes water. She had plans for the bitch.

"I need some information before I start."

They talked for a few more minutes as Emma scribbled in her logbook. *One bullet for fifty-million dollars?* Easy peasy, lemon squeezy.

Chapter 62

Noah remained in the shadows until the vehicle drove away, then he picked up the burner phone. A weight lifted off his shoulders. Not many people had that much money and therefore that option, but it was worth it.

He had spent an entire day working with the lawyer to liquify the properties and investments on the computer. There were losses as he accumulated the payment, but he could afford it in the end. Noah wasn't bankrupt by any means. Quite a few contracts could not be closed so easily, and he left them alone. They would still generate a profit down the road.

Noah crossed the baseball field and headed toward the back fence, where he met Dickinson.

"I'm guessing everything went as planned?" She held a 300 Win Mag over one shoulder and a collection of pistols in her left hand—two were tucked into her waistband.

"All good. That should be the last of them. Although, I didn't get a receipt."

Angie grinned. "There's probably no refund anyways."

Only one field had a good position for distant observation, and they had guessed correctly. Noah took his only advantage and chose the meeting place. The military had trained him well—ground dictates the situation.

"Do you want to drive first or second?" Noah wanted to arrive in Washington by morning. Angie placed the rifle across the backseat and the pistols on the floormats. Noah struggled to get the ballistic vest off, and he needed help.

"You can drive first. I think I could sleep." She piled the vests on top of the weapons and covered them with the backpacks. "What do you want to do with this?"

Noah had been transporting Leslie Taylor's pack across the country. A brief inspection revealed survival gear, rations, and a change of clothes, with no weapons or electronics. He shrugged. "It's all she has left. We'll keep it for now."

Within a minute, they were heading north to the interstate. Paying off the hit team was the easy part. What was coming next made Noah nauseous when he thought about the many things that could go wrong.

*****

Amanda grew aware of a jagged stone digging into the side of her face as a warm liquid dripped across her lips and into her mouth. The metallic taste of blood made her stomach roll, and she struggled to spit it out. Sharp pain from the broken ribs on the right side made her grin as the memory of the fight flooded back.

She still managed a front snap kick to the woman's groin when the beating started. As her attacker groaned in pain, Amanda laughed. The second kick to the throat would have ended the fight had her leg been an inch longer. Fifteen years in judo and six years in karate had paid off. She knew how to maximize damage with priority targets. However, being handcuffed to the post was her downfall.

In the end, Amanda tried to protect her face and torso from her masked abductor's barrage of strikes. Balaclava notwithstanding, she believed she would recognize those hazel eyes if seen again. They were cold with black specks and were permanently engraved in her memory. Every five-foot six-inch woman would be subjected to scrutiny.

Bitch.

Amanda struggled to open her eyes, but both were swollen shut. It was then every nerve ending began to scream, and she groaned once before blacking out.

Chapter 63

Angie had managed to curl up on the front seat despite being six-foot-one, and her gentle snore made Noah chuckle. I-95 was becoming a familiar sight as he made his way north and entered North Carolina. By one in the morning, they passed Fayetteville, and Noah's eyes were getting heavy.

Half an hour later, the signs for Smithfield showed gas stations and coffee shops, and he knew it was time to stop. The tank was less than a quarter full, and he may as well top it off.

It was then that he made a mistake.

After taking the ramp to the Market Street exit, he turned left over the overpass and accidentally hit the cruise control's resume button. The Navigator accelerated to sixty-two miles per hour, then remained steady. Soon as he passed the Waffle House on the north side, a familiar sight appeared in the rearview mirror. Red and blue lights flashed from a police cruiser.

Noah almost chuckled. It had been nearly two decades since he'd been pulled over.

As he signaled and braked, Angie woke. "What's going on?"

"I was going a little over the limit."

She sat up, wide awake, and slipped on her shoes. "How much over?"

"Too much. I should have known better."

Noah lowered the window and shut the vehicle off with the hazard lights on. He glanced in the backseat and was relieved to see the weapons were covered from view. While there was nothing illegal, he didn't need the hassle. With both hands on the steering wheel, he waited.

The cruiser parked properly behind, two feet to the side, to block. As the officer stepped outside, he adjusted the wide-brimmed trooper headdress. Noah watched from his side mirror as the man casually laid his right thumb on the Navigator's brake light before approaching. The flashlight flicked over the side of the car, backseat, and Dickinson before resting on Noah's chest.

"Morning. Do you know why I pulled you over?"

The man stood six-foot and was older than Noah by fifteen years. His tanned face was lined with deep wrinkles and a bright white mustache. The oval, frameless glasses suited him.

Noah nodded. "I have an idea."

"I've clocked you going sixty-two miles per hour in a forty zone."

"I'm not going to argue that. I accidentally hit the cruise button, and it resumed highway speeds." Noah winced.

"Honesty is appreciated. License and registration."

"Wallet's in my back pocket." Noah waited until the officer nodded before moving. During a traffic stop, making sudden moves in the middle of the night left him on edge. He caught the nametag on the uniform; *Barton.*

Noah held the APPD badge up chest height as he passed over the Wyoming identification. "If you could, I'd appreciate some professional courtesy."

Barton studied the photo on the card and made sure Noah matched the picture. "Have you been drinking or drugs? Either of you?"

Angie shook her head. "Neither."

"Nothing."

Noah knew a practiced eye studied them and the Smithfield officer gave them a slight grin. "Good to know. I'll verify your ID and be right back."

As he walked back to the cruiser, Noah smiled. "That'll teach me."

"How far are we from Washington?" Angie stretched and cracked her neck.

"Four hours or so. We need to fill up, and we'll be there when the sun comes up." Noah noticed Barton returning. "That was quick."

"I'll drive from here. You can catch some sleep."

Noah held up a finger to forestall further conversation. A chill washed over him as he looked in the side mirror.

He could see the officer's side and empty holster. Barton's right arm was stretched straight down. Instead of approaching the window, he stood ten feet back and at the thirty-degree angle.

"Keep your hands where I can see them. I'm confirming you are Noah Hunter of Arrow Point, Wyoming?" the officer's voice was cool and calm.

Confused, Noah turned. "Yes. That is me."

"Son, we can do this two ways. You seem like an upstanding young man, so I'm not going to mention the second method. Step out of the vehicle with your arms in the air."

Before he opened the door, Noah showed two empty hands. "Not a problem. Can you tell me what's going on first?"

Barton raised his pistol chest height. The weapon never wavered. "There's a federal warrant for your arrest."

Fuck!

"Walter Scott," Angie whispered. "Asshole."

Noah thought of various scenarios and came up short as Angie drew a sharp breath. "I'm opening the door. Slowly. You'll get no problems from me over this mistake."

He stepped out of the Navigator and raised both arms above his head.

"Face the side of the vehicle."

Noah was quickly frisked. "Do you have any sharp objects in your pockets or on your person that could harm me?"

"No."

His wallet and coins were placed on the front seat. His right arm was secured with one handcuff, and the left remained free. They wouldn't fit over the brace. Barton was about to escort him to the cruiser when Noah held back.

"Before we go, may I say a few quick words to my partner?"

Barton paused, then nodded. "Very brief."

Noah leaned in the driver's door and whispered for ten seconds. Dickinson was about to say something but simply nodded. Her eyes flashed toward the officer with controlled anger.

"You'll be fine." Despite the turmoil, Noah wasn't going to cause any problems to a man just doing his job.

"Let's go." Barton radioed in the call and opened the rear door for Noah. Once he was inside, he secured the other end of the cuff to the handle on the passenger door. "You have the right to remain silent …"

After his rights were read, Noah's shins were tight against the front seat as the door slammed, locking him in. He watched as Dickinson climbed behind the wheel and closed the driver's door. She would be fine. Now.

For the first time in his life, he was on the other side of the Plexiglas divider. He laid his head back and wondered who would get to him first? The real FBI, CIA, or someone working for the council? Regardless, the sudden shift in plans would put Dickinson out of harm's way. The anxious feeling lowered once he realized Angie would be safe. Noah knew the farther away she could get, the better.

Chapter 64

Walter Scott unbuckled, raised the starboard window shade, and squinted at the rising sun. At thirty-two thousand feet, the crisp blue skies were a sight to behold, no matter how many times he'd seen it. On occasion, the cloud cover cleared, and the dark Atlantic Ocean would appear.

The London security chief briefing had been cut short. He received information that Miriam Davis accepted the transfer and was back in the CIA. Walter should have known better, and he had fallen victim to the most dangerous opponent known to man. Complacency.

It wasn't the first time the council had been split or a grab for power been thwarted, and it wouldn't be the last. However, it was the first time someone had come back from the dead and taken a promotion. Fucking bitch had more tricks up her sleeve than a magician. After four and a half decades of playing the game, Walter knew he would be just as difficult to take down—if not impossible. Safeguards had been in place for many years, and he would see any attempts coming long before it happened.

The arrangements for Miriam's replacement on the council had been narrowed down to a select few, and by all reports, another opening would soon occur. Dennis would not last much longer. Walter expected to hear of his passing any day now. The opportunity to stack the council with two more loyal to him boded well. He wasn't about to give up the first chair. It was a position earned over the years, and he had grown accustomed to being the puppet master. Controlling the strings behind the scene suited him perfectly.

"Mr. Scott, you have a phone call." A young man, Jeremy, in a navy blazer, stood from the rear seating of the jet. He passed a secure satellite phone to his boss.

Walter nodded and held out his hand.

"Go ahead."

"I hope you're sitting down." Cameron sounded excited.

"I am. What's going on?"

"Noah Hunter has been apprehended. He was caught speeding, of all things, and was arrested with the federal warrant."

Walter chuckled. "About time that thorn in our side was pulled. Do we have someone nearby to handle it?" He glanced out the window when the Gulfstream shook with minor turbulence. The fastened seatbelt chime sounded, and he ignored it.

"I'll adjust the paperwork to transfer Hunter to the Seattle holding facility. From there, he'll be taken care of within a day. A carton of smokes goes a long way, and shit happens."

"At this point, I don't care if it looks like an accident or not. Just get it done. I'm on my way home so that we can deal with the second chair." Walter couldn't keep the annoyance out of his voice. "She has nine lives."

"I thought I was going to be second?" Sean couldn't keep the near-whine out of his voice, setting Walter's teeth on edge.

"You *are*. I have to make her retirement more permanent. In Miriam's new position, she will be overseas within a month. Flights get lost all the time." Walter couldn't help but glance around at his current mode of transportation, and the desire to knock on wood was strong. However, only his notes were sitting on top of the briefcase next to him. It would have to do.

"I have to go, but I'll see you soon." Walter disconnected the call, his mind already turning to arrange the need for Miriam to take the flight. He would also have to cancel the contract on Noah Hunter, and then he had to arrange a meeting with a rising star at the bureau. Walter had no idea how the country ran without him at the helm.

Chapter 65

As they drove through the small town of Smithfield, North Carolina, Noah studied the streets and buildings. The sinking feeling in his stomach wouldn't settle, and he couldn't help but recall what his commander in the infantry used to say. You can plan for an operation all you want, but unknown factors can force change—learn to adapt and overcome. His right arm shifted, and the links on the handcuffs rattled. Noah wasn't sure how he could adjust the new circumstances to his advantage, if at all.

Traffic in town was almost non-existent at one o'clock in the morning. Barton drove north through a residential section and turned left on East Market Street. The area was a mix of farmland and tracks of forest, with homes or businesses scattered. They entered the downtown core after passing an industrial set of buildings on the left and going under an overpass. Small businesses and restaurants lined the main road, and Noah saw a large sign for an Aqua Center. They turned south after passing Tucker Furniture and then right into the police station's rear parking lot.

The building was a long, single-story structure that reminded Noah of the Richmond Hill PD, and he was glad the carnage wouldn't be following him to this small town. Too many lives had been lost.

He tried to move the fingers in his left hand, and the thumb and index finger could now touch but not press together. The swelling was gone, but he was far from being fully functional.

Barton drove in a loop so the passenger side was beside the back door to the station where another officer waited. Once the door opened, Noah was escorted inside for processing.

"I guess you're going to be familiar with what will happen next." Barton brought Noah into a small four by four-foot room and had him stand facing the wall. The second officer stood outside.

"Yes, but not from this perspective."

Noah went through a secondary search, including inside his shoes, underwear, and genitals, and his hair was examined. "I'm going to remove the splint to exam it properly."

"Go ahead."

It didn't take Barton long, and he left it off for the moment. "After, I need to take pictures of any injuries."

Noah was led into the main processing area, where his mugshots were taken and then he was fingerprinted. The days of rolling a person's fingers in an ink pad, then paper were over.

Noah's hands were cleaned with an alcohol swab, then once dried, were placed on a scanner. The left hand was difficult to put in position, but once the screen chimed, he gingerly lowered it. The palm and fingerprints were good and saved.

"Okay, before I put the splint back on, I need to record your other injuries."

Noah pulled the T-shirt over his head. "Hope you have lots of film."

The bruising from being bounced off a moving truck had blossomed into an array of yellow and green swaths across his back. A dozen wounds where gravel had embedded in his shoulder blades had healed without infection, but the mass of scabs made Barton wince.

"Did you get the name of the bus that hit you?" The camera clicked as several pictures were taken. When a person was brought into custody, any prior injuries were recorded. If not, they could state that they were subject to police brutality and the injuries were sustained after arrest. It forestalled any legal actions and the CYA procedure—*cover your ass.*

"Close. It was a truck. I was trying to apprehend a suspect after he killed two cops in Richmond Hill." Noah winced as he slid his arms overhead and back into the clothing.

Barton lowered the camera and turned Noah about in the small room. "Were you under a truck, by any chance?"

Noah tried to read the officer's face, but it was like stone—no expression. Slowly he nodded. "Yes. How do you know?"

"Were you also at the Richmond Hill Police Station?" Barton ignored Noah's question and asked another.

He wasn't sure where this was going but nodded.

"Stay here a moment."

Barton escorted him back to the small room, closed the door, and whispered to his partner outside. Confused, Noah looked around and spotted a small camera with a solid red light in the corner of the ceiling. Other than that, the room was empty.

Five minutes passed, and when the door opened, a tall man stood outside in a dress shirt and tie. Captain bars were on his collar, near the points, and he was clean-shaven with short thinning hair.

"Captain Matt Pike. Step outside and raise your arms out to the sides."

His pale green eyes were piercing and followed Noah's every move. A thick belt was wrapped around his waist, with a single link out front. Prisoners wore them for transportation, and a chain usually went through the link to connect the ankles and wrists.

Once it was locked at the small of his back, the single handcuff was closed in front. Noah nodded. It was the best solution to secure a one-armed man. With a broken wrist, they had to minimize any risks.

"Follow me." Pike led the way deeper into the station. Two rows of standard government-issued desks lined the room, with a single large wooden desk at the end. A metal chair was arranged before the wooden desk, and Noah sat. Barton stood behind his shoulder.

Half a dozen officers were working, but when Noah passed, they grew silent, and eyes followed. The feeling of unease grew with everyone watching. Noah had booked hundreds of people for almost two decades. Never had he brought someone to see the shift captain.

Pike sat down at the desk, punched away on the keyboard, and clicked a few times with the mouse before turning the monitor to face Noah.

It took a few seconds before he could figure out what it was. Someone's hand shook initially, but it stabilized once it was pressed against the glass window. The video zoomed across the parking lot and lingered on the police car for a few moments before tilting the angle to include the pickup truck. A man climbed in the back with a shotgun while a figure crouched low in front of the grill. As the man walked forward and onto the cab, the man in front slipped underneath. When the truck drove away, the woman filming gasped. The man beneath had clung to the underside carriage of the truck as it took off down the road.

Captain Pike then clicked the mouse a few times, and it went to an interview outside the police station, where an off-duty police officer had killed an armed assailant. The reporter was behind the barricade tape, but she identified the man sitting on the back of the ambulance as the off-duty officer who took down a rampant killer. The camera zoomed in on Noah Hunter, wrapped in a wool blanket, staring at nothing on the ground.

The woman faced the camera, and Pike turned on the audio. "It is times like this where an unspoken hero stands up to evil and triumphs. Without his courage, many more could have died."

Noah didn't look up when the officers behind him stood and began to clap. *I wasn't a hero. I was scared shitless and did something that needed to be done.*

"Detective Noah Hunter, I think it's time we talked." Pike leaned forward on the desk when Noah looked up. The captain had a sparkle in his eyes.

Despite the situation, he felt a flicker of hope.

Chapter 66

While Noah remained secured, Captain Pike escorted him to the staff lunchroom. The coffee pot could have been a relic from the 1940s—battered and stained, but the coffee was hot. Barton poured him a mug before they sat. If Noah leaned forward, there was enough play in the cuffs to take a sip.

"I had a chance to run a background check on you. Why is there a federal warrant for such a decorated officer?" Pike grabbed a coffee for himself and sat at the pale, yellow-chipped table.

Noah looked over his shoulder. The large officer waited outside the room. It was just Barton and Pike. No cameras or recording equipment.

"I'm not going to bother with the usual 'this is off the case' opening, but I would appreciate what I'm about to say goes no further."

He didn't turn around, but Pike's eyes flicked up to Barton and then back before a slight nod. "No promises. It all depends on how much my bullshit detector registers."

"Fair enough." Noah took another sip of his coffee before beginning. "My first major case happened eighteen years ago. A little girl was kidnapped but never found. Recently, a document was sent to the station. It had the missing girl's fingerprints recorded but as an adult. Angela Taylor was alive after all this time. I reopened the case, and that's when the problems started."

Barton shifted behind him, and Pike could have been carved from stone—there was zero expression on his face as he listened.

Noah told how he was ordered off the case by the mayor's office and subsequent findings. "Angela's parents were sleeper agents, and their daughter was kidnapped to force them to comply with CIA demands."

"I thought the CIA didn't have any jurisdiction within the states." Pike's brow furrowed, and a finger tapped the tabletop.

"This all started seventy years ago. The president made a mistake, and this is what happened." Noah knew this would be a hard pill to swallow, but he didn't hold anything back. It took almost thirty minutes for him to finish, and the coffee was long since cold.

The captain leaned back in the metal chair and shook his head. "I don't doubt you believe everything, but I'm lacking one thing."

"Proof." Noah turned to Barton. "I'll give you a phone number for verification." The officer pulled out a notepad and wrote down the eleven-digit number before leaving. Dennis had arranged through his secretary to have any calls from Noah forwarded through to him, no matter the time of day.

"Even if what you said is true, there's the matter of the federal arrest warrant. I can't legally let you go. Even if it were issued in error, it would be for the courts to decide." Pike shrugged and looked at his watch. "Your arrest has gone through the system, and the FBI has been notified. However, there are certain things I can do to ensure there's a level playing field. If you are up for it."

When you are cast adrift in the ocean, any lifeline is welcome. "I don't want anyone having issues or troubles on my account. But I'll gladly accept."

*****

Amanda Taylor awoke as the sun rose, angled down the steps into the cellar, and warmed her face. The door to the basement was directly opposite the dining room window, and for fifteen minutes each morning, the sun would shine down the old wooden steps. Her right eye wouldn't open, but her left took in the beam of light and the dust motes suspended in the air, and she smiled.

I'm alive.

313

Despite that declaration, her body didn't feel like she should be alive—enough ribs were cracked that breathing was painful. When Amanda tried to move, shooting pain from her left leg narrowed her vision to a small pinpoint of light and threatened to send her unconscious. Ligaments were torn, and bones had broken in her lower leg.

Amanda had been driven and focused on achieving her goals—from martial arts to schooling throughout her life. If one door were closed, she would open another even if she had to kick it down. Her left leg wasn't responding well, but her right was fine.

When she sat up and leaned back against the post, the broken links of the handcuffs rattled. She had been beaten hard enough that the cuffs had broken. But she was now free.

As she ground her teeth together, a few were loose, and a molar was missing altogether. While keeping her weight on the right leg, Amanda ignored everything to crawl up the stairs. The pounding headache made the world spin as she froze.

A noise from the kitchen was subtle, but it carried down the hall—a muffled thump.

There was no chance of running or putting up a fight in her condition. When Amanda crawled forward, the noises were coming from a door next to where the stove would have been. A pantry. After brushing away a pile of broken plates and garbage, she opened the door, expecting the worse.

"Brian?"

A figure lay bundled with a sack over his head. Lengths of a thin green cord were coiled about the large figure, from shoulders to his ankles.

"Give me a second. Stop moving."

Amanda dragged herself alongside him and focused on loosening the knots at his feet, then wrists. Amanda pulled the hood off his head with the last bit of reserve energy and removed the gag.

Brian's eyes watered with relief, but she didn't notice. A black wave of unconsciousness dragged her back down into its embrace.

Chapter 67

On Friday morning at nine o'clock, Noah sat on the bed and laid the breakfast tray underneath. He had difficulty falling asleep in the holding pen but still managed a few hours. It would have to do.

The stainless-steel toilet was behind a forty-two-inch partition wall and was missing the lid. The cold metal woke him up more than any coffee would have. The standard room was five by nine feet with a single cot bolted to the floor. The room was empty, except for a sealed light on the ceiling and a small drain on the floor. Arrow Point's holding cells were similar, but the walls were a uniform gray. In Smithfield, someone had painted the walls a bright pink.

It made Noah chuckle as he ran a hand along the surface.

"It's supposed to be calming. The chief had read a report and ordered it done. Not too sure if it works or not."

Captain Pike stood on the other side of the bars with a tablet in his left hand. He wore a dark blue blazer over a shirt and tie. Despite being awake all night, he looked full of energy and not tired in the least.

"I'm guessing the feds are on their way." Noah leaned against the wall.

"They'll be here in five minutes. Ready?"

Noah's right hand tucked in his T-shirt and glanced around the empty cell. "All packed."

"I've looked through your personal effects and see no reason for you not to retain it. Here you go." Pike passed Noah's driver's license through the bars. The captain glanced over his shoulder at the camera in the hallway, recording audio as well. "We've misplaced your jacket, but we'll provide you with a sweater. Hope you don't mind the Smithfield PD crest."

"That works for me."

A second officer stood down the hall with the sweater in hand and acted as backup to the captain. The same rules apply to most law enforcement across the country—two men for one prisoner.

Pike called out down the hall. "Open bay two."

"Opening bay two," a woman's voice responded.

With a click, the door swung back with one finger, and the captain gestured for Noah to step outside. He was brought to the small containment room where Pike helped remove the splint and dress. Once completed, the brace was replaced and strapped in place. The sweater was oversized and allowed the sleeves to be rolled up. "It's time. Good luck. We'll be right back."

Noah leaned against the wall to wait. His insides were in turmoil at the thought of what could happen next. It wasn't for his own concern but that Walter Scott would be getting away with his crimes. If he orchestrated a kidnapping and blackmailed the parents—regardless if they were foreign agents or not—what else had he done in the name of justice?

Captain Pike closed the door on the small room and stepped to the side. Noah knew the transfer papers would need to be signed and identification verified before turn-over. He had done the same process countless times at his station. However, the need for verification was usually waived if he knew the attending officers. Charlie from the Natrona Sheriff's Office handled most of the transfers and had done so for a dozen years.

Fifteen minutes later, the door opened, and a tall man stood on the other side in the expected dark blue suit. They must issue them to all the agents straight off the rack. The man was young but looked like he played football or lifted cars for a living. He was clean-shaven and had a serious demeanor.

"Special Agent Bishop, FBI." Thick fingers flipped open a wallet to show the badge, then identification. The baritone voice had a hint of a Southern accent. "You're in my custody for transport."

Bishop produced a set of cuffs from the small of his back and glanced down at the brace on Noah's left wrist. The agent turned to the police captain. "Injury was before arrest or after?"

"Prior. That and other injuries were documented properly." The captain handed over a folder containing the police report. Copies would have been sent electronically as well.

"Let's go."

Noah was led down the short hallway to the station's back door. Parked in front was a Ford Interceptor SUV. The vehicle was missing the light bars on the roof and decals. Otherwise, it could have been used by any police department across the country. The rear bench seat left little room between the front and the back seats. A wire mesh separated the front seat and was bolted to the roof.

Bishop opened the rear passenger door, and as Noah sat, his right arm was handcuffed to the door handle, but he barely noticed. He stared across the parking lot and scanned the rooftops. Nothing. All the vehicles in the parking lot were empty, and no pedestrians were in the area. *Maybe I was wrong?* Before the door closed in his face, Noah glanced upward at the blue morning sky.

As Bishop climbed behind the wheel, Noah smiled.

Chapter 68

Smithfield, North Carolina, under normal circumstances, would have been a town that, if you blink, you would have missed it. The sign stated a population of thirteen-thousand people. However, Noah couldn't help but scan rooftops and around each corner as they turned right on East Market Street.

"Expecting someone?" Bishop's eyes followed him through the rearview mirror.

"Pike didn't tell you?" Noah tried to see inside a minivan that passed on the left. A small child in the backseat stared him down while the driver ignored him.

The FBI agent shook his head. "Tell me what?"

Noah remained silent. The real story wouldn't be believed, and he didn't know which side of the fence Bishop lay. If he were sent through Walter Scott, nothing he could say would make a difference. Bishop shrugged and kept his eyes on the road.

While being more discrete, Noah waited.

Miriam and Dennis had agreed on one thing. Despite paying the full contract, they doubted Noah would be considered one-hundred percent free and clear of danger. Scott would keep pushing or follow up—others could be hired from different organizations. Walter had garnered a wealth of contacts throughout the years, and it would not be difficult. Noah's resources, on the other hand, were all but gone.

Mid-morning traffic hour was light as they drove into the morning sun and approached the edge of town. East Market Street ended at the I-95 on-ramp, and with the morning sun in their eyes, they didn't have a chance to see the shooter on the rail overpass.

The first round went through the windshield, and the impact sent the bullet tumbling.

Instead of a straight trajectory, it veered to the side, over Bishop's right shoulder, and through the backseat, missing Noah by six inches. The slight deflection saved the federal agent's life. The wind noise followed the pop through the hole.

"Get down!" Bishop swerved the SUV.

Noah ducked as a second round punched through the roof and out the rear window. A hole the size of a softball appeared in the tempered glass, and cracks radiated outward.

"Jesus Christ!" Bishop kept low while peeking over the dashboard. Luckily there were no other cars in the area. He swerved in the opposite lane as another round hit the windshield. It would have sprayed gray matter over the interior if Noah had been sitting upright. He didn't have to look to see how close that had come. The bullet *tinged* off the wire barrier.

When Bishop swerved to the opposite side, Noah slid across the bench seat until the handcuff pulled tight against the handle. "Get under the bridge! They'll have no target then."

Noah had enough of being a human pinball. Using his teeth, he pulled the Velcro straps back on the brace until he could slide out his hand. The SUV was approaching the overpass and safety. At best, the shooter would have to reposition to fire underneath—temporary protection. He peeled back a small tear in the fabric on the underside of the brace and removed a long-handled handcuff key. As Bishop kept up a zig-zag pattern, the cuff on his right wrist opened. While painful, he had enough strength in his left hand to turn the key.

"Are you hit?" Noah realized he was screaming, but Bishop answered the same way.

"No. You?"

"I'm good. Get undercover. Call it in!"

Another round went through the roof and into the seat behind the driver as the angle closed. "Fuck, that was close!"

The moment stretched on for an eternity, and both men could see a figure dressed in black stand with a long rifle. Bishop parked in the middle of the road, under the overpass. He drew a Sig Sauer P226 and stepped outside the vehicle as he pulled out a cell phone. The pistol shook in his hand as it swept the area.

While he was distracted, Noah slipped the key back into the brace and wore it again. "Open the door. Get me out of here!" The last thing he wanted to be was a stationary target. There was zero doubt in his mind that the shooter was after him and not the agent. He would be easy pickings unless he could get out. "Hurry up!"

Bishop was yelling on his phone as he spun in circles. Noah brought up a foot and slammed it into the door to get the agent's attention. When the agent flicked the handle to open the door, all hell broke loose.

Chapter 69

A dark green object, the size of an apple, plummeted from the overpass toward the road. Noah's eyes grew round as he followed the descent. It bounced once with a metallic *ping* and rolled a few inches toward the car. Noah had both feet on the ground and was about to stand when it registered.

"Grenade!"

Bishop dove toward the front of the vehicle as Noah tucked his feet back in the Ford and turtled on the seat. The explosion rocked the SUV, and what was left of the rear window blew inward and pelted over Noah. The glass in the back door blew outward, and the inside panel was riddled with fragments of metal and asphalt. Despite being sheltered, Noah's ears rang from the concussive force.

He groaned, and he quickly frisked himself, looking for injuries. Nothing. However, Bishop was outside. *Fuck!*

Outside, small fragments cascaded onto the ground and sounded like hail. Bishop groaned as he rolled in front of the hood. The majority of his body had been protected, but the lower right leg had been hit. The dress pants had three holes from shrapnel, and blood was pooling on the road.

Noah darted forward and rolled Bishop onto his back. Awkward fingers loosened the tie and pulled it free.

"Be quiet," Noah whispered. "They haven't left yet."

Bishop nodded and tried to sit. Hunter pulled up the pant leg. Two of the wounds were shallow, but the third was bad. A twisted-triangular piece of metal had buried an inch deep, just below the calf muscle. Before Bishop could see or object, Noah pinched it with his fingers and gave it a quick yank. The federal agent started to scream before he caught himself.

"It's out." Noah let the wound bleed a few seconds to flush it before wrapping the tie three times about the leg as a quick field dressing. The Sig Sauer lay a foot from Bishop's right hand. He was tempted to go for it, but now wasn't the time.

"Jesus Christ, that hurts."

"Can you stand?" Noah scanned the area, but there was no sign of the shooter. Yet. The ringing in his ears had lessened but wasn't totally gone.

"Help me up."

After standing, Bishop leaned on the hood. He also kept an eye on the area. They were not done yet. "We have to leave."

"Fish in a barrel," Noah muttered as he passed Bishop the pistol. "Do you have a backup?"

"No." Bishop paused and looked at the backseat, then Noah. His eyes widened. "How the hell did you get free? If you're part of this, you're going to be in jail a *very* long time."

"I have nothing to do with this, but—"

The sound of falling gravel came down the embankment behind, and Noah helped Bishop to the driver's side. The federal agent held the pistol with two hands and used the roof to steady his aim. The far slope led up to the tracks, and it was too steep to climb. The rocks were the size of two fists and were used to prevent erosion. A small stone, the size of a golf ball, bounced down the incline and rolled on the road.

Noah frowned, and as he turned to look behind him, a thin man in a balaclava crouched beside the overpass, twenty feet up the slope and fifty feet away. The man had a rifle slung over one shoulder and a pistol in a two-handed grip.

Noah didn't have time to yell out a warning before being shot.

The round struck his right shoulder blade and sent him sprawling over the hood of the Ford. Bishop spun about and calmly squeezed the trigger. Eight rounds were fired, and five found their mark. The man jerked and spasmed as each bullet landed. He dropped face-first on the stones and slid down the incline to land in a jumbled heap at the bottom.

"Fuck!" Bishop swore and kept the muzzle pointed at the corpse. The shooter's pistol skidded across the road toward them.

Noah groaned. "I'll never get used to that."

"What the hell?" The federal agent stared as the police officer stood and rolled his head back and forth before stretching.

Noah lifted the dark blue sweater Captain Pike had given him. Underneath was a ballistic vest with ceramic plates forming a second layer above the vital organs. Smithfield Police Department was embroidered on a Velcro tag on the chest and upper back.

The Sig Sauer swung about and aimed Noah's face. "You better fucking explain what the actual *fuck* is going on!"

"The vest is my insurance that I'll make it to wherever you are dragging me." Noah took a deep breath and twisted. He would have another fantastic bruise on his back, but nothing was broken.

"Insurance?" The pistol never wavered despite Bishop's confusion.

"Someone placed a contract out on me, and I thought they were dealt with, but another group may be trying to collect." Noah winced as he stretched.

Bishop took a step back to gain some distance between them, and the 9mm lowered. "Who took a contract out on you?"

Noah's eyebrows raised in surprise. "I thought you knew. The man in the shadows, who apparently controls the FBI and CIA. Walter Scott."

Chapter 70

After five minutes of listening, Bishop shook his head. "I don't know. It sounds a little far-fetched. Even if it is true, it's several paygrade levels above me."

"Just call in, and ask for the nature of the arrest warrant. Who's the authorizing signature?" There were several requirements for a warrant to be issued. An affidavit from a law-enforcement officer under oath must provide enough factual information to a judge or magistrate that a crime has been committed in order for the warrant to be considered legal. Should a warrant be issued without it being justified, any arrests would be regarded as invalid and open the issuing authority to litigation—a career-ending move on many fronts.

Bishop holstered the Sig Sauer and limped over to the body. He slid the rifle off and placed it to the side. Underneath the balaclava, a young man was revealed. He was a teenager with a shock of dyed white hair and facial tattoos.

"ID?" Noah had joined him.

Bishop felt for a pulse on the side of the neck before checking the pockets. He pulled out a stack of crisp bills, wrapped in the brown paper banded from the bank—ten thousand dollars.

"No wallet, just the money."

"Uh ... Bishop." Noah shuffled to the side until his heels hit the rifle. An older white Toyota truck had parked sideways across the road into town, one hundred feet away. Two men sat in the front seat, and as the driver's window lowered, they pulled dark ski masks down. "We have company."

"I've called my supervisor at Quantico. Help should be arriving shortly." Bishop kept his eyes on the truck as he stood.

"I don't think we have time to wait." Noah picked up the rifle and confirmed a round was chambered. "Take this. It needs two hands."

The truck's engine revved, and the tires squealed as it lurched forward. The exhaust popped and sounded like a tank as the truck accelerated.

"Fuck!" Despite the panic in his voice, Bishop wrapped his left forearm around the sling and seated the rifle into his right shoulder. At sixty feet, he fired. The new black Remington 700 was accurate, and the first round went into the front grill of the Toyota. However, it did nothing to slow the truck.

The passenger leaned out of the window with a pistol in his right hand. The sharp retort of small-arms fire sounded like firecrackers going off. *Pop, pop.*

Bishop knelt and used his knee as a brace for his left elbow. His right hand flicked the bolt rearward, and a spent casing flew out. The next round fired went through the windshield an inch above the steering wheel. The driver jerked once as he died, but it was too late to stop the truck.

Noah grabbed Bishop by the shoulder, and the rifle fell. "Move!"

The only safe direction was up. They scrambled over the body as the passenger tried to grab the steering wheel. The truck ran over the shooter before colliding with the side of the gravel slope. The vehicle didn't have enough clearance, and it crashed two feet below Noah's heels. The shock vibrated through the gravel, and Bishop lost his footing, and if not for Noah's grip on his shoulder, he would have fallen. Inside, the passenger was thrown against the dashboard when the truck's front end hit. Had the Toyota been going faster, Noah might not have made it.

When the engine shut down, Noah heard the man inside groaning as he held his head. "We have to go. More will be coming."

Bishop may have been shocked at the close call because he simply nodded. Hunter helped him down and around the truck toward the Ford. Despite the explosion and bullet holes, it would run.

With his right leg injured, Bishop couldn't drive. Noah helped the agent into the passenger seat. As he climbed behind the wheel, they heard yelling. The man in the truck held a cell phone and tried to get out of the cab. The impact damaged the front end, but the doors were fine. Noah didn't have time to wait.

The Ford roared to life, and he didn't waste any time. Within a quarter-mile, he pulled onto the ramp for the interstate and merged with the traffic. The wind howled through the front windshield and out the rear window.

"Do you have your cell phone?" Noah's heart had calmed to normal rates, and he started thinking again.

Bishop pulled it out of his jacket pocket. "Yes. I'll update my supervisor and—"

Noah plucked it out of his hand and threw it out the window. "They'll be tracking us with that. Sorry, but I can't chance it."

"What the hell!" Bishop's fist clenched. "You're still under arrest, Hunter."

Noah grinned. "Sorry, you can consider this an official escape from custody. You have failed to provide adequate security to safeguard my safety, and I must take matters into my own hands."

"Is that your official story?" Bishop barked laughter. "How about I just shoot you?"

He shook his head. "That's what I'll be going with, yes. I have time to take care of your leg before I leave. If you were going to shoot me, you would have done so already. I'm not worried."

"There was a hospital in town. Turn around." Bishop's hand relaxed and stayed away from the holstered Sig.

Noah grinned. "Sorry, Agent Bishop. It's too risky, and others will be hurt or killed. Relax. We'll be there in less than an hour."

Instead of continuing north on I-95, Noah took the bypass and drove north-west on I-70. The first sign read forty-five miles to Raleigh, North Carolina.

Chapter 71

The Raleigh-Durham International Airport had a five-story, long-term parking garage next to Terminal Two. Noah pulled up to the barricade and pressed the button for his ticket. The yellow control arm was raised to allow him entry.

"What the hell are we doing here? I doubt there's a doctor that can give me stitches and antibiotics." Bishop had remained mostly quiet throughout the drive, for which Noah was thankful. The less he was involved, the better chances the agent would have to survive. They had looked at the wound, and Bishop was correct. It would need to be professionally looked at with infection setting in. While it stopped bleeding, several courses of antibiotics were in his immediate future. It could have been much worse.

"You will be rid of me soon, and then you can call it in. Cover your ass." Noah drove through the parking garage and took the ramps to the next level until he reached the top, open-air parking. He slowed and went up and down each aisle.

"You are probably on the no-fly list. You won't get far." Bishop hadn't tried to escape or hinder Noah despite the pistol on his right hip.

When he backed into a vacant parking space, he held up a hand to forestall the federal agent. "Stay here for a second. I'm going to get something for your leg."

Unsure of what was happening, Bishop nodded.

Noah stepped out of the Ford and looked around at the roof-top parking level. It was about one-third full. Not many wanted to leave their car parked long-term outside. The weather, however, was nice, and the overhead sun felt good.

Bishop turned in the seat to follow him. Noah stepped behind the vehicle parked next to him and knelt behind the SUV's bumper. He fished the keys out of the tailpipe and unlocked the rear lift of the Navigator. Everything was laid out before him, just as he left it.

Dickinson had flown home and left the rental waiting for him as a backup plan. Noah was adamant about her going when he was arrested, and they only had a few seconds to come up with a plan. There were still enough weapons inside, along with cash and supplies. Right now, Noah was more interested in the small ablution bag inside his pack.

When he opened the passenger door to the Ford, Bishop had drawn his pistol, and it sat on his lap. "Are you still trying to tell me this whole scenario wasn't planned?"

"Having my rental vehicle here was planned in case of emergency. My partner flew home early this morning. I didn't think I would have a chance to get my things, but I'm glad it's here."

Noah ignored the Sig Sauer and knelt next to Bishop. He removed the tie and opened the case. Iodine was used for flushing the wound, and he cleaned up the dried blood with alcohol swabs. The jagged edges were already turning a dark red and looked puffy.

"Here, take two of these." Noah handed him a prescription bottle. "General antibiotics, and here are some Aspirins."

Bishop gave him a funny look before swallowing the pills. "Thanks."

Noah pulled out two butterfly bandages and secured the deep cut. "That will hold until you can see a doctor."

The federal agent glanced at the Navigator. "Where are you going now?"

"First, I will help you into the backseat before I call the local police to get you. After that, I'm going to arrest the person responsible for a kidnapping eighteen years ago and put them in jail."

Bishop's brows furrowed, and he shook his head. "Sorry. I sympathize with you, but I can't let you go."

As the agent raised the pistol, Noah pulled a loaded Glock out of his waistband. "Place your weapon on the dashboard. Slow movements."

"I don't think you are going to shoot." Bishop placed his gun on the dash and raised his hands regardless of his statement. Noah stepped back and gestured for the agent to sit in the backseat.

"Lock the cuff on your wrist, and pass me the keys in your pocket." After he complied, Noah unloaded the Sig Sauer and placed the magazine with the pistol under the Ford. He left the handcuff key on the hood. "Make sure you retrieve the gun. I'll make the call in five minutes. It's been an interesting day."

Noah closed the door on the grinning agent. Moments later, the Navigator pulled out of the parking spot as Noah looked at the time. He had just over thirty hours and eighteen-hundred miles to make sure all the pieces were in motion.

"Time to get started."

Noah opened the armrest and found the cash and his wallet as he left the parking garage and airport. Angie had taken enough to cover her flight home, which left him more than enough.

True to his word, he activated a new burner phone and called 911 to let the local police know where agent Bishop was secured. When the call was done, he tossed the phone out the window. "Good luck tracking that, guys."

It took fifteen minutes to get to downtown Raleigh, and Noah picked up some sandwiches and a coffee from a café before he was ready.

"Time to kick the hornet's nest."

He parked outside a bank and pulled out his debit card. At the ATM, he punched in his PIN, and instead of a withdrawal option, the screen flashed *one moment, please.* After a minute, the screen read *card invalid.*

Noah grinned and flipped a middle finger toward the camera lens above his head before walking away. Once he was back in the Navigator, he drove west.

Chapter 72

Walter Scott pulled the reading glasses out of his breast pocket to see the report on the computer. The more he read, the more his blood pressure increased. He controlled the urge to throw the laptop across his office and leaned back in the leather chair.

He opened the second drawer and removed an encrypted satellite phone. There was only one phone number programmed, and he dialed.

Mother answered on the second ring. "I've been meaning to call you."

"Update." Despite the emotional rollercoaster inside, Walter's voice was calm.

"With lack of current data on Hunter's whereabouts, we sub-contracted out to increase the pressure. However, I believe we are getting close to wrapping this up."

Walter closed his eyes and tried to control his breathing, slow and steady, to calm his heart rate. "We *had* him in custody, but *you* fucked up, and he escaped. There's yet another mess for me to clean up. I'm not pleased with your performance."

"That was one of the sub-contractors. Their dealings with us are terminated. It won't happen again." The woman sounded nervous, as well she should be. The amount of money and contracts he had thrown their way over the years was quite substantial. Despite the excuses, the rage flared.

"Of course, it won't happen again because they are *dead*! I have two bodies in Smithfield and a missing federal agent, but no Noah Hunter." Once again, the urge to hurtle something across the room made his hands shake.

"From my last update, I believe they are closing in." Mother must have been typing. Walter could hear fingernails tapping on a keyboard.

"You have twenty-four hours until I terminate the contract and all our future business dealings." Without ceremony, he disconnected. There were other such mercenary teams for hire, and he never had a problem with the English group over the years. Not only were they currently hitting a roadblock, but the collateral damage left in their wake sent ripples across the law-enforcement community. It was only a matter of time until the shooter's identity in the police station became known. Once that happened, a trail *could* lead back to his office. He had worked too long and hard at the job to let that happen. Even further measures had to be taken, even if he had to do it himself.

It may be time to hire a second team to take out the first organization. That would be expensive but a better alternative than sitting in jail.

Walter had a chime from an incoming text on his personal phone from Cameron. *Check your email.*

Curious, he quickly read the reports and scanned the attached pictures. Noah Hunter had escaped custody and was located in downtown Raleigh, North Carolina. Traffic cameras had followed him through the city and lost him at the interstate. Noah was headed east toward Washington, D.C.

He was not worried, but Walter ordered a security detail and then informed the US Marshals. The marshals excelled at capturing escaped fugitives. The state police could also set up roadblocks, and an APB would be sent out. Hunter would be entering the most heavily patrolled state in the country. Walter set the play in motion.

*****

Alexander tugged on the leash, and the golden retriever puppy came to heel. One of the conditions of having a pet: walking him before and after school and cleaning up after him. His mom was firm, and Alex would have agreed to almost anything. Soon as the school bus dropped him off, he took the five-month-old pup for a walk. The twelve-year-old brushed the hair out of his eyes before ensuring the poop bags were in his pocket. Not that he was going to use them. He had a plan.

"Kody, put that down."

Alex was ignored as the dog carried a long stick along the rural road. He wasn't sure, but it could have been the same stick from yesterday. Kody always found them.

"In here, boy." Alex turned into the driveway of the old Miller house. No one had lived there for a long time. Most importantly, Kody could do his business in the yard, and he didn't have to pick it up.

He unclipped the leash and threw the stick up the driveway. Kody's ears flopped as he chased it. "Good boy!"

However, instead of running to the stick, the puppy kept going right up to the house's front porch. "Kody, come on!"

Alex ran after him, then stopped twenty feet away. There were two adults on the porch, and Kody was barking. Something was wrong. It looked like the man and woman had survived an accident. There was dried blood and cuts over their faces, and neither moved. Alex wasn't sure, but they looked like corpses. The man lay halfway out the door, and the woman sprawled across his legs.

"Kody. Come here," he whispered.

The puppy ignored him and started to lick the woman's hand. When she stirred and saw what was happening, a smile spread across her face. Despite the swollen eyes, she focused on Alex. "Do you have a cell phone?"

Alexander swallowed the lump in his throat. "It's for emergencies only, though."

Her smile grew wider, and he relaxed. "If you could call us an ambulance, that would be great. Trust me. This is an emergency."

Kody laid down beside the woman and continued to clean her hand. Alex pulled the phone out of his pocket. He dialed 911.

"What's your name?"

"Amanda." She rubbed the puppy's ears. "And thank you for saving us."

Chapter 73

Noah lost time when he circled north around Raleigh, but he knew the Navigator would be tracked from the bank machine onward. Over the last eight hours, he had stopped to fill the tank and pick up a thermos of coffee. The small cups were only good for so long and frustrating. When he arrived in Lexington, Kentucky, he drove thirty minutes north of the city before pulling over at the first rest stop. Despite being used to going for twelve-hour shifts, he still needed to stretch his legs and use the bathroom. That was when he was fresh and not injured.

He took the time to remove the ballistic vest and bring a change of clothes inside. Most importantly, one of the burner phones. Once dressed, he felt better, and Noah sat on a bench in the lobby to make the call.

Cameron answered on the fourth ring. After a quick chuckle, he spoke. "Noah Hunter, to what do I owe the pleasure?"

"I want to make a deal. I want my old life back and you guys to call off the hounds." Noah had ensured the interior didn't have any security cameras, and no one sat in his immediate area.

Sean asked. "Why would I want to do that?"

"I'll hand over the files I have on Walter Scott and the Taylor's. I made copies of the voice recordings and videotapes, and you get everything. I want assurance that Angela Taylor will not be hurt and you guys will leave me alone. That's it." Noah glanced at his watch.

Cameron remained silent on the other end, and Noah couldn't tell what was going on.

"Well? Deal?"

"I'll call you back, and—"

"I'll call *you*. You aren't tracing this phone."

Noah disconnected the call. He waited until the bathroom was empty and hid the cell inside the paper towel dispenser, activated, but on silent mode.

There were no files or video recordings on Scott or anyone else, but Sean Cameron didn't know that. Even if he suspected Noah made that up, he couldn't take the chance—he would make the call. It would be like kicking an anthill.

Seated in the Navigator, Noah drove south on the interstate, *back* where he just came, before heading west. Going an hour out of his way still left an eighteen-hour drive. One knee kept the wheel steady as he poured more coffee into the paper cup. He had enough fuel to keep going—it was what waited for him at the end that worried him the most.

344

Thirty minutes later, a flatbed truck parked sideways across the rest stop entrance with orange lights flashing on the roof. Two men jumped out and placed orange cones warning approaching vehicles that the rest area was closed.

There was only one vehicle in the back parking lot by ten o'clock at night. A black semi-truck and trailer had stopped, and the driver woke when high winds made the cab rock back and forth. A helicopter had landed in the parking lot, and the rotor wash sent plumes of dust and dirt flying into the surrounding trees.

Six men in full tactical gear exited and dashed into the building while two men covered the truck. The driver pulled the curtain closed soon as their rifle muzzles swept across his windshield. The red laser dots were easy to spot at night.

The men blocking the entrance moved the cones aside to allow the police cruisers and three unmarked vehicles inside. A flurry of activity happened when the building was cleared, and within a minute, the search began.

An older man with deep lines on his face found the cellphone in the men's bathroom. It was quickly passed to a technician who set up an office on the hood of a Chevy Tahoe. A laptop connected to the phone as a computer program went to work.

"This is the phone that made the call."

"Pull up a map of the area."

After a series of clicks on the laptop, several men gathered to study.

"I thought Hunter was going to Washington D.C.?"

"He's running. But to where?"

There were two options. The FBI agent tapped the screen, and it zoomed into the city north of their position. "He was heading there. I want roadblocks leading into the city and eyes in the air. Close the interstate down. Move."

As his orders were being carried out, the US Marshal Brooks wasn't sure about Cincinnati. "The hunter has become the hunted. See you shortly, Noah."

Chapter 74

Noah suppressed the urge to speed as he merged with the traffic on I-64 eastbound as he took stock of the supplies remaining. He was down to two burner phones, still in their packages. The money situation was good, with thousands left in cash, but any attempts to use a credit card would put them on his trail within seconds. Something to be avoided at all costs. For now.

Noah resisted the temptation to pull over and close his eyes despite the late hour. Later on, he may have no choice, but he had to keep going for now. Passing east through St. Louis slowed him down. Even at one o'clock in the morning, traffic had slowed to one lane in either direction with the construction.

As the morning sun rose, he drove into Kansas City. More coffee and fast food were on the agenda, and top off the tank. He loved the Navigator, but it wasn't the most fuel-efficient. Noah opened the packaging for a burner phone and pulled the plastic tab to activate it. It already had a fifty-percent charge. Perfect.

After completing the running around, Noah walked into the largest Walmart Supercenter he had ever seen. It took a few minutes to find the electronic department, and once there, he dialed.

Cameron picked up on the third ring. "Change of mind? Ready to come in, Noah?"

"Not a chance." Noah leaned against a massive DVD discount bin. "I get my life back, and I won't release any of the intel I have on your organization. I need a decision within the minute."

"This decision is above me. I'm bringing someone else in on this conversation, just a sec."

As Noah was placed on hold, he knew it was a stalling tactic, but he wasn't positive when a familiar voice spoke.

"What's the deal, Hunter." Despite a series of background traffic and wind noise, the voice of Walter Scott was recognizable.

"I get my life back without retribution. You get all copies of the documents, video files, and witness statements. Hell, you can even have the fingerprint sheets back. I only have one condition."

Walter let out a sharp bark of laughter. "You're not in a position to make any conditions."

Noah ignored him. "You leave the girl alone, but fill her in on everything that's happened. Let her live her own life. She's still a kid."

Sean Cameron remained silent, but there was no doubt he was still on the line. *There would be others listening in as well.*

"I can guarantee there will be no further action against Amanda Rawlings. As to the remainder, I would need to confirm the material. I wouldn't buy a home without visiting it at least once."

"That can be arranged. I'll be in contact shortly."

After hanging up, Noah pretended to dig through the pile of DVDs. At the bottom of the large bin, he stashed the burner. On the way out of Walmart, he stopped at the Cell Phone Store and bought two more pre-paid phones before leaving.

*****

Their response time was better than at the rest stop. Within twenty minutes, police had each exit of Walmart covered while police officers swept through the store. K-9 teams stood at the front and rear exits. The same marshal arrived a few minutes later with his team.

US Marshal Brooks guessed the target had either gone north or west. After splitting the team, he wasn't far out of Kansas City when the call came.

The store manager's office had access to the security system, and they scrolled through the footage. Once Brooks located Hunter, they followed the timestamp on different monitors. The phone call was made at the rear of the store, and afterward Noah dug through a display.

Brooks paused the video and turned to a waiting police officer. "Go dig in that bin. Phone's probably in there."

Brooks resumed the surveillance without waiting to see if his orders were followed. Hunter then went into a store within the larger store. "What's this place?"

The cameras didn't follow him inside. The kiosk was blind.

A middle-aged woman with the nametag *Sandra* pinned to a blue vest was the acting manager. "They sell phones and monthly packages. Walmart doesn't own the store, but they operate inside."

Five minutes later, the US Marshal talked with the young man who ran the shop. Business hadn't been so busy that he couldn't remember the man and what he bought—two pre-paid cell phones.

Brooks picked up another phone in the package and asked. "Are these sequenced by lot number?"

The salesman sorted through the remaining three packages on the shelf and nodded. "The lot numbers are the same. The phone numbers would be sequential, I'd guess. But I have no idea if they were before or after these."

The federal agent didn't have time to go through financing and approval. He pulled out a credit card. "I'll take them all. Open them up. I need to get the numbers now."

As Brooks called the team to rally back in the parking lot, he got on the phone with Sean Cameron. The NSA could monitor the whole lot of numbers at once. Soon as Hunter activated the burner, they would know within seconds.

The marshal pulled up maps and scouted possible areas of interest but came up short.

Hunter's running, but where?

When the possible answer hit him, Brooks scrambled for the phone. The first chair would want to know immediately.

Chapter 75

The featureless landscape of Nebraska was overshadowed by massive cloud formations which charged across the sky like battleships as Noah drove west along I-26. The southwest wind brought the promise of rain. He was getting close to Wyoming, and that alone kept him going. The hours of driving and lack of sleep were taking their toll, and Noah tried every trick in the book to stay alert. The windows were lowered, and he found a talk radio station with an annoying announcer to keep him occupied.

Nebraska was uneventful as usual. However, the farther west he drove, the more apprehensive Noah became. The lack of sleep and nerves felt like a brick had settled in his stomach, and despite the cool fresh air, sweat beaded his brow.

Soon as he crossed over the Wyoming border, Noah opened the pay-as-you-go phone and made a call.

Tracey began her career with the NSA straight from MIT, and her skills had only sharpened. Curly red hair and freckles fooled many, and they doubted her ability to navigate the computer world. For her, it was a simple matter of creating a program to monitor the series of cell phone numbers—to ensure success, Tracey increased the numerical range by a thousand, bracketing the target.

At the end of her twelve-hour shift, the audio alert sounded. Excited, she located the cell tower to pinpoint the location. The signal lasted long enough to trace the call, and the resulting match popped up on a close-contact list.

"Mr. Cameron!" Tracey called out to the open office door. The excitement in her voice brought her boss running.

"Where?"

With two mouse clicks, the overlaying map filled the center monitor. "Westbound."

The target didn't show on the map, but the cell towers were clearly marked. The signal had just jumped and confirmed the direction on I-26 West.

"Cameras in the area?" Cameron traced the route with a finger and shook his head. "Never mind. There wouldn't be."

The screen flashed red.

"Signal lost. Ninety-eight seconds duration." Tracey tried to ping the number from the contact list, but it wasn't available.

"The target called this location from one-hundred and forty miles away."

A fingernail with chipped polish tapped the screen.

Arrow Point, Wyoming.

"Good job." Cameron pulled out a cell phone and began giving orders as Tracey tried a few more tricks. The warm glow of satisfaction plastered a grin on her face, and the others in the office groaned. They knew she would rub it in. Of course, she would. It was the best part of her day.

Chapter 76

When the call came in, teams scrambled into action. Four men remained inside Noah Hunter's home, while twelve others relocated to set up roadblocks into town. There were only two ramps off the interstate, and by eight o'clock Saturday night, traffic was being checked vehicle by vehicle. The FBI worked in a coordinated effort with Homeland Security to outward appearances. The Arrow Point police were absent from the operation.

Walter Scott received updates every ten minutes during his flight to Los Angeles. When Sean Cameron called to let him know Hunter's location, he diverted the flight to Denver, Colorado. Golfing at the Bel-Air Country Club could wait while he pulled the thorn from his side.

There was no evidence to the best of his knowledge, and even if there were, it wouldn't make any difference. He could squash and spin the narrative to suit the situation. Walter had learned a few tricks during his many decades in the government and could handle bad press. When he was done, Hunter wouldn't see the inside of a courtroom.

*****

The fatigue vanished when Noah drove through Casper. The sun was inches from disappearing below the horizon, and he kept one eye on the traffic and another in the air. The familiar sights did nothing to calm the turmoil inside, but he couldn't hold back a grin when he spotted the Hills Road overpass. It wasn't the bridge but the vehicle that waited underneath—a Ford Police Interceptor.

Hills Road was the eastern boundary for the APPD.

Noah lowered the passenger window as he pulled alongside the black cruiser. Dickinson got out and leaned inside.

"You don't have much time. Feds are everywhere." She passed Noah his cell phone and an extra-large coffee. "Phone's charged, and I thought you could use this."

"You have no idea how much I need that. Thanks." Noah opened the armrest and passed her a white envelope. "Hold onto this."

Angie frowned. "What is it?"

"My will. There are no guarantees in life and too many moving parts right now. I'd feel better if you held onto it."

She tucked the envelope inside her vest and frowned. "I can leave the cruiser here and go with you …"

356

Noah held a finger in the air and canted his head to the side. When his head snapped forward, he had a visual. "Helicopter."

The chopping sound was subtle but carried for miles, and the setting sun made it easy to spot. A thousand feet in the air, a black-bodied Bell UH-1 hovered over the interstate off-ramp to town.

"I have to go. Thank you for everything." Noah held out a hand across the passenger seat, and Angie's hands shook as they embraced.

"Hopefully, I'll see you soon." The rasp in her voice and watering eyes made Noah's heart lurch.

He reluctantly let go and winked.

Noah engaged the four-wheel drive, and instead of merging onto the interstate, he cut in front of the cruiser and into the ditch. After a hard right, the SUV climbed the incline. Hills Road overpass was a prominent location to the APPD and a favorite spot to set up a speed trap. Noah had sat here for countless hours over his career. ATV and snowmobile trails paralleled the main road for miles and had worn a path.

The undercarriage scraped when the right side dipped low, but the vehicle was more than up to the challenge. Noah kept one eye on the helicopter and turned right on the overpass. The device vibrated after he turned on his phone and nearly had a meltdown as several dozen notifications dinged.

When he turned west on the county road, he activated the phone's GPS. "Come and get me, assholes."

The county road paralleled the interstate for six miles. There was only one active farm in the area and acres of vacant land. When the helicopter swung out over the interstate, Noah stepped on the accelerator and raced toward it.

Four minutes had passed since he activated the phone. "Not bad."

Noah swore and pounded the steering wheel when he passed the old Campbell farm. His first instinct was to keep going and ignore the hitchhiker dressed in patrol blues.

There just wasn't time.

However, despite the time constraints, he hit the brakes and stopped fifty feet past the extended thumb. When Steve Hutchings climbed inside, Noah didn't wait for the door to close before taking off. The staff sergeant slammed the door shut as he was thrown back in the seat.

"Thanks. It's hard to get a ride with all the G-men around." Hutchings buckled in, and Noah remained silent.

The helicopter descended to five-hundred feet and swung about in an arc, pacing the Navigator. The gig was up.

"I can still let you out. Last chance, old man."

Hutchings snorted and helped himself to Noah's coffee. "Ah, perfect temperature."

The SUV was flying along the straight road. Noah stopped looking at the speedometer when he passed ninety. He refused to cave in and ask the question.

Sixty seconds later, he couldn't stand the silence.

"Okay, I give up. How the hell did you know the way I would be coming in?" Noah's white-knuckled grip kept the vehicle steady. "Hold on. Turn coming up."

Hutchings chuckled. "Who do you think taught you about Hills Road?" He held the coffee on an angle as Noah turned north on a little-used fire road. The engine hummed under the abuse, and the tires found purchase on the gravel road. Any doubt the helicopter was following them disappeared as it turned north as well. The thumping noise drew closer.

Dickinson had talked to Hutchings, and the old man figured it out. Lovely.

"If you finish my coffee, you *are* getting out to walk." His left wrist was doing better, but it would still need a full month of rest to be whole. He gingerly steered and held out his hand.

"Don't worry, rookie. I gotcha covered." He passed over the drink.

Noah only had time for a quick sip before turning west once again on Concession 4. "Open my phone up to the security application."

They were two minutes out from Noah's home.

The ten-acre property used to be part of a farm on the outskirts of town. As Arrow Point grew over the last twenty years, other farms had sold out to developers, including the former owners. All that remained of a one-hundred-acre parcel of land were ten acres, a barn, and a farmhouse. Noah enjoyed the privacy. It felt like he was in the country while still within the city limits.

"Alarms have been activated inside the house." Hutchings scrolled through the video footage. "They are still there."

Noah finished the coffee and glanced in the rearview mirror. "Anything for zone two?" The helicopter had disappeared, but they could still hear the thumping noise.

"It says secured, and the icons are green."

"Click on disarm and open zone two. The code is 44174417."

Noah slowed as he entered the residential streets.

One minute out.

"Seriously? That's just your badge number, twice."

"Easy to remember," Noah chucked. "Open the door."

When the helicopter eased off, the background noise had shifted. Wailing sirens were drawing close, and a black Chevy Tahoe whipped around the corner in pursuit—one hundred yards behind.

The massive Douglas fir tree on Noah's front lawn came into sight.

"Hit the trunk side." Hutchings braced himself against the dash and gripped the door handle.

A navy-blue SUV blocked the end of Noah's driveway, and when the front end of the Navigator hit, the smaller vehicle didn't stand a chance. They barely slowed, and the sound of twisting metal sounded like an explosion as they drove up the driveway.

A man in full tactical uniform had stepped out of the side door when Noah roared by. The man didn't have time to bring the rifle to his shoulder when the Navigator missed him by inches. He fell back inside the house.

"Get ready."

One hundred yards into the field, lights inside the barn outlined the large opening. The crack of a rifle sounded, and the rear window of the Navigator shattered. Noah ducked as low as possible as he hit the brakes.

"Now!"

The abused Navigator drove inside as the reinforced gate swung closed behind. The sound of bullets striking the side of the barn steadily increased, but none hit the vehicle. The motors swung the door shut and the locking pins settled into the steel frame. Red Knight Security had turned the barn into a fortress, and it would be even harder trying to get inside the second structure.

The three-room bunker resembled an igloo with two other domes attached. Steel reinforced concrete could easily hold off gunfire and explosions. When the five-inch steel door closed behind the Arrow Point police officers, Noah punched in the code on the panel and locked them inside the bunker.

Chapter 77

The barrage of bullets tapered off as more agents arrived. Noah sat at the control center and flicked through the different camera feeds.

"There's a buried cable for power and the security system. The air filtration has a battery backup. You can even check your email."

Hutchings nodded. "Got it, rookie. Get some sleep."

They had set up two cots in the front room, and Noah didn't have to be told twice. He had burned the candle at both ends, and unless he had some downtime, he wouldn't last. The adrenaline rush had faded, and Hunter could barely keep his eyes open. Time to pay the piper.

Hutchings watched the drama happen in real-time on the large monitor. A command location was erected between the house and barn behind a large, armored step-van, with vehicles to either side. None of the federal agents had thought to disable the cameras, and Steve had full control. "Too bad there wasn't audio."

Agents nestled in the field, watching through the rifle scopes for any movement. Noah briefed him on the barn, and while the door and bunker had been updated, the overall structure hadn't been. It wouldn't take much effort to pry a board or two out and slip in through the back. It would take hours of drilling to get inside the bunker. The barn could burn down around them, and they would be fine.

Spotlights were erected, illuminating the field. The camera over the barn door only showed a white glare.

"Jesus Christ."

Three vehicles drove past the house into the field and parked in an extended line. Black-armored plating and a narrow windscreen made the Humvees resemble tanks more than SUVs.

The big boys have arrived.

Hutchings leaned back in the chair and crossed his arms when the sound of Noah snoring filled the bunker.

"Rest up, buddy. You're going to need it."

Despite the situation, he couldn't help but grin. He had waited eighteen years, and it was almost over.

*****

US Marshal Dean Brooks didn't have to give the pilot instructions. He followed the vehicle and relayed instructions to the ground support. Brooks was surprised when the Navigator pulled ahead on the country road, but the helicopter didn't need to travel in straight lines.

"We need machine guns mounted underneath," Brooks muttered. Although they could track Noah Hunter, they could not do anything to halt his progress. As the fleeing vehicle turned west, his phone rang.

After a brief conversation, Brooks turned to the pilot. "Change of plans. We're going to Denver, refueling, and coming back."

"Yes, sir."

A few minutes later, Brooks received an update that Noah Hunter was trapped inside the barn. Orders were given to gather information and to make sure he went nowhere. They would breach in the morning.

Chapter 78

"You shouldn't have let me sleep that long." Noah sat on the edge of the cot and rubbed his eyes.

Hutchings handed him a coffee. He had all night to explore the bunker and found the butane stove and supplies. "It's instant, but not too bad. You needed the rest, so get over it, rookie."

Noah sipped, changing into a navy blue APPD T-shirt with *police* across the back in white letters. "Any action?"

The staff sergeant set up a folding chair and sat facing him. His uniform wasn't rumpled, and Noah guessed his former partner stayed up all night like a mother hen.

"A helicopter landed an hour ago. There must be thirty men outside from four different branches of the government. Maybe more, I couldn't tell."

Noah glanced at his watch. "When do you think they'll take action? Sunrise?"

Hutchings nodded. "Yeah. Twenty minutes or so."

"Let's start our day."

A small room in the middle had enough space for a composting toilet and not much else. Afterward, Noah sat at the command console and powered on his phone.

"When the shit hits the fan, I want—" Noah was cut off as an explosion rocked the bunker. He scrambled to remain in his seat. Hutchings ducked with one hand on his holstered pistol. Dust filtered from the ceiling and hung suspended in midair before gently falling all around.

Noah waited for armed men to storm inside, but nothing happened except another attempt at the door. Three consecutive thumps made it feel like he was in a metal drum. The door remained sealed.

"Sounds like they are getting antsy." Hutchings examined the entrance. "They're not getting in this way."

"Put your hand on the door. Let me know if there are any warm spots."

Hutchings followed the instructions and shook his head. "Nothing."

"Okay. Right now, they're probably trying to find a drill or cutting torch to break in." Noah checked his phone, but there was no signal inside.

Suddenly, the overhead light and computer system shut off, and the bunker was thrown into complete darkness.

"Shit."

The background quiet hum from the ventilation fan shut off, and the only noise was two men breathing heavily. Noah could hear the pounding of his increased heartrate.

After fifteen agonizing seconds, the lights returned, and the ventilation resumed. "Battery backup kicked in. They must have killed power to the surrounding area, not just the house."

Safeguards were built into the security system, and it drew electricity *before* the panel to the home. The barn's electrical had its own breakers, and they weren't tripped.

"Leave your gun here." Noah glanced at his watch and finished his coffee. "Play it cool."

"As a cucumber." Hutchings finished their old saying, unloaded his Glock 19, and left it on the desk.

Noah waited until the computer system was back online and recording before moving to the bunker door. *44174417*

The thick steel door creaked as it opened outward. The explosion had shifted it slightly but caused little damage beyond a layer of paint. A lingering smell of cordite filled the barn as Noah stepped outside. At first, he thought he was alone, and when a figure turned in the open barn door, a rifle barrel swung up, and a red laser danced across Noah's chest.

"Hey! You're trespassing. Get the hell off my property."

It took the federal agent two seconds to process the audacity before calling out. "Get on the ground! Get down!"

Moments later, the barn was filled with men, and all manner of firearms were pointed at the two Arrow Point police officers.

A man, the size of a refrigerator, tackled Noah and pinned him to the ground with his weight. The brace was ripped off his left wrist, and he struggled to breathe with three hundred pounds over his lungs. Noah's hands were wrenched to his lower back, and plastic riot cuffs zipped closed by another that rushed in to help the first.

Hutchings was treated similarly, but he let out a constant stream of curse words at the rough handling. A few of them were new to Noah. For Hutch, this was playing it cool. "Get the hell off me, you greasy, bloated, fourteen-sandwich-eating bastard!"

Without his feet touching the ground, Noah was hauled outside. The pain in his wrist caused his eyes to water and grind his teeth. Too much was going on to pay it much attention.

They were brought through a crowd of agents, all similarly dressed: bulletproof vests, tactical helmets, assault rifles on combat slings, and Sig Sauers in a thigh holster—each one stared the bound officers down with cold disdain.

When they turned the corner behind the black step-van, a voice called out. "Ah, Noah Hunter. Thank you for seeing reason. You've saved us a lot of time."

As the sun crested the horizon, Walter Scott, dressed in a golf shirt and khaki pants, stepped out of a crowd of suits. The wolf grin plastered across his face was anything but reassuring.

Chapter 79

Two men lowered Noah until his feet touched the ground, but their iron grips remained wrapped around his upper arms. The M4 carbine digging into his back ensured he wasn't going anywhere. Hutchings was treated similarly and was brought to stand beside him. Not that going anywhere was a possibility with a small army of men filling a corner of Noah's backyard. Ten acres was more than enough room for several vehicles and the helicopter.

"Brooks, I think we should arrange a private moment so we can talk with Mr. Hunter." Walter turned to a middle-aged man with the US Marshal badge hanging around his neck. Brooks had the tell-tail bulge under his suit jacket from a holstered pistol. When the marshal studied him, a chill ran down Noah's back.

"I think we could step inside the barn. Lots of privacy there." Brooks grinned, and the gesture didn't reach his eyes.

Noah knew if they took him to the barn, he wouldn't come out unless it was feet first.

"I'm good. We can talk right here."

"Hey, dumbass one and two. How about you read us our rights and show us a copy of the arrest warrant? Otherwise, this whole circus act would be considered illegal, and you know it." Hutchings wasn't intimidated by the rough handling.

Walter Scott addressed the men holding Hutchings. "Take him over to the side. We'll deal with him later."

"Free me, and we'll see who the tough guy is, asshole." Hutchings struggled but was helpless against his escort. They carried him around the step-van, out of sight.

A man ran over dressed in the tactical uniform, without any identifying badges or rank. "The bunker is secured. We found a dozen weapons and a computer security system. Everything has been recorded, but there are several blind areas."

Scott nodded. "Let's go inside, Hunter. I'd love a tour of your safe room."

Noah twitched and tried to pull his arm free, but the bonds were too tight, and the ache from his wrist made his teeth ache. "I'll send you pictures. I'd rather talk out here."

"I wasn't asking. Let's go." Walter gestured to the men holding Noah to follow Brooks across the lawn.

Noah tried to dig in his heels, but they just lifted him off the ground once again. Ignoring the pain in his wrist, he thrashed to break free, but his captors were too strong. Noah was carried a hundred yards toward the barn like a pig to slaughter.

When they approached the front door, Brooks stopped, and so did the men who held him. At first, Noah couldn't hear it, but then it became clear.

"What the hell is going on? Get him inside. I have a golf date that I plan on keeping." The agitation in Walter's voice was ignored as Brooks turned about.

The familiar chopping sound of a helicopter increased in volume, and everyone turned when the Sikorsky VH-3D Sea King flew over Noah's home and circled once around the field. The downwash flattened the grass and sent dust flying as men turned their heads away and covered their eyes. While everyone's attention was on the landing, many missed the parade of six Suburbans as they drove onto the field and blocked in the other vehicles.

Trees lining Noah's property swayed violently back and forth with the buffeting winds as the large craft's landing gear swung down. The large helicopter rotated so the port-side door faced the barn.

Walter Scott swore. "What the *fuck* did you do, Hunter?"

The American flag above the door was prominently displayed, and the *United States of America* was written down the side toward the tail-end.

Marine One, the presidential helicopter, had just landed.

Men in suits ran across the field and turned to face the crowd as the stairs were lowered. There was no doubt in anyone's mind who was on board when the marine appeared in his dress uniform, with white belt and cap. He marched down the

371

stairs, performed a left turn, smartly marched around the landing gear, and opened the aft staircase. A second marine stepped outside, and together they stood at the bottom of the stairs, one to each side, and waited.

The agent that held Noah's right side mumbled, *oh shit,* and Brooks turned to Walter Scott. "What do you want us to do?"

"Nothing can happen. Relax. He has no real authority." Despite his reassurance, Walter looked pale, and a beat of sweat crossed his brow.

Twenty-five men and women in suits stood in a circle fifteen yards from the helicopter, and a bald man in sunglasses stepped outside. He scanned the area, looked over his shoulder, then nodded.

Miriam Davis was the second to disembark. She wore a dark dress suit underneath a long tan coat. From a hundred-and-thirty yards away, Noah spotted the thick black ankle monitor on her right leg before it was hidden.

The marines snapped to attention, performed a crisp salute, and held the position as President James Monroe stood at the top of the stairs. He took a moment to survey the array of forces before him before joining Miriam. Monroe returned the salute and made his way across the field.

More secret service and two men hastened to follow after leaving the helicopter and joined the others in forming a protective ring about the president. Several men directed the agents into one area, away from the procession.

President Monroe, a former republican senator from Arizona, over four decades in politics and fifteen years of Naval service, had arrived. There was no sign of age or frailty in his rigid posture and short dark hair. His usual Hollywood smile was absent, and a rugged look caused the lines on his face to deepen. Broad shoulders stretched the suit as he fixed his gray tie. Miriam had a deadpan look, and Noah couldn't read it.

The bald secret service agent with sunglasses arrived at the barn, and Walter Scott tensed at the confrontation.

"You two. Disappear." The bald agent pointed toward the two men holding Noah.

They dropped Noah's arms and stood back, but Walter rose a hand. "Hold on. They don't work for you and don't need to listen."

"But they do work for me, and they *will* listen." A man in a brown suit joined the group. FBI Director Ernest Clarke pointed to the side, and the two agents promptly left.

"Thanks, Ernie." President Monroe and Miriam Davis arrived.

"Mr. President." Clarke nodded and stepped back. He didn't want to stand in the line of fire.

"Before we start, Mrs. Davis has something to say." The president gestured for Miriam to step forward.

"Walter, it gives me the greatest of pleasures to inform you that you're fired." Her grin was all teeth, giving Noah the sense of a predator closing in.

Walter Scott chuckled. "I don't think—"

"That's obvious," President Monroe cut him off. "We're just getting started."

A secret service agent stepped behind Noah and cut away the plastic cuffs. Miriam turned and called out, "Where is Sergeant Steve Hutchings? Bring him over."

Noah heard a familiar laugh from behind the truck, and Hutchings's voice carried across the field. "You guys are fucked. Good luck."

A brief smile quirked across the president's face before disappearing. Noah rubbed his wrist to get the circulation going as Hutchings was escorted by a man and woman dressed in tactical gear. Homeland Security was written across the ballistic vests in bold white letters.

Hutchings reached behind his back and pulled out a set of cuffs. "Walter Scott, you are under arrest for kidnapping and abducting a police officer. There will be other charges, but that's enough to get started. Turn around. You have the right to remain silent …"

Chapter 80

Noah couldn't describe the feeling as the cuffs closed on Walter's wrist. Each ratcheted *click* sent a warm glow of satisfaction in his chest, and the tension eased in his shoulders.

"This is only temporary. Nothing I'm concerned about." Noah wanted to punch the smug look off Walter's face.

For the first time, a twinkle appeared in President Monroe's eyes as he reached inside his suit jacket and pulled out a folded piece of paper. "You should be concerned. I've been busy the last few days as documents were pulled from the National Archives. I've had the AG go over President Truman's executive orders, and we came up with a solution."

The president opened the folded paper to show Scott. "I signed an executive order that canceled and nullified Truman's."

"You can do that!" Walter's face was turning red, and he stepped forward. Hutchings yanked back on the cuffs and turned him over to a waiting FBI agent.

"The only one that could have any legal argument against this decision has been dead for fifty years. There is only *one* executive branch, and for now, that's me."

President Monroe nodded to the agent, and Walter Scott was taken to a waiting vehicle.

Miriam spoke up. "We have heard from Amanda Rawlings. She was taken and beaten quite severely but is expected to recover. Another charge Walter is going to have to account for."

"Sergeant Hutchings and I want to thank you, Mr. President. We've waited a long time to close this case, and we have never given up hope the child would be found." Noah patted his friend on the shoulder.

"There may not be good news for Leslie Taylor. Now that she has been compromised and is a known foreign agent, she will undergo extensive questioning and could even face deportation." Miriam gestured to the FBI director. "Between us and the DOJ, we'll figure out the best course of action."

"I would like to thank you both for your efforts and dedication to justice. You and others from Arrow Point have gone well and above the call of duty." President Monroe extended a hand.

"I'm sure none of this will be in the press?" Noah asked.

"No photo ops, please." Hutchings stepped forward to shake the president's hand, then Noah.

"Sorry, much of this will be confidential due to national security, but I would love to invite you to the White House for dinner along with Sergeant Dickinson. I have heard that—"

Many things happened simultaneously, and time slowed to a crawl for Noah.

The woman in the tactical gear that had escorted Hutchings stepped forward, and her right arm rose parallel to the ground. The Browning 9mm pistol was steady, and her finger was on the trigger.

"Gun!"

Secret service agents moved faster than Noah thought possible and swarmed the president, protecting him with their bodies.

Noah was about to move when he stared into the woman's eyes and recognized her. It was the same woman that drove the truck from the shoot-out. She had a few cuts across her nose and dark circles under her eyes, but it was her.

When the pistol fired, Noah was already in motion.

Hutchings tackled him, and they fell to the ground next to the president.

Agents also swarmed the shooter, and the gun was pried away within seconds. Secret service agents picked up the president and sprinted toward the helicopter.

Noah wrapped his arms around Hutchings. "Thanks, man. That was close."

Hutch whispered in his ear, "I gotcha, rookie."

Noah pulled his hand from Hutchings's back when the weight suddenly settled on his chest. It was bright red with blood.

"No ..." Noah scrambled to roll his friend to the side, but he couldn't move him. "Help!"

Many hands rolled Steve Hutchings, but it was too late. Slickened, blood-covered fingers fumbled to find a pulse but failed. When Noah's eyes filled with tears, he could barely see, and he screamed for a medic.

"Come on, Hutch. Shake it off. You can do it."

Gentle hands guided Noah to the side as the doctor from Marine One arrived, but nothing could be done.

Chapter 81

The next few days were a blur to Noah, and he moved about in a daze as the realization sunk in. Angie Dickinson stayed by his side as he recovered.

Arguably one of the best doctors in the country had been at hand, and there was nothing that he could do to save Hutchings. That didn't stop him from trying his best. POTUS had returned to the scene after it was secured to offer his condolences. The woman had been arrested along with Walter Scott. The agents Scott had commanded were being dealt with in their respective command structures.

Miriam had kept Noah updated on the developments for the first few days as they dismantled the council. It would take many years to comb through Walter Scott's actions and make reparations, if possible—let alone deal with his predecessors. She was on a short leash but eager to help.

"Do you want another?" Angie sat beside him on the couch and picked up the empty coffee mug.

"No, thanks. I better get over to Hutchings's house and meet with the realtor." Noah rubbed the plaster cast on his left wrist and tried not to scratch. The doctors had reset the bone, and that hurt worse than when he broke it in the first place. He was on desk duty for the next few months as acting staff sergeant. "I'd like you to come with me if you can."

"Of course." Angie had been more than helpful and talked Noah into seeing the councilor through the station. She was seeing him, herself.

As he was about to stand, his home phone rang, *unknown caller* on the display. Countless people had called over the last three days, and as a general rule, he didn't answer.

"Hello?"

"Mr. Hunter?" The woman sounded young. If it were a reporter, Noah would hang up.

"Yes, how can I help you?"

"We've never met, but I wanted to thank you for everything you've done for my biological mother and me."

"Amanda?"

"Yes, it's me. I also wanted to let you know that the FBI has granted my security clearance. Right now, I'm still healing, but I'll be fine for next semester. I've always wanted to be a police officer, and even more so now, after what you've done."

"I'm not going to lie. It can be a very rewarding job, but it also comes with costs. If you ever have any questions, don't hesitate to let me know."

"Will do. I'm allowed to see my biological mother, Leslie, and that's pretty important to me. Thanks again."

After disconnecting, he glanced at Dickinson. Her eyes were watering. "It does come at a cost. Was it worth it?"

Noah closed his eyes for a moment and thought it over. Steve Hutchings should have been asked that question, and even if he were asked it, Noah knew what the answer would have been.

Life's not fair, rookie. Nobody gets out alive.

His eyes opened, and he nodded. "It was."

Angie smiled, and her dimples made an appearance for the first time in days. "I think so, too."

Noah stood and grabbed the keys to his truck. The Navigator was returned to the rental company, and for the first time, he was glad for the extra insurance. "Come on. Let's go check out your new house."

Dickinson wiped her eyes clear as her jaw dropped. "What are you talking about?"

Steve Hutchings had left Noah as sole beneficiary and executor of his will. He may have had some distant cousins in Florida but no immediate family. Everything went to Noah.

"What am I going to do with two homes?" He chuckled at her expression. "I'm sure Hutch would want you to have it."

The dark fog that hovered in his mind and clenched his heart had lifted. It wasn't totally gone, but it would with time.

"I don't know what to say. Thank you!" Angie gave her partner a rib-crushing hug.

Noah chuckled. "Not a problem."

When she pulled back, his face flushed as he studied her eyes, mere inches away. Angie's dimples made another appearance, and her cheeks grew red as well. "We better get going."

Noah wiped away a lone tear making its way down her cheek and nodded. The cost was worth it because friends and colleagues demanded it. They knew the risk and were reminded of it daily when they wore the uniform. Upholding the law came with a price. One he and many others were willing to make many times over.

A genuine smile made the corner of his eyes crinkle, and he tried not to sigh as they separated. "Come on, rookie. You're driving."

1

Sneak peek of

Hunter's Gambit

The Noah Hunter Series, Book 4

David Darling

Chapter 1

Jordan Gent slammed the rear doors of the transport container closed, and the inspector crimped a cable seal through the locking mechanism. An airhorn sounded from an off-shore ship, and it was taken up by a chorus of waiting vessels across the Port of Vancouver. The sound of the Pacific was temporarily drowned out as the inspector glanced at his watch.

"Yup. Midnight on the dot."

Jordan verified the information matched the shipping container and handed the clipboard back. In his mid-thirties, he was an unassuming man with dark brown skin, clean-shaven and short black hair prematurely going white. The streaks made many revise their opinion of his age on a constant basis. From a distance, the slim five-foot-five-inch man appeared to be elderly.

"Why do they do that?" Jordan had a deep bass rumble that resonated and was more suited to James Earl Jones than a slim Native American.

"Usually, ships signal when leaving port to alert other vessels. However, these guys do it at midnight to make sure we're awake and not sleeping after the nightshift." The older inspector chuckled. "Mostly because they're assholes."

"Gotcha. Thank you. Have a good night." Jordan tipped his baseball cap and climbed inside the semi-truck cab.

As the rig pulled away, he punched a green button on the dash. The ten-inch screen spun in a whirling display matching

the logo on the side of the truck and rust-colored container—
DTS Medical Disposal, a yellow biohazard symbol on a stylized
blue garbage bin. The approved eastbound route rotated, so the
three-dimensional map was orientated to the ground.

In eleven hours, he would arrive in Lethbridge, Alberta,
and unload the container before driving bob-tailed back to
Vancouver. Jordan had completed the same route four times
now, and it was easy money.

Jordan was still new with the company, and the first rule
was to follow the route and *no* deviations. He had to be at certain
checkpoints on time, and if he were more than five minutes
behind schedule, he was to press the red button on the computer
screen. He would be connected with a company operator and
report on any issues. DTS drivers were allowed one fifteen-
minute break every four hours. Rumors spread about his
predecessor falling asleep and being fired on the spot. The
money was good, and he couldn't afford to lose the position. It
was all he had.

At his first break, Jordan pulled over, watered the tires,
and kept going. When he pulled into the DTS compound a mile
outside of Lethbridge thirty-seven minutes ahead of schedule, a
smiley emoji appeared on display and, *well done*, scrolled across
the bottom.

Lethbridge was a hub for the medical disposal company,
with the main shipping run to the Clearwater, Oklahoma,
processing plant. DTS mainly dealt with radioactive and
hazardous waste materials from hospitals and treatment facilities.

4

There were many methods for making the waste material safe. However, long-term storage was the safest method, as radioactive decay makes the material inert.

The shipping manager, Raymond, waited on the docks as he backed in. Ray was a short bald man with a thick dark beard, and the ever-present coffee travel mug waved him over. "Good run, Jordan. I have a bit of a problem. Can you help us out?"

He shrugged. "If I can."

"Our Stillwater driver called in sick, rather last minute. Are you up for the Oklahoma run?"

Jordan glanced at his watch. "I'm supposed to rest after eleven hours. The logbooks, you know."

Ray ran a hand over his head and winced. "Don't worry about the logbook. I'm in a tight spot. How about double-time pay for the run, plus a day off after the haul?"

"If I can sleep for an hour before heading out," Jordan did the math in his head, and the promise of the extra pay decided for him. The Stillwater run would be a twenty-three-hour drive— long, but doable. "I may need to sleep a wee bit on the route, but not much. After that, I'll be burned out."

"Thanks, man! I'll schedule an hour break at the halfway mark. Will that work?"

"Yes, sir. I'll be in the cab. Knock when ready."

Jordan had time to clean up and eat in the cafeteria before closing his eyes in the snug sleeper. He didn't stir when the forklift ran in and out of the forty-five-foot shipping container,

5

switching the cargo. The shipping manager knocked on the truck door. He woke up, recharged, and ready.

Ray passed him a new logbook. "This shows you've just started your shift after being off a few days. Your onboard systems have been updated. Thanks for helping us out, man. It won't be forgotten."

Moments later, Jordan pressed the green button, and the new route appeared on display. Ray raised the travel mug in a salute as Jordan drove through the security gates.

*****

An ominous cloud stretched across the horizon like a mountain range, bringing the promise of rain as the wind made the treetops dance back and forth. The humidity had steadily built over the last few days in the early June weather and had not yet reached the breaking point. High in the branches of a white pine, a gray squirrel chattered in disapproval when a stick broke below. The high-pitched tirade was brief before it darted into a nest.

The bull elk was easily spooked by the change in the weather and did not stop to eat. The rut was over three months away, but the need to seek new feeding grounds was compelling.

Hours later, after the breeze shifted the rainclouds north, a stillness settled on the countryside. An evening mist flowed out of the woods and rose from the ground. Visibility dropped to fifty feet, then twenty as a thick fog blanketed a hundred-square miles of Wyoming.

As the elk traveled south toward Colorado, occasionally, the thirteen-hundred-pound animal paused and bleated. The call carried through the rural area and sounded like a squeaking bugle.

The animal was magnificent and stood six feet tall at the shoulder. The antlers were eighteen inches long and covered in a soft layer of velvet that would shed later on in the summer. The impressive rack would branch out to seven points and a four-foot spread by late fall, weighing twenty pounds each. Even now, the protrusions were useful in battering aside branches and formidable as weapons if required.

Droplets of mist collected on the thick dark mane and trickled down his coat. At midnight, he stepped out of the underbrush and onto the shoulder of the interstate.

The nine-year-old bull would have lived another five years had he stopped to browse on the fallen aspen branches, but after shaking off the water, he proceeded across the four-lane road.

Chapter 2

Jordan had no problems driving through the Canadian/US border. The DTS shipments were known, and the biohazard signs on the side of the shipping containers were enough of a warning. The average customs agent was not qualified to inspect the cargo, but the paperwork was in order, and he drove through without hassle. And most importantly, on time.

When he drove through Billings, Montana, the rains had started, and the display screen flashed with a route change due to the weather and an obstruction ahead. I-310 would take him south through Wyoming and east on I-26 before resuming the original route east of Casper. Jordan noted the change would add thirty minutes to his original route, but he knew better than deviating.

After an hour, the rain stopped, and once the sun had set, the traffic became almost non-existent. However, Jordan had a problem when he turned east on I-26. The fog restricted visibility, and despite his best efforts, he had to slow down.

Without hesitation, he pressed the red button next to the display screen.

"DTS Control, go ahead." The woman's voice came through the radio system and reminded Jordan of a waitress he once met from New Jersey.

"Thick fog at my location. It will increase my time."

"One moment, please."

8

He dropped to twenty miles an hour and turned on the four-way flashers.

"Once you are east of Casper, the weather pattern changes. Your arrival time has been adjusted accordingly. Drive safe."

Without fanfare, the woman disconnected. The GPS sent by-the-minute reports to control, and had he not pressed the button, they would have called him. Better to be safe than sorry.

He drove through patches that forced him to slow to a crawl, and other times the fog lifted enough that he could make up some time. The local weather reports were not helpful, and Jordan turned on a local country station.

The fog lifted during an elevation change, and he coaxed the truck into a steady seventy-five miles per hour. Despite nearly twelve years of long-distance driving, Jordan's reflexes had slowed with the lack of sleep and the weather.

When the interstate took a dip, a thick wall of fog suddenly appeared around the next bend.

"Jesus Christ!" He allowed the Jake-Brake to slow his progress, but it wasn't enough to avoid the elk crossing the road. Had the large animal not jumped at the last second, the sixty-thousand-pound truck would have dented or smashed the headlight assembly and sent the beast flying with minimal damage.

However, the elk jumped enough to clip the front left fender on impact, and the momentum flipped it over the hood. The beast crashed through the windshield in an instant as Jordan held an arm up across his face. He didn't have a chance to react as he was covered with tempered glass and a thirteen-hundred-pound elk almost in his lap.

The animal screamed, but while injured, it wasn't dead. Jordan tried to gain control and steer, but a flailing hoof smashed his head into the driver's window and knocked him unconscious.

The elk thrashed in pain as the truck drove straight for another hundred feet before the right tires sunk into the soft shoulder. Seconds later, the front grill smashed through a green city sign with an explosion of wood and metal before careening across the off-ramp and into the side of an overpass.

There was no chance for Jordan or the animal when the truck hit a stone wall at fifty-five miles per hour. The shipping container flew forward, flattened the cab, and then hit the overpass. The corner of the container had rusted from constant exposure to the salt air and tore open like a bag of chips as it flew free and landed on its side, blocking the right lane on the interstate.

Two dozen stainless-steel boxes had broken open and spilled the contents across the road. Instead of medical waste material, armaments were flung across two lanes. Many of the weapons looked like movie props but were on the edge of advanced technology and not available to the public.

The XM-25 Grenade Launcher had its own onboard computer and increased the soldier's ability to target effectively by three hundred percent. Two self-aiming rifle scopes (TrackingPoint XS-1) were worth almost twenty-thousand dollars each, and part of a precision firearm system had landed in the far ditch next to a crushed beer can. New CornerShot rifles lay next to Digital Revolvers—neither could be used without the appropriate biotech-smartwatch it was paired with and fingerprint recognition.

Eight cases of like-wise weapons remained in the container, held in place with steel bands and locked into the floor rails. Untold millions of dollars in weapons lay next to the twisted wreckage as the GPS unit broadcasted a distress call to DTS control of an accident.

What remained of the green *Welcome to Arrow Point* sign swung back and forth like a pendulum as the night sounds resumed. The creaking was accompanied by the sounds of oil, transmission fluid, and blood steaming off the truck's hot engine in a black cloud before dripping to the ground below.

*****

Sensors relayed the accident through the 5G network to an office tower in Montgomery, Alabama. The first four floors of the black-mirrored building were rented out to a real estate company, and Checkmark Investments LLC owned the fifth floor (and building).

The company bought stocks in businesses when prices were low instead of index weighing. Hot stocks, purchasing low, and selling high, are not part of their practice—Checkmark Investments looked for long-term financial guarantees as they

11

managed over thirty diverse portfolios. Minimal investments were eight percent on the low end, fifteen percent on average— that alone guaranteed them a solid clientele.

Thirty portfolios were in the books, but several were not.

Last year's acquisition of DTS Medical Disposal gave Alan Donaldson and Mark Carson fifty-one percent control of the operation and access to its logistic capabilities. Another company dealt with shipping to a Shenyang incineration facility for weapons in China.

Many of the containers never leave the dockyard before they begin the return journey across the Pacific.

Alan Donaldson found a shipment had been returned by accident, and it was not accounted for by the Canadian Border Services Agency (CBSA). Twelve months later, the two middle-aged men were moving weapons at an increasing rate as word of their capabilities grew. For Mark, it was about the risk and reward as he was pushing into new territory, while Alan wanted to disappear with his family and quit while he was ahead.

The latest shipment was for Saudi Arabia out of Miami in eighteen hours. When Mark's assistant called in the middle of the night to wake him, he knew it wouldn't be good. Disappointing his new clients could have severe repercussions.

Mark, in turn, couldn't call without Alan's wife answering, so he called the third, silent partner. Fredrick Luciano would handle it.

Chapter 3

After a detailed look inside the cab, Noah winced, and when the light breeze shifted, he wanted to rub some Vicks under his nose. The cloying scent of blood, excrement, and vehicular fluids baked on the engine clung to every surface, and he had to take slow, shallow breaths through his mouth to avoid gagging.

The Highway Patrol was short-staffed, and the weather caused a chain reaction of accidents throughout Natrona County. Arrow Point police were told that technically, the accident was within their jurisdiction by mere feet, and the Highway Patrol couldn't attend as they were overwhelmed.

The fire department took ninety minutes to extract the driver's remains and another thirty minutes to separate the elk parts from the human's. The police had other matters of concern on their hands, and the first officer on the scene called in reinforcements as she closed the interstate.

Bright road flares cut through the low visibility and redirected traffic to the off-ramp on the eastbound lane. After Noah arrived, he promptly closed the westbound. Dressed in jeans, a white dress shirt, and a dark suit jacket, the detective directed the scene with apprehension. Every discovery twisted the knot of tension in his guts and shoulders.

By five-thirty in the morning, the rising sun began to burn off the fog, and the accident scene continued to develop.

"Got another one!" Sergeant Angie Dickinson set up a yellow numbered placard in the far ditch. "I think it's a pistol."

Noah joined his partner and studied the silver-bodied weapon. A digital display ran the length of the body to the squared-off muzzle. "Do you think it's real?"

Angie documented the find with a few pictures, then picked up the weapon, pulled the slide, and held the action rearward. "Real as it gets."

A shower of sparks from the rear shipping container doors arced outward to fall on the road. The digital lock was removed with a cordless grinder, with help from the fire crew.

After safe readings were announced, he needed to see inside. Noah assessed the weapons and discounted the chance of transporting hazardous or radiation materials. While DTS appeared legitimate, there was nothing legal about shipping arms.

"I'll add it to the pile." Dickinson carried the futuristic pistol to the back of a squad car and stored it in the trunk. She wore nearly the same outfit as Noah, jeans and blue dress shirt, but had forgone the suit jacket—her badge and holstered gun rested at her right hip. Angie stood two inches taller than Noah at six-foot-one and kept her sandy-brown hair in a braid. Despite turning twenty-nine years old a month ago, she looked much younger with freckles across her cheeks and dimples.

"Detective Hunter!" A firefighter called Noah over.

The lock shackle was cut through, and the door swung open to land on the ground like a drawbridge. The contents

14

should have shifted with the shipping container on its side, but the stacked crates on the end blocked entry. Each container was marked with a biohazard logo.

Noah pushed on the top box, but it didn't move. Dickinson swore and climbed on the wreckage with a flashlight in hand. The rough opening was six feet long and two feet wide. Mindful of the sharp metal, Angie poked her head inside and flicked the flashlight back and forth.

"Holy, Jesus Christ!"

Noah closed his eyes. *This can't be good news.*

"What do you see?" He wasn't the only one interested. Her words carried to the other police officers and the remaining firefighters.

"We have another body." When Angie yelled inside the closed space, he could hear a strange echo to her voice, but he caught the intensity. "Those boxes on the end are part of a false wall. There has to be a switch."

"Where are you hiding?" Noah tapped each box and found the bottom wasn't made of cardboard or wood but metal.

When he pulled on one side, a toggle latch was revealed. After lifting the end, a wall of boxes fell back and down. It would have swung inward like a door had the container been upright.

It took a few seconds to process the interior. The remaining thirty-five feet of cargo space looked like a trailer park after a tornado stopped to say hello. Four-foot olive green boxes with thick hemp rope handles were haphazardly piled in the middle, and a cot and sleeping bag lay on top. Stainless steel boxes the size of a briefcase were in the mix, along with black Pelican waterproof crates lining the back row. They reminded Noah of the barrack boxes he had in the military when on deployment. Several were cracked open, and he could see more weapons.

Dickinson's flashlight shone on the twisted corpse against the far wall—an arm and leg were bent at an impossible angle, and the neck appeared to be shorted with the head resting on the shoulders. The man wore black cargo pants and a white T-shirt that showed off his muscular physique. All the weight lifting and muscles had done nothing to save him when the truck hit the bridge, and he bounced around inside like a human pinball.

"Detective, is it safe to go inside?" the young fireman had a radio in hand, ready to call in more help. The nametag on the jacket read, Weathers.

"Yes, go ahead." Like the driver, he would have died because of the impact, not related to any foul play, or it would have been a crime scene and not an accident. According to the red smear on the far wall, the man must have been hit headfirst.

Two firefighters stacked the crates to the side and made a path to the body. Pictures were taken, and the dead man was carried out on a backboard. There wasn't any form of identification found, but Noah thought he looked like a soldier, with the short haircut and the lines on his face didn't relax upon

16

death—a hard man. Dickinson joined him as they made sense of the interior.

"He was living back here while traveling." Noah found a bag of food, bottled water, and a bucket for a toilet.

"What's the point?" Dickinson searched through the sleeping bag but found nothing.

"Added security. I'm not sure what the weapons' value would be, but someone wanted an extra set of eyes on it, that's for sure." Noah opened a wooden crate, and nestled inside were six HK416 A5 rifles. With fifteen boxes in total. "These rifles are not available to civilians. Military or law-enforcement only."

"What are we going to do with all this?" Angie shone the flashlight over the hundreds of weapons. "Oh, fuck. Hunter ..."

When Noah dropped the lid on the crate, his eyes followed the beam of light. "I think I'd better make some calls. Quick."

Against the ceiling, currently the left sidewall, a black dome lit up when the electronics inside came to life. A whirling of gears caused the camera to orientate, and a red light blinked as the lens focused on the police officers.

Author Notes

When I started writing The Tipping Point, I had no idea that there would be a second, let alone a third novel, in the series... but here we are! I'm already well underway on Hunter's Gambit (book four in the series) and have plans for book five. When will the series end? Right now, I have no idea. Long as the ideas are fresh and the inspiration is there, I will keep writing!

What is real and not real within Course of Action? It's true that President Truman created a taskforce to deal with UFO rumors, and a leaked document in the early 70's gave them a name—MJ-12 (Magic 12). However, any Air Force investigation into MJ-12 couldn't prove it was valid. Of course, the government was doing the investigation.... Once I heard that story, I wondered what would have happened (if they were real) that they didn't willingly give up whatever powers they had. That gave formation in my mind, to the shadow government or 'deep state' and premise for the novel.

Regardless, I hope you enjoyed it! Hunter's Gambit (book four) is underway and if you are interested in an ARC, there is an email address **within** the pages of *Course of Action.* Write to the email address and you will be entered into the contest!

If you could also take a moment and leave a rating/review for this novel, it would be appreciated. I enjoy reading the comments. Your kind words and encouragement motivate me to continue writing.

David Darling, April 2022.

About the Author

David grew up in a small town east of Toronto, Canada. He has had many interests throughout the years, including the military, martial arts, playing guitar, and reading, and in his mind, he is quite an excellent fisherman. David is married and has one daughter, and he still misses his chocolate lab beyond words.

Feel free to write to David Darling at:

author.david.darling@gmail.com or check out his website www.daviddarlingbooks.com

CPSIA information can be obtained
at www.ICGtesting.com
Printed in the USA
LVHW081917120522
718422LV00014B/381